The Ice Box

THE GLENMERE BOX MYSTERIES, BOOK #2

Lisa Adair

FriesenPress

One Printers Way
Altona, MB R0G 0B0
Canada

www.friesenpress.com

Copyright © 2024 by Lisa Adair
First Edition — 2024

All rights reserved.

No part of this publication may be reproduced in any form, or by any means, electronic or mechanical, including photocopying, recording, or any information browsing, storage, or retrieval system, without permission in writing from FriesenPress.

ISBN
978-1-03-831070-5 (Hardcover)
978-1-03-831069-9 (Paperback)
978-1-03-831071-2 (eBook)

Fiction, Mystery & Detective

Distributed to the trade by The Ingram Book Company

Disclaimer

This is a work of fiction. Unless otherwise indicated, all names, characters, businesses, places, events and incidents in this book are either the product of the author's imagination or used in a fictitious manner. Any resemblance to actual persons, living or dead, or events is purely coincidental.

If you can dream it, make it happen!

Chapter 1

**Friday, September 20, 1985
Glenmere, Saskatchewan**

Officer Randy Doyle stepped carefully onto the slippery sidewalk leading up to the 1940s two-bedroom, two-story home, relieved to be home again. He shared the house with his new wife, Samantha, and their German Shepherd-cross, T-bone. The home was situated a few blocks from his in-laws, George and Beatrice Petersen. Rushing eagerly into the kitchen, Samantha and T-bone greeted Randy as he walked in.

"T-bone, get down!" Samantha giggled, kissing Randy firmly and turning away toward the refrigerator. "One of these days, I will beat him to the door when you come home."

1

"I doubt it. The dog can hear me before you can."

She popped her head out from behind the open door of the fridge. "Are you hungry? I am making breakfast."

"No, just tired. The night shift was long and filled with paperwork," Randy said, hanging up his police uniform jacket and unbuckling his utility belt. "It is freezing and damp outside. The weather is miserable. It will be snowing by lunchtime."

"That doesn't sound very good. My parents are going to Saskatoon this morning to talk with their accountant. Mom phoned to tell me that my niece, Amy, might need a ride home from work tonight if they don't return. She doesn't want her to walk home in this weather."

"I'm sure they will be back to town before she's done her shift at the Family Grocers, but I can swing by the store during my night shift if she needs a ride home. There's no need for you to go outside in this weather," Randy said. "I'm heading to shower and then into the darkroom for some sleep." The tiny home had two bedrooms on the second floor. One room was the main bedroom; the other served as a black-out room to accommodate Randy's shift work schedule, allowing him undisturbed sleep with total darkness at any time.

"Long shift? Were you busy fighting crime last night?"

Randy hesitated, knowing that Samantha didn't like him working on dangerous cases. "I told you that I'm not assigned to any big cases. I am overrun with paperwork, rescuing cats in trees and helping old ladies to cross the street." He nudged her jokingly. "The only exciting thing I did today was file some parking violations and stop a few people for ignoring the four-way stop. Nothing serious."

Samantha smiled, "I would rather you spent time doing that than work in the city where bad guys shoot at the police. It was scary to think that you were almost in a drive-by shooting this summer. Good thing you weren't in any danger." Randy wrapped his arms around her, hugging her close. If only she knew how much he craved the excitement of the real crime investigations of big city police units.

His focus drew him back to the August events that had given him a taste of real police work. Randy felt his heartbeat quickening with an adrenaline rush, remembering that day a month earlier, when he'd accompanied Officer Gerard to question a notorious gambler charged with murder who had just made bail.

"I think the address is the yellow-brick apartment building up the block on the left. Watch for it. I hate the congestion of busy cities," Officer Gerard complained, craning his neck and looking for a suitable parking spot. "The Saskatoon police think that our guy, Bobby, is part of their ongoing investigation into some big shot money laundering scheme. We are here only as a courtesy to listen to the Saskatoon detectives ask him some questions. I guess no one expected him to make bail at his hearing today, otherwise we would be meeting everyone at the jailhouse. Afterwards, we will come back to that deli we passed on the last block for a sandwich before we leave the city for home. The aroma of smoked meats is still making my stomach rumble."

Officer Randy Doyle spotted the guy they knew as Bobby. He was dressed in a rumpled brown suit, fitting his short and skinny frame, casually leaning against the metal railings at the top of the cement stairs and smoking a cigarette. Two smartly dressed detectives in dark suits were talking to him. One detective was advancing up the steps. Randy squinted, not recognizing the detectives from the Saskatoon Police force. "Yeah, I see them. I don't see any parking yet. This area has too many apartment buildings with only one parking spot per unit. I'll be surprised if you find a spot on this block. I hope they don't start questioning our suspect before we find parking."

Officer Gerard suddenly slammed on his brakes, jerking Randy against his seatbelt and locking him into position. Randy turned and looked through the windshield. The brake lights of a red pickup truck flashed on and off, coming to a near stop. A flashy yellow car cut in front of it in the middle of the intersection. "That was a bit aggressive. That guy is lucky we are here to follow up on an important case, or we'd pull him over," Gerard mumbled, continuing to scan for a parking spot. "That is, if we had jurisdiction. I'm not willing to stretch my neck out for traffic violation stops on behalf of the Saskatoon Police Force."

The brake lights of the red truck flashed again as the yellow car out in front slowed. Gerard unrolled his window, leaning to see around the truck more easily. A quick succession of shots echoed off the buildings as the detectives scrambled on the steps of the apartment building. The impacting bullets caused the shattered glass doors to rain broken shards down on top of one of the Saskatoon detectives and Bobby as weapons fire propelled them backwards. Without hesitation, Officer Gerard flipped the switch to the lights and siren of the Glenmere police cruiser, yelling, "It's a drive-by shooting! Doyle, radio City Police for backup! Tell them we are in pursuit!"

The 1982 Plymouth Gran Fury police cruiser lurched forward with sudden acceleration and braking, alternatingly pushing Randy into the headrest and against his restraining seatbelt. Grabbing the radio and pressing the talk button to call out to dispatch, Randy tried to brace himself against the jerking motion of the vehicle, yelling into the handpiece, "Shots fired! Shots fired! Officers and civilians down at an apartment building near Avenue T South. Send ambulances immediately. Glenmere Unit 879 in pursuit of a shooter driving a yellow, um, Chrysler... headed East on Twenty-second Street. Send all units to intercept!"

"It's an early 1970s Chrysler Imperial LeBaron. Tell them the plate! The plate!" Officer Gerard yelled, instructing Randy while he weaved in and around vehicles in pursuit of the shooter.

His heart pounding in his chest, echoing in his ears, Randy focused on relaying the vehicle's make and model, "Plate number bravo-alfa-victor," he craned his neck, trying to see the plate around the traffic that kept getting in the way. "Three-five-six. Do you copy? Over."

"Yes, I copy. Sending all units now and running the plate," the female dispatcher voice over the radio confirmed. "Stand by."

Officer Gerard swerved his police cruiser around a small blue Pontiac crossing through the intersection across the police cruiser's path, screaming, "Get the hell out of the way! Lights and sirens, you fucking moron!"

The radio came to life with rapid instructions addressing all police units, "Attention all units, all units! Glenmere Police Officers are in pursuing a stolen, yellow 1973 Chrysler Imperial LeBaron, licence plate bravo-alfa-victor-three-five-six. The driver is involved in the shooting of police officers and presumed armed and dangerous, heading east on Twenty-second Street towards Idylwyld Drive. Number of passengers is unknown. Over."

"Copy. Unit 936 en route. Over."

"Copy. Unit 721. Over."

"Unit 144 as well. Over."

Traffic was starting to get difficult to navigate the closer they drove toward Idylwyld Drive. "What's going on here?" Randy anxiously wondered, pulling the radio mic towards his mouth and pressing the button. "Glenmere Unit 879. Traffic is starting to slow down on Twenty-second Street. It's going to block us!"

"It doesn't matter," Gerard said. "If it slows us down, it will slow that guy down, too. Keep your eyes on the yellow Chrysler."

Releasing the radio talk button, Randy responded, "I see him! He's two cars ahead in the middle lane. I hope he doesn't turn off."

The radio crackled continuously from other units trying to get into position to block the Chrysler from various streets and avenues, trying to narrow escape routes. "Unit 879, are you still in pursuit? What is your position? Over," a male voice asked over the radio's emergency channel.

Randy pulled the microphone back to his mouth, pressing the button, "We're still in pursuit. We are on Twenty-second Street headed east, about three blocks west of Avenue F. Traffic is slowing us down. I have eyes on the target."

"Unit 879 units are setting up roadblocks and redirecting traffic away from your upcoming intersection; however, reports indicate that a southbound train is headed towards the Twenty-second Street crossing. Watch for tactical maneuvers. We are going to try to secure the vehicle into a box. Over."

"Copy that." Randy frowned, wondering which tactical maneuver while hooking the microphone back onto its holder and looking through the window where he last tracked the yellow LeBaron. "Shit! I lost sight of him!"

"I got it! He changed lanes ahead of the white Ford truck. Watch for him to sneak out through the lights at the next intersection!"

The flashing lights belonging to two police cruisers blocking the right and left lanes, with officers directing traffic, drew Randy's attention. The open middle lane created the illusion of an escape route for the driver of the LeBaron with hopes he would take the chance.

Gerard slowly moved into the middle lane, preparing for the chase. The LeBaron tires squealed as it swerved out from in front of the white truck across the intersection between the parked cruisers. Blue smoke momentarily obscured Randy's view. "We got you!" Officer Gerard grinned, pressing hard on the gas pedal, throwing Randy back into the seat. "Get ready. This could get messy fast! The railway crossing lights are starting to blink. The train is coming! Unbuckle your belt to bail if it looks like it will be too close."

Randy hesitated, questioning if he should unbuckle his belt, but decided to risk it. His eyes were glued to the rear end of the LeBaron, watching it release blue smoke with increased speed, crossing to the other side of the tracks under the boom barrier dropping down to stop traffic from proceeding. The arm of the boom grazed the top of the LeBaron, ringing and shaking with the impact. Leaning forward, placing both hands on the dash, Randy craned his neck to the left, watching for the oncoming train. It was speeding towards the intersection with blasts from its whistle mixing with the clanking of the train crossing signal. "There it is! The barrier is down. We aren't going to make it!"

"The bastard is not getting away with this!" Gerard yelled over the long frantic blasts of the train whistle, gripping the steering wheel tighter. He leaned forward and intently focused on the yellow car on the other side of the tracks. "I'm crashing through the barrier!"

Randy gripped the door handle, bracing himself. The big Plymouth crashed through the first barrier, smashing the lower half of the windshield and bouncing over the roof. Randy squeezed his eyes shut as time moved at an impossibly slow pace, feeling the sensation of the police car catching a rough, jarring bump when its tires hit the rise of the tracks. Randy felt his body rise weightlessly from the seat. The sound of squealing train wheels shrieking in his ears mixed with the sound of his rapid heartbeat. Opening one eye, he watched the grill of the police cruiser ram through the second barrier. Time fast-forwarded again as the police car landed with another jarring bang, hitting the pavement on the other side of the barrier and propelling Randy toward the dash before the car's sudden upward momentum jerked him back into place. The long blast of the train whistle roared behind them.

While trying to slow the pounding drum in his chest by taking deep breaths, Randy looked through the severely cracked windshield at the yellow LeBaron. Three police cruisers were blocking all lanes at the far end of the block with officers standing behind them. Randy quickly unrolled his window to lean out for a better view, noticing that a spike belt was rolled out. "Spikes! The LeBaron is about to roll over the spike belt unless he can stop before it!"

"I see them!" Officer Gerard slowed his pursuit. "He does, too!"

The brake lights of the LeBaron lit up and the rear tires locked into a sideways skid. With impressive skill, the driver managed to spin the car around, causing smoke to rise from the tires as he hit the accelerator, changing directions almost one hundred and eighty degrees. The smell of burning tires and exhaust smoke assaulted Randy's nostrils. Taking a deep breath through his mouth, Randy screamed, "Gerard! He's getting away!"

"Brace, Brace, Brace! We are going to hit!" Gerard yelled, steering his cruiser head-on into the yellow LeBaron. Anticipating the collision, Randy fumbled with the seatbelt, but managed to click it into place. The impact of screeching metal and popping glass was ear-piercing. The seatbelt jerked Randy back against his seat, causing pain across his sternum and pushing the air out of his lungs. Gerard hit the other car almost head-on, giving Randy a face-to-face look at the driver, aiming his gun out of his unrolled window at Randy.

"Gun!" Randy yelled, unclipping his side arm and pulling it out of his holster. Unbuckling his seatbelt with his other hand, Randy reached across his body to quickly open his door, keeping his gun aimed at the driver with a weapon targeting Randy.

Saskatoon Police officers surrounded the vehicles, drawing their weapons. Randy's ears, ringing from the sudden impact, registered muffled shouting. "Drop your weapon! Drop it. We have you surrounded. Drop your weapon on the ground! Put both hands out the window!"

Trying to take a deep breath, Randy focused on maintaining eye contact with the driver and holding his steadily aimed firearm, but pain in his chest only allowed for quick, shallow breaths. Time stood still. Randy's vision started to blur. Finally, the man dropped his gun, putting his hands out of the window.

"Open the door from the outside and slowly step out of the vehicle," an armed officer instructed. Randy struggled to keep his gun trained on the assailant as the driver moved slowly. "Face down on the ground! Arms above your head."

Unmoving, Randy kept his gun pointed at the driver until the man was fully restrained in cuffs by several City Police officers. He released a shaky breath he didn't know he was holding and slowly re-holstered his weapon. He became vaguely aware that Officer Gerard was now standing beside him.

"Good work, rookie," Officer Gerard praised, patting Randy on the shoulder. "Let's find out who this guy is and determine if he has anything to do with our case, then we will get some takeout from the deli while we file our paperwork. I'm glad you did not have to fire any bullets. That's paperwork I never want to show you how to do if I can help it." Gerard slapped Randy on the back.

Randy smiled, his body starting to feel the abuse of the seatbelt as the feelings of excitement and adrenaline started to leave his system. "This is why I became a police officer," Randy responded, smirking.

"...Hey, did you hear me?" Samantha brought Randy back to the present, patting him on the back.

"What? I'm sorry. I'm exhausted. What did you ask me?"

"I said, I'm glad we came back to my hometown of Glenmere, where things are peaceful and safe."

Randy held Samantha by her shoulders, looking down into her blue eyes. "I told you, crime happens everywhere, even here. The public doesn't see what all goes on around them."

"That's a bit scary, don't you think?" she pouted, casting her eyes downward.

"You have T-bone to guard you when I am not here. When I'm here, you have your own police protection," Randy smirked, pushing Samantha's brown hair back away from her face. "You don't need it because nothing ever happens in this pint-sized town."

"That's not funny." She walked out of his reach. "Go have your shower."

Randy shrugged. He didn't know what else to say. She knew he was training to be a police officer when they met at a club in Regina. *What did she think their life would be like if they got married? I only put Glenmere as one of my options on my posting request so that she could be near family if I were working long hours,* Randy thought, pulling a fresh towel out from under the bathroom sink.

Chapter 2

Sitting in history class, Amy could see large flakes of snow starting to float down towards the dry ground. An early snowfall gave the residents of the small Saskatchewan town of Glenmere a glimpse of winter. Snowfalls in September usually don't stay around for more than a few days, but sometimes a snowstorm could be so fierce that it could threaten to be the beginning of an early and relentless winter. Amy hoped that it was just a few flurries that would interrupt the cool days of autumn temporarily. She was planning for a warm evening in front of the television, drinking a mug of hot chocolate with a plate of Granny's fresh cookies, when she remembered she promised to work for another cashier at the Family Grocers after school. She had to walk directly to work from the high school when classes were let out to make it in time for her shift.

Hopefully Amy's friend Sarah was also working tonight and they could walk to work together.

Amy met up with Sarah at their lockers after the final bell rang. "Do you work tonight?" Amy asked.

"Yes, I am covering for Anna. I don't know why she needed it off, but she traded me for Sunday. I think she's getting the better deal out of it. I'm losing payable hours working the shorter shift. What about you?"

"I'm working for Brenda tonight at the store. She is going to a family wedding out of town this weekend. Imagine getting married in this weather!" Amy shrugged.

"I think Anna said she had a family emergency," Sarah replied.

"Funny, I don't remember her sister, Leah, mentioning that she had a family emergency when I worked with her yesterday at Frankie's Diner," Amy frowned, trying to remember the conversation she had with Anna's sister. Amy had picked up another casual shift last night at the diner as the dishwasher. She talked to Leah in the kitchen about the staff shortage while they worked together, tackling the mountain of dishes from the lunch and supper rush. Amy never turned down the owner, Frank, when he asked her to pick up a shift because she benefited from a free meal at the diner whenever she wanted one.

"It's snowing and blowing. My hair is going to look like crap when we get to work. Is your grandpa picking you up today?" Sarah asked hopefully. "Maybe we could swing by the Circle K and grab a slushie before going to work? Everyone had slushie drinks this morning and I have been craving one all day."

"No, I wish we could get one," Amy said, rolling her eyes. She closed the door on her locker, turning the lock. "I am walking because Grandpa drove Granny to Saskatoon to meet with their accountant. They'll return to pick me up after work tonight."

"What about your uncle? Could he give us a ride?"

"Uh, no," Amy said. She was barely familiar with her uncle and she didn't want to draw more attention to herself than she had last month. No, Amy didn't want to feed the town gossip if she was seen riding around in her Uncle Randy's police cruiser again. She shuddered at the thought of being connected to another police investigation. *No, thank you, not today, not ever again,* she vowed.

"Oh. My mom will pick me up tonight after work. Do you need a ride?"

"No thanks. My grandparents will be picking me up."

"I guess I'm going to change into my high tops in case the snow gets too deep." Sarah frowned, pulling her new L.A Gear high-top sneakers with pink and green laces out of her locker. "Do you think I have time to switch in my sparkly laces?" She held the shoes up, framing her face.

Amy laughed, looking at her wristwatch. "No, we don't. You don't want to be late for work. You are still a new employee; Dan can fire you just for being late too often."

Wet snowflakes swirled around their heads as the two teenage girls walked briskly to work, trying to keep their hands warm in the small pockets of their thin jackets. "My socks are getting wet! The snow is getting in my shoes!" Amy complained. "If we walk a little faster, you will have time to fix your hair when we get there." Amy was thankful that her colourful scrunchie was holding her frizzy, brown hair into a high ponytail, as usual. Her hairdo would hold up against this weather quite easily.

"Is it just me, or is the sky getting darker?" Sarah wondered, shielding herself from the swirling bluster of wind and snow.

Amy and Sarah rushed through the front doors of the Family Grocers, shaking the wet snow from their jackets and stomping their feet on the large mat in the entranceway. Dropping their backpacks on the benches in the staff room, they hung their wet jackets on the pegs. Both girls reluctantly changed into their frumpy blue uniform pants, checkered blue blouses and matching vests to start their shifts.

Amy left the smoky staff room to stand at her position on register one. She started ringing in customers' groceries while watching people racing through the front doors to escape the storm. The skies continued to darken prematurely before sunset. Amy shivered, attributing her chills to her still-damp feet and the icy wind coming in with each opening and closing of the front doors. She looked towards the other cashiers and wondered why Sarah was on register three, as she was covering for Anna Labrash, the cashier who usually worked register one closest to the doors. Usually, Amy worked on register three, where the owner mounted the wall phone. The drawback of working in that position was answering the phone during the shift.

The front end of the store was quieting down. The casual shoppers who were trying to warm up inside the store found somewhere else to be. Amy thought people might have gone home to snuggle up in blankets in front of the television. The phone rang on the wall near register three, alerting Sarah to answer it. Gloria, the cashier on the second register, slid her closed sign onto her turntable. "I'm taking a smoke break!" She called, pulling her purse from under the counter and heading towards the staff room.

Amy sighed, resting her hip against the counter. The hair on her neck stood up when a group of teenage boys boisterously strolled through the doors on their way to the snack aisle. She recognized one of the boys as Liam, Anna Labrash's boyfriend.

Sarah appeared next to Amy, giving her a jolt when she spoke. "Your grandpa just phoned to say that they won't make it back to pick you up from work tonight but hope to make it home later. Like, maybe midnight. The roads are slick with freezing rain and snow. I guess it will be slow driving. You are supposed to call your uncle Randy for a ride." Sarah looked towards the cereal aisle and said, "I'll be right back! I think I saw Anna. I want to talk to her."

Amy remained at her register, ringing through the occasional customer. Eventually, Gloria emerged from the staffroom. She instructed Amy, "Go to the back room and get the mop. The floor is gross. It's mucky by the front door and around the registers."

Amy slid the closed sign onto her turntable, walking towards the door leading to the back room. In front of the produce counter along the back wall, Amy could hear Sarah arguing with Anna about their shift changes.

"What are you even thinking? You told me it was really important!" Sarah shoved Anna into the produce cooler, grunting with exertion.

"It is! I'm not lying! I need your help or I wouldn't have asked for it. I'm in a lot of trouble and don't know what to do!" Anna complained, pleading her case. "I just need to talk to him and then I'm out of here."

Amy rolled her eyes, pushing the swinging door into the back room to avoid getting sucked into the heat of the argument. The last thing she wanted was to find trouble for herself. She had had enough of that last summer with her involvement in Glenmere's big criminal investigation and being the main topic in the town's gossip mill. Shaking her head back to the present, Amy noticed that the back door was partially open, allowing the snow to sneak in. She opened the door wider to see if someone was outside putting something in the dumpster. The wind bit at her cheeks and all she saw was darkness. Someone turned off the outside light. She flicked the light switch on and off, but nothing happened. "The bulb must be burnt out," she mused. Seeing no one out there, Amy slammed the door shut. It bounced back open, making her push against it a second time. Locating the mop and yellow bucket on wheels, she used it to wipe up the water by the back door before heading up front to clean up the floors.

There weren't many customers after 7:30 pm because the snowstorm was still raging, leaving the stockboys battling to maintain the parking lot with shovels with little effect. Gloria, the more senior cashier, said, "When you finish mopping around the front area, you can work on straightening up the product on the shelves in aisle one. I will tell Sarah to start on the opposite side of the store."

"Ugh, the first aisle with the pickle jars is the worst," Amy mumbled. "The last time I faced that aisle, I broke two jars." Amy worked slowly and carefully in the first aisle to get the jars neatly from the back of the shelving to the front. When she finished that aisle, she checked her watch, surprised to find that it was almost closing time.

At the front of the store, Gloria was standing idly at register two. Looking up at Amy, she said, "If you will man your register, then I will take my till to start my cash up."

Amy looked around the front of the store and down the first three aisles. "What about Sarah? Where is she?" Amy asked, realizing she hadn't had the chance to talk to her since she saw her fighting in the produce aisle with Anna about switching shifts.

"She just came up to the front. I sent her to the office to start her cash up. I'm going to help her tonight so that she doesn't take all night trying to figure it out," Gloria stated. "I don't think I want to wait around for her tonight. I might do it for her. The roads are going to be bad. Are you okay with me leaving as soon as I'm done?"

"Go ahead. I'm good."

Amy watched the clock slowly tick out the last few minutes until the store closed. At nine o'clock she left her position on register one, walking along the front of each aisle to check for lingering last-minute customers. At the other end of the aisle she could see Greg, one of the stockboys, keeping pace with her and doing the same thing. When they both reached the last aisle, Amy called, "Anyone else in the store?"

"No one here! Lock the front doors. All of the boys are leaving out the back door to catch a ride together so it will be just the girls up front," Greg called from the back of the store, running his hands through his green Kool-Aid coloured hair.

Amy walked over to the main front doors, looking at the blowing snow through the window. She turned the lock on each door to keep customers from sneaking in after closing. Pulling her till drawer out of the register, Amy carried it upstairs to the office to start the reconciliation and ready her deposit. Amy was surprised to see that the office was empty. She was sure that Gloria and Sarah would still be here working on their deposits because she didn't see either of them leave. Amy shrugged, fighting her feelings of abandonment, beginning to count the cash in her drawer. She shook her head, reminding herself that she had to let go of those negative feelings and past trauma like her therapist told her. "Get it together! The sooner you get this done, the sooner you can change into pajamas," Amy encouraged herself, pushing herself to focus on the present.

Finishing her cash out, Amy walked downstairs towards the staffroom, surprised that someone had already turned most of the lights off. The store was eerily dark and quiet. Her shoes squeaked on the floor as she walked. She fumbled to turn the lights back on in the staff room before retrieving her jacket and backpack. Finding her belongings slightly damp from the walk to work, Amy remembered that her grandpa would not be picking her up to drive her home tonight. Amy unhooked the front door key she needed for tomorrow's opening from the staff bulletin board and turned out the lights.

She walked to the main entrance doors, watching the snow swirl across the parking lot. Hesitating, Amy debated if she should call Officer Randy Doyle, who she had recently found out was her uncle, to pick her up for a ride. Amy looked around the darkened store, deciding she wouldn't be caught dead in another police cruiser. She didn't want to draw unnecessary attention to herself again. Committed to walking home, Amy flipped the lock and stepped into the cold. She pulled the heavy door shut, inserted the key and engaged the deadbolt. Amy walked home, slipping the key into her pocket and trying to duck her head against the howling wind.

Chapter 3

Saturday, September 21, 1985

Amy yawned as she prepared the store for opening. It was early Saturday morning at the Family Grocers; her body was tired from working last night's close shift for Brenda. Amy began to feel that trading the Friday shift wasn't getting her the best deal; maybe being this tired wasn't worth it. Longing for her warm bed, Amy shuffled her feet, pushing the mop bucket with her as she tracked water on the floor from the front area to the freezer aisle. Discovering a leaking freezer, Amy glided her hand across the cold water running down the front of the glass doors. Someone had left the door to the third freezer slightly ajar, frosting up the inside of the glass. Grabbing the handle to open the freezer door and seeing what was interfering, Amy blinked a few times before her brain registered the frosty hand sticking out from under the frozen bags of peas. Amy's jaw dropped open, releasing a gut-wrenching scream from somewhere deep within.

Suddenly, two large hands grasped her by her upper arms, pulling her away from the freezer door and turning her away from the scene before her. "Amy! Stop screaming! What is wrong?"

Amy closed her mouth, unmoving from her place before looking up at the tall stock boy holding both of her arms. "S-Shane," Amy stuttered. "I-I-I am alright. Go call the police station immediately! Someone has put a dead body in the freezer!"

Shane's eyes widened behind his thick glasses and moved slowly up and over Amy's head at the scene behind her. "Holy shit! I will be right back. Don't go anywhere!" he growled, pushing his wire-rim glasses up and turning away. He inhaled deeply, walking purposefully towards the front of the store to use the phone next to the registers.

Amy's legs buckled beneath her as she sank to the floor. She doubted she could go anywhere even if she wanted to; her legs felt like heavy lead weights. Her eyes stayed fixed on the hand with dark pink nail polish holding the freezer door slightly ajar. Amy did not know if she was brave enough to look at the person, obscured by condensation, but morbid curiosity drove her. She mechanically crawled across the aisle, as if pulled by a wire, towards the dead body. Her brain barely registered her blue uniform pants getting wet, dragging through the water as she crossed the cold floor on her knees. Amy slowly placed her hand on the door panel, holding her breath. She jolted back to awareness suddenly when she kneed the freezer's kickplate, feeling a sharp prick. Looking down, Amy found a gold earring stuck into her right knee. She gingerly pulled it out, placing it in the small pocket of her uniform vest, with fleeting thoughts of depositing it later into the lost and found.

Amy slowly opened the freezer door, her eyes travelling from the pink-nailed fingertips up the arm of the body and over to the victim's face. Someone had carefully buried the girl's body up to her chest in bags of frozen vegetables. Whoever put her there had spent a lot of time packing frozen goods around the body. Somehow, Amy's hands reached out to gently cradle the girl's chin and lift her face upwards. Amy gasped, snatching her hands away. *Anna! What are you even doing here? Sarah worked last night's close shift for you,* she thought.

Amy reached up to the freezer door's handle, using it to pull herself up off the floor. She gently moved Anna's hand out of the way, setting it inside the freezer so that she could close the door, almost as if she was tucking her in for bed.

Standing two feet away from the freezer, Amy shivered, staring at the frosty glass and waiting for Shane to come rushing around the corner into the aisle. "The police will be here shortly. Stay clear of the freezer so you don't disturb anything while we wait for them."

Looking down at her hands, Amy realized she had just touched the freezer door and the body. "Uh-oh! Too late. I just closed the freezer door."

Shane frowned, "Why would you do that?"

"I don't know! This is kind of, like, my first dead body!"

"I am going to go stand by the front doors to watch for the police," he paused, watching Amy nervously twirl her hair with her fingers. "You should probably come stand by the front doors, too. The rest of the staff will be wandering into work soon. We should probably keep the customers out. I'm sure old man Brookes will show up and want to roam around the store, complaining about the cost of groceries. Today is not a good day to entertain him."

Amy numbly followed Shane to the glass doors of the main entrance. As fellow employees walked up to the doors, Shane let them in, telling them to stay near the front of the store while waiting for the police. Amy ignored all of the questions being asked around her, trying to remember every detail of the night before. Still, she could not erase the vision of Anna lying in the freezer under frozen vegetables. Shifting her tired body, Amy leaned against a glass window. She closed her eyes, allowing her weight to pull her down to a cold spot on the floor.

Replaying this morning's events in her mind like a horror movie, Amy felt like she was stuck in a continuous, terrifying loop that she didn't want to watch or star in as a main character. How did she get herself mixed up in another murder investigation? Amy hoped to give her statement soon so she could put everything behind her and return to her warm bed. She was still exhausted from working the late shift last night.

What could she do to help? She shook her head, desperately trying to focus, when she realized that Dan, the store manager, had just arrived. His usual ruddy complexion turned white when he was told why the staff were gathered around the front doors, waiting for the police to arrive. Someone said something to him that made him turn and look at Amy. She looked away, avoiding the accusing look in his eyes. Amy suspected the gossip would travel among the employees and be all over town within a few hours. She shuttered, remembering how hurtful words had stung her during her last time in the spotlight.

It didn't take long before the parking lot was lit up, red and blue flashing lights bouncing off the icy snow from yesterday's storm. Officer Gerard and several uniformed police officers pushed through the front doors, followed by young Officer Randy Doyle. Shane, the tall, skinny stock boy with glasses, led the officers and Dan to the freezer aisle where the body was discovered.

After several minutes, Dan returned to the front where the staff were silently waiting, "Anyone who did not work yesterday or was not here before eight o'clock this morning can go home for today, but give your names to the police. The store will be closed today and tomorrow to allow for the investigation. Everyone else needs to stick around until you talk to one of the police officers.

Remember, we don't need rumours flying around town before the authorities notify the family. Maybe don't talk about it. If you know anything, even if you think it could be nothing, please tell the police." A blast of frosty air floated around Amy, sending shivers up her arms, as a few staff members happily exited through the main doors, noise in the foyer increasing with whispers and giggles. "The rest of you, sit in the staff room until one of the officers dismisses you. Someone needs to make a pot of coffee. I'm going to call in the staff from last night," Dan said, loosening his blue plaid tie and unbuttoning the top button of his blue uniform dress shirt.

Amy entered the staff room to claim a spot on the bench against the wall. Someone tried to hand her a mug of hot coffee, but she shook her head in disgust at the black liquid. Smoke began filling the small room as a few staff members lit up cigarettes while they discussed meeting up at Frankie's Diner for breakfast. One by one, as staff members were individually called out to talk to the police and dismissed, the chatter in the room died down until only Amy and Shane were left in the lingering smoke of the staff room.

Shane broke their awkward silence. "I'm sure I'm next. I wasn't here last night. There is not much for me to tell them besides what happened after I heard you screaming. I found you with a dead body and then called the police."

"I didn't kill her and stuff her in the freezer if that's what you are thinking," Amy frowned, glaring at him. "I will be the last one the police will call to be questioned.

My granny makes meals for the police in this town all the time. One of them will give me a ride home hoping to score a home-cooked breakfast. It will most likely be Officer Gerard or Uncle Randy. I'm sure I have nothing to worry about." Amy sat silently, thinking about the trouble that surrounded her last month when she first got to know the town's police officers. Once struggling to make ends meet and hoping for an inheritance, Amy now lived with her newfound grandparents in a dream world of white picket fences and homemade cakes and cookies, not a care in the world until this morning. The discovery of Anna's body ruined the icing on the cake, putting Amy right back in the middle of another investigation. Amy sighed, regretting that she'd had to work this morning.

"Are you saying that Mrs. Petersen bribes the police with food to allow you to get away with anything you want?"

"What?" Amy huffed, blowing her bangs out of her eyes. "No! That's not what I am saying! Officer Randy Doyle is the Petersen's son-in-law, my uncle. My granny cooks for him and the other officers when they come over because she wants to feed everyone walking through the front door. The cookie jar on the counter is always full of freshly baked cookies. What's your favourite? She would make them if you asked."

"Are you asking me to come over and eat cookies? I think I'll wait and see whether or not you are a suspect in this investigation before answering that question," Shane teased, raising his eyebrows above his glasses. Amy glared, mocking his ill-attempted humour. "Glenmere isn't as peaceful and boring as everyone once thought. I'm sure you don't need me to bring up what happened last summer."

Amy sighed; she didn't want to think about anything that happened in August. How could she get away from the gossip and live her life in peace? She focused her attention toward the empty door, waiting for an officer to call her name. "I guess you will have to wait for the six o'clock news to find out, unless you are friends with Denise Schnieder, the biggest gossip in town. I'm sure she will tell everyone that I stuffed Anna in the freezer last night after my shift so that we could all have the weekend off!" She crossed her arms in front of her, looking at her shoes and noticing that her laces were untied.

Police Officer Hanson entered the staffroom, calling Shane to come out for questioning. When they left, Officer Gerard and Officer Doyle entered the staff room. Sitting across from Amy, Officer Gerard flipped his notepad to a new page. "Amy, before I start asking you to tell us what happened during your shift yesterday, do you need a drink or anything else?" Amy shook her head no. Officer Gerard began questioning, "Start with the beginning of your shift. Try to be as detailed as possible, even if you don't think it's important."

Amy tried to give as much detail as she could, but it didn't seem like anything out of the ordinary happened last night that would lead to finding a dead body in the freezer this morning. "Gloria had gone to help Sarah cash up. I was alone at the registers. I checked the store at closing time before locking the front doors and going to do my cash up."

"What were the other staff members doing at close-up time?" Officer Gerard questioned.

"The stock boy, Greg, checked the aisles for customers at the same time as me. I was at the front and he was at the back. He said all of the boys were leaving out the back door. When I went to the office to make up my deposit, Gloria and Sarah were already gone."

"What time did you leave the store?" Randy asked.

"I think it was around 9:30 pm," Amy stated, watching Officer Gerard scribble notes into his little notebook. "I'm not quite sure."

"Who gave you a ride home?" Randy asked.

"No one. I walked home. I got a call from my grandparents that they would be late getting back to town because of the snowstorm," Amy answered.

Officer Gerard looked up from his notebook, "When did they see you? Did you see them come home?"

"I didn't see or hear them get home. I was tired, wet and frozen. I had a hot shower and crawled into bed when I got home."

"What about this morning? Did George or Beatrice tell you when they got home last night?" Officer Gerard asked, opening his eyes wider with suspicion.

"Neither one of them was awake when I left this morning, so I didn't ask," Amy supplied.

Both officers exchanged glances. Randy leaned forward, "This is very important, Amy: When can someone from last night confirm that they saw you, and what time this morning can someone confirm seeing you?"

"What do you mean?" Amy shuddered, knowing that she didn't like these questions. She thought that if she was on Miami Vice, the answers she was about to give would put her in handcuffs. Crossing her arms defensively, she asked, "Are you looking for an alibi?"

"Please answer the question, Amy. I need to rule you out as a suspect." Officer Randy Doyle rubbed his hand across the stubble on his face, sighing, "You should have called me for a ride home last night."

"Greg saw me at nine last night when we did the final check for customers, but I didn't see anyone after that. I think that I was the last to leave the store. Most of the lights were already off when I came down from the office," Amy said, trying not to rush her answer while she twirled a strand of her brown hair. "How much trouble am I in?" she asked. "Why did I walk home?! If I would've asked for a ride, then I would have an alibi. Right?"

Refocusing on the investigation, Randy sighed and asked, "How did you get to work today?"

"This morning, I walked to work because my grandparents were still sleeping. I had a key to the front doors because I closed up last night and it was my turn to open up the front end today. Shane is the first person that I saw. He must have been on the open shift for the back. I didn't see him come in; we met up in the freezer aisle." Amy looked from one officer to the other, waiting for one of them to say something. "I was already standing in front of the freezers when he came up behind me. He heard me screaming."

"If there is nothing else that you can remember, Doyle will take you home. He can ask George when they got home last night to see if they can verify that you were home. I am taking him off the case until we can rule you out as a suspect." Officer Gerard flipped through the pages in his notebook; looking up at Amy, he said; "I'll have Hanson assist me with this case. We will need to talk to your co-worker, Sarah; you and another employee both said that she was in an argument with the deceased last night."

Randy stood, shaking his head, "Are you sure you want me off the case? I'm sure I am as anxious to discover what is happening here as Jeffrey Hanson. I thought I proved myself useful on the last big case."

"We all are concerned when a crime happens in Glenmere. I know you aren't directly related to Amy; everyone just found out that she is related to the Petersens. Still, until we can get a better handle on this case, I can't doubt the evidence collection." Gerard sighed, tucking his notebook into his breast pocket and slipping his short pencil beside it. "The store owner told us that the security camera is fake. We have nothing to back up Amy's story. If Amy or the Petersens say anything to you, whether incriminating or not, I expect you to report directly to me or Jeffrey Hanson. Are you clear on this?"

"Yes, sir," Randy stiffened his posture, making his lips form a tight line. "Come on, Amy, let's get you home.

I could use a good cup of coffee and a hot breakfast. I finished the night shift two hours ago. Your grandpa will want to talk to me, but I can't answer his questions, he has to answer mine."

Nodding slightly, Amy dutifully followed her uncle out of the staff room and into the store's foyer. They followed the muddy tracks the officers and the staff left behind this morning. With her eyes downcast, she almost ran into Shane, the tall, skinny stock clerk.

"Amy, do you want to go for a milkshake at the diner?" Shane pushed up the glasses on the bridge of his nose.

Amy looked up, startled, "Um, Officer Doyle is driving me home to talk to my grandparents. I think I will go get breakfast at home." She brushed past Shane and out into the Family Grocers parking lot, wondering why he was asking her to the diner. *Was he hoping to get a free milkshake?* Most people have already figured out that diner staff didn't pay for meals, making Frankie's Diner a hot spot for employment applications.

Opening the door for Amy to pass through, Shane said, "We can meet later to talk about this morning if you want."

Amy raised her hand, waving goodbye in a non-committal way as she climbed into the passenger seat of Randy's police cruiser. She trembled, pulling her light jacket tighter around herself.

Chapter 4

Randy parked his police vehicle in George and Beatrice Petersen's driveway, reminding himself that the Petersens are good, understanding people. Yesterday, George mentioned that he was taking Beatrice to Saskatoon and would need him to check to see if Amy needed a ride home from work. Mentally kicking himself, Randy tried to push down his sick feeling, letting out a deep breath. Maybe it's his fault for not arriving at the store at closing time, giving Amy an alibi. He looked over at Amy, who seemed to be lingering inside the vehicle with him, "I'm sure it will all work out in the end. I have known George and Beatrice since I started dating my wife, Samantha, several years ago. They will be concerned about the situation, but will not be mad at you. If anything, your granny will be like an overprotective mother hen! If anyone gets in your way, she will protect you at all costs."

"That's what I'm afraid of." Frowning, Amy absently twisted a strand of her hair that had escaped its high ponytail, a nervous habit. "I have only been living with the Petersens for about a month. Although they are my biological grandparents and my guardians, I'm only just getting to know them. Now I am bringing trouble to them again! I will need you to start talking. I don't know how to begin."

"Okay, I will start, but you will have to answer my questions truthfully even if you have already answered them. Your grandparents need to know what happened. If anything, George will blame me for not picking you up at work. "You should have called me." He paused, reaching for the door handle and pulling it open. He hoped one of his in-laws could provide Amy with an alibi for at least a part of the evening. She was in a lot of trouble.

Amy sighed heavily, rolling her eyes. She wanted to tell him that she was trying to avoid being seen in police cars and the speculations it would cause, but instead she said, "I didn't want to bother you at work."

"I was only doing paperwork," Randy stated. "As usual, there wasn't much happening. The towing company was the only one getting emergency calls last night. A lot of people were stuck in the ditch."

Randy entered the front door into the kitchen of the Petersen house, inhaling the smell of fried bacon and pancakes. "Good morning! How was the trip to the city yesterday?"

Looking up from the newspaper before him at the round kitchen table, George smiled, "Good morning, son. Are you just getting off now? Have you had any breakfast? Coffee?"

"Actually, I could use some coffee; the stronger, the better. It has already been a long day for me. I was on the night shift, about to head home, when Gerard called us all out unexpectedly this morning," Randy rubbed his hand over his face, sighing. He realized that Officer Gerard had just taught him another lesson: police work is difficult when the people involved in the case are your family. But how is he going to learn about working big cases if he doesn't get assigned to them?

Beatrice entered the kitchen, apparently overhearing the greeting. "Good morning! I will get you your coffee and breakfast. Sit down, Randy." She grabbed her frilly apron, tying the strings behind her back. "Amy, I thought you were at work. Did you get sent home? Are you not feeling well, girlie?"

Randy jumped in, noticing that Amy was signalling him with her eyes to explain the situation. "That's why I am here. I brought Amy home from the Family Grocers. A staff member called the police early this morning to deal with a difficult situation. I helped question the staff and sent them home," Randy hedged, clearing his throat. "I need to ask the two of you some questions to follow up on this new case."

"We have been out of town, you know that. What could we possibly know that can help you?" George frowned as he folded his newspaper to set it aside. He leaned back as Beatrice set a full plate of pancakes, eggs, bacon and hash brown patties before him. "Looks delicious, Bea."

Randy's throat was constricted with words he knew would be challenging. Beatrice slid a steaming cup of coffee with cream and sugar before Randy. He picked up the hot coffee, prepared precisely how he liked it, taking a tentative sip to clear his throat. Maybe if he had more experience as a police officer, this would be easier for him. Randy decided to use the direct approach that his mentor, Officer Gerard, preferred, "I need you to be very clear about three things: what time you came home last night, what time you knew Amy was home and what time she left this morning for work." Using a fork, he reached across the table to steal a piece of crisp bacon from George's plate.

"What does Amy have to do with anything?" Beatrice asked as she busied herself, measuring flour to make more pancake batter.

"I'm not saying that she did or didn't do anything. Please give me those answers and we can talk more. There is only so much that I can say, but a serious crime was committed last night. We need to verify all of the statements we collected this morning, not just Amy's." Randy picked up his mug, blowing on his caffeine-beverage before taking another sip. "I'm trying to follow standard police procedure."

"I don't know; we got home just after midnight. Amy was already in bed. Her door was closed. What time did she leave this morning, Bea?" George stated, looking to

Beatrice to provide the information. "I was still asleep, tired after our long day."

"It was a quarter past twelve when we got in last night. We were quiet not to wake Amy. We both overslept. I didn't even prepare the coffee maker before going to bed. Amy was already gone when I got up this morning. I didn't hear her leave at all," Beatrice popped some bread into the toaster as she fried sliced ham and eggs. "I don't have much more bacon, but I am frying some ham. I hope that is okay."

"It smells wonderful already!" The smell was making Randy's stomach gurgle in expectation, and he tried directing his questions to get what he needed. He stole a half of a piece of toast from George's plate, dunking it into his coffee and biting into it. "Did you actually see Amy asleep in her bed or talk to her at all?"

George and Beatrice both paused, looking at Amy. Frowning, Beatrice responded, "No, but her bedroom door was closed when I went to bed and it was open when I got up this morning." George nodded in agreement to her statement.

Randy swirled the crumbs floating in the hot liquid in his cup before looking up, "Sadly, we need to verify Amy's whereabouts."

"It sounds an awful lot like you are investigating our girl, Amy, for something. What's the basics you can tell us about this case?" George asked, pointing his finger at Randy.

"This morning, Amy and one of the stock boys found a victim of foul play in the store. Amy is one of the suspects until we find evidence to prove otherwise or lead us to other suspects. The victim was last seen by several employees at the store yesterday evening. This morning, she was found dead by Amy and another staff member."

"Oh, how horrible!" Beatrice said, leaving her pancakes on the grill to rush over to Amy. "Are you alright?"

"Yes," Amy squeaked out, motioning to Randy to say more.

"Bea, get the boy some food before he eats all of mine!" George protested.

Randy chuckled softly at George's comment, looking over at Amy expectantly, knowing that she will need to say something to her grandparents sooner or later. "We will have to wait for the autopsy report to narrow down the cause and time of death, but the situation is baffling. Until we get more answers, it is difficult to say what direction this investigation might take us."

"I don't want to talk about it," Amy groaned, putting her head on the table. "I just want to eat and go to bed. I want to hide under my covers until this mess is all over."

Beatrice returned to the stove, filling up plates. She set two plates of food and a stack of toast on the table. "Nonsense! I told you to stop ignoring the hard things you don't want to face. Sit up and eat some breakfast. You will give your condolences to the family. Randy, I'm sure you will keep us posted on the investigation and let us know how it's going."

"Actually," Randy reached for a buttery piece of toast, adding it to his plate of pancakes, eggs and ham. "Gerard is making me move on to other things so I don't sway the investigation. But don't worry, the truth always reveals itself. We have to wait for more evidence, but if anything comes up, you need to tell me and I will pass it on to Gerard or Jeffrey Hanson. You have met Officer Hanson, right, George?"

"No, I haven't met him yet. I only know he is the new transfer to join the unit. Gerard talked about him over coffee at the diner a few weeks ago," replied George, swallowing the last of his black coffee and pushing a bowl of raspberries toward Randy. "What is he like?"

Not wanting to reveal his true feelings toward Officer Hanson, Randy lied, "He is a good police officer. He has my complete trust while helping to solve this case." Randy lifted his coffee mug to his lips, hiding his grimace.

Chapter 5

Amy walked into Frankie's Diner, stamping the wet snow from her sneakers onto the floor mats before the main doors. She greeted Frank Demmans, the owner, looking over the orange booths as she walked by his station at the front desk, "Is Leah working today?"

"No, actually. I got a call this morning from her auntie. Leah needed a leave of absence for a family emergency, leaving me short-staffed. Any chance you can work some extra shifts? I don't know how long she will be gone, and I have a catering gig coming up and need some extra hands. I don't want to have to hire a new trainee; they get in the way at big catered events. Interested?"

Amy knew she couldn't refuse to help Frank at the diner whenever she could. She felt an obligation to him for all of the free meals he had sent her way in exchange for working a shift or two once in a while. "I'm sure we can work things out. Did Leah's aunt say how long she would be off?"

"Her auntie only told me that it was a family emergency. What did you hear from her sister, Anna, at the Family Grocers? She must be off, too." Frank asked as he leaned his large frame forward, almost falling off his stool.

Not wanting to get into a conversation about what she saw at the Family Grocers, Amy hedged, "Must be something important, anyway. They are both very reliable. I will help if I can, but remember, I am back at school so no dayshifts or any really late shifts. I have to do homework and get good grades. I can't live in this town forever."

The cold wind and the jingle of the bells over the door signaled Sarah's arrival, "I'm here! I've been craving a thick chocolate shake since you called me. Let's grab the last booth by the front windows." She hooked her arm through Amy's, dragging her away from Frank and to an orange vinyl booth next to the window.

"Where have you been? You left the store without saying goodbye to me and then I couldn't reach you this morning. The phone rang forever!" Amy punctuated each word with her finger.

"Calm down! I'm fine; I slept in. My mom took my brother to the rink to sign up for hockey. I had the whole house to myself! It was so quiet." Sarah grinned, looking at the door.

Amy panicked, turning towards the door to see if Sarah had invited anyone else to the diner to join them. "Are you expecting someone else?"

"No, not this time, but it's a pint-sized town. You never know who might come in to join us." Sarah smiled, coyly playing with one of her hoop earrings.

Frowning, Amy asked, "Who is it? I thought we said on the phone that we were meeting to discuss last night's shift and stuff."

The interrogation was interrupted by a young waitress, Carly, wearing the blue and orange frilly apron uniform of the diner. "Hey, did you know what you want?"

The girls ordered milkshakes and french fries with gravy. Amy waited until Carly was out of earshot before pressing, "Are you expecting someone? Yes, or no?"

Sarah grinned, backcombing her bangs with her fingers. "Well, yeah, kind of."

"You always do this to me. Why can't the two of us meet up for a change like the old days?" Amy played with the napkin on the table faking a dramatic pout.

"We aren't little kids anymore. I just turned seventeen and feel like I need to find a boyfriend. Maybe you will feel the same way when you have your birthday."

"I can't believe you think that in a few weeks I will change my focus from getting my grades up so I can go to university and get a career in the city to just settling for finding a boyfriend. I don't have time for that! What's the big pressure?"

Sarah scrunched up her face, "Fine. I find this town to be so... small and boring. Well, you know. Don't you think we should have a little more fun? And Matt is planning on going to university, so he won't be stuck in this place forever."

"I want to get out of Glenmere just as much as you do. I get it. Nothing happens around here, but a boyfriend isn't going to do that for you, you have to do that for you," Amy said, widening her eyes and raising her eyebrows.

"Okay, but something did happen! Now the big question is this: what in the hell happened to Anna, anyway?"

Exhaling slowly, Amy gladly accepted the change in subject, realizing that the police must have already talked to her. "You tell me. I saw you with her last night arguing by the produce section. What happened next?"

"Just a second, here come our milkshakes," Sarah whispered, drifting her eyes towards Carly as she delivered the drinks. She smiled sweetly at Carly, "Thank you."

Amy waited until Carly left the area; there would be no use in feeding the town gossip mill about the events this morning. Looking over her shoulder to see if the coast was clear, Amy spotted someone else entering the diner. "Oh no, looks like you will have to tell me later. Your want-to-be boyfriend is here."

Sarah quickly smoothed her crinkle-crimped hair, moving closer to the window to allow Matt Macklin to slide into the booth beside her. Sarah said, blushing a little, "I was wondering if you would come. Did you walk over by yourself?"

Suddenly, Shane, the tall, skinny stock boy from the Family Grocers, appeared next to the booth. "No, I drove him. He told me you two ladies would be here and offered to treat me if I drove. You've started with milkshakes! I feel like I was talking about milkshakes earlier today. When was that?" He waved at Carly to come take their order as he pushed his way onto the bench, forcing Amy to move over, nudging her arm. "Oh, yeah, at work when the police cut my hours because of a police investigation." Amy couldn't leave his retort unanswered, but didn't want to comment. She fiercely glared at him instead.

"I was hoping to say my condolences to Leah. I don't know why I thought she would be working today," Amy said, playing with the plastic straw in her milkshake. "I need to find her. Have you seen her?"

Carly bustled over, "Well, hello boys! Are you hungry today? Kimberley just finished icing a white angel food cake. It is served with glazed strawberries for a delicious treat!" The young waitress smoothed the front of her orange and blue apron as she worked her charms on the teenage boys.

"Funny, I don't remember you telling us the specials when we came in," Sarah sweetly batted her eyelashes for a sarcastic effect while Matt and Shane placed their orders.

"What's your problem today?" Amy mouthed at Sarah. Sarah smiled. Annoyed, Amy looked out the window at the police cruiser pulling up to the curb in front of Frankie's Diner. Officer Gerard and Officer

Hanson emerged from the vehicle with severe expressions. *The police must be done questioning everyone,* Amy frowned with concern. *What are they doing here?*

Blushing, Sarah pointed out the window, "Oh, look, it's Officer Handsome! He has these gorgeous icy blue eyes. He came to my house just after I rolled out of bed this morning. I was mortified! I hadn't combed my hair, and I was still wearing my pajamas!"

"It's Hanson. He questioned me at the store. I hadn't met him before," Shane said, turning to gawk out of the window. "I think he's fairly new in town. I'm not sure how long he has been a police officer, but he seemed pretty cocky with himself. He is one of the new officers added to the department after last summer's messy crime wave."

Amy turned around to watch the two officers stroll into the diner. They stopped in front of Frankie and started speaking in hushed whispers. Frankie covered his face with his hands, shaking his head in misery. Amy imagined that her soft-hearted friend, Frankie, was hearing about Anna's death, but she did not know why the officers needed to tell him. *It is Leah who works for Frankie, not Anna... unless the police officers are looking for Leah too,* she thought absently, watching the stock clerk, Greg, squeeze past the officers to grab a booth. "I wonder what the purple-haired freak is doing here?" Amy muttered.

A bell rang in the pickup window, signalling that their orders were ready. Carly rushed the orders to their table, practically slamming the plates down in front of everyone in her hurry to get closer to eavesdrop on the conversation between Frank and the officers at the front desk.

"Oh, I forgot to mention that Dan scheduled you to work at the Family Grocers tomorrow. We will not all have the day off after all," Shane announced, shoving the last of his hamburger into his mouth.

Amy dipped her fry into her gravy bowl, "Damn, I was hoping to have the day just to do nothing. I had originally switched shifts with Brenda to work Friday instead of Sunday." She watched Officers Gerard and Hanson start to move about the diner, occasionally stopping to speak to a staff member before heading into the kitchen.

"I don't know what you are complaining about, I'm the one who has to clean out that freezer after the police tossed the spoiled food back into it," Shane explained, slurping on the remnants of his milkshake. "The freezer was unplugged and everything in it thawed out. Dan asked them not to throw anything out because the product needed to be inventoried for the insurance claim. We can't sell food that may have touched a dead body!"

Amy's throat constricted, making her food get lodged in her throat. She was shocked, making it difficult to swallow. Amy's tears started running down her cheeks before she could speak, "That's a horrible thought!"

"I'm glad you feel that way, because I volunteered you to help me inventory the entire freezer bank and throw it out. We need to clean and sanitize the freezer and order new stock," Shane said, nudging Amy with his elbow as he took a few fries off of her plate. "Dan called everyone to find out who was available. Greg can't come to work tomorrow to help and the other boys will be busy packing groceries and putting out freight. I know you like to get extra shifts and I thought you would appreciate the gesture since you lost today's wages."

Amy looked around the diner, trying to spot Greg's colourful head of hair, but she couldn't find him. "I'll do the paperwork part; you can do the heavy lifting," Amy answered, eating another french fry as Carly came over to check on them.

"Anything else? Cake? Just the bills?" Carly said, looking at the boys for verification and taking the empty plates.

"Just the bills. Make a separate one for each of us. Thank you," Matt answered for the table.

Carly promptly returned, placing a bill slip in front of each person at the table. Amy picked up her bill, frowning. Frank had never charged her for meals; she would give him the bill on her way out. Amy was sure their long-standing agreement to pay her $2.50 an hour in cash for any casual shift and waive all charges for meals was still in effect. She had talked to him about helping out with more shifts just an hour ago, after all. Slowly, Amy turned over her bill and stared at the unfamiliar, cramped scrawl someone had written there. *Watch your back! Do not trust him.* Amy looked around, searching for Carly and wondering who she was being warned about. She glanced over at Shane's bill, confirming that it was written in Carly's flowery cursive script with her signature, unlike the handwriting in her hand. *Who wrote this warning? Was it Greg?* Amy wondered. She folded the bill and slid it into her blue jeans pocket, thinking that she would find out the next time she picked up a shift at the diner, which would likely be soon if Leah took a leave of absence following her sister's death.

Chapter 6

Sunday, September 22, 1985

Amy held tightly onto the clipboard and pen, trying to focus on the task required: to take inventory of the freezer's contents. Shane called out manufacturer and product names and the number of items as he unceremoniously tossed each frozen bag into a nearby grocery cart. Occasionally, another stock clerk would replace the full cart with an empty one. Amy shuddered, thinking about all the wasted food hitting the dumpster at the backdoor, knowing what it is like to go hungry.

Taking a deep breath, trying to uncramp her hand, Amy asked, "Are we just about done? My hand is hurting from all the writing."

Stretching to his full height at just over six feet, Shane pushed up his glasses, "I will remove some of the bottom shelves, and then you can use the little dustpan and brush to sweep the crumbs off the bottom of this unit."

"Why me?"

"Because you are short and I don't feel like bending down that far to do it," he smirked, wiping his hands on his blue striped apron bib. "I will get the dustpan and brush for you as soon as I take this last cart to the back room."

Amy waited, staring into the shelves still in the freezer while waiting for Shane to trade her clipboard for a dustpan.

Shane returned, talking with authority and saying, "The stock crew is packing groceries at the registers. I will empty that cart into the bin while you sweep the crumbs. Use this rag to wipe it when you're done. We need to start figuring out what we have in stock in the freezer before we start an order sheet."

Amy waited until Shane left her alone in the aisle before she started doing as he had instructed, thinking that she would choose to clean the stinky staff bathrooms over this task. She laughed as she began sweeping the wet crumbs off the bottom of the freezer. Amy never really thought cleaning bathrooms was preferable to this, but this wasn't just an ordinary job. Amy sobered as she thought about finding Anna's body in this freezer.

After Amy finished sweeping as much as she could, she reached into the far back with the rag to start wiping out water off the bottom tray. The water was cold, even though Dan had unplugged the freezer sometime yesterday. Lost in her thoughts, Amy knelt down and leaned in further to clean the bottom tray with a soapy rag. She jumped when something in her vest pocket poked her in the ribs. Frowning, Amy swiped a finger into her vest pocket to see what the problem was. After some maneuvering, the item pulled free of the tangled blue thread, producing a shiny gold earring with a diamond dangling from a small hoop. Amy stared at the piece of jewelry in stunned silence.

Realizing that she was sitting there gawking, Amy muttered, "Oh, for heaven's sake. It's just a dumb earring." She slipped it into her blue uniform pants pocket to take it to the lost and found bin after her shift. Intent on finishing her task, Amy stood to wipe the condensation off the inside of the doors, wringing the rag into a bucket. When she removed the props holding the doors open, she noticed the floor needed a mop to finish the clean up and headed to the back room to get it.

As she pushed through the swinging doors into the back room in search of the large mop and yellow bucket, Shane came in through the back door, slamming it shut. As it had on Friday night for Amy, the door bounces open again. "Son of a bitch! What's with this door?" Shane inspected its hinges before looking at its latch. "Who is the idiot who crammed something into the plate? No wonder the striker doesn't want to catch and keep the door shut." He pulled out the wadded-up cigarette package that was wedged into the space of the strike plate, tossing it into the open garbage bin before securing the door shut again.

As Shane turned the lock on the handle, Amy's eyes widened, "Oh, my God! The door was like that on Friday night. Someone could have easily come in the back door with Anna after closing, killed her and stuffed her in the freezer!" She looked up at Shane, waiting for confirmation.

Shane hesitated, saying, "It's possible, but this isn't the first time that I have removed something to keep the door from locking shut. It happens quite a bit! The asshole who keeps doing it needs to learn to turn the lock to the unlocked position while taking out the garbage and then re-locking it once he comes in again."

"This is happening all the time? What if the paper wad isn't removed? The backdoor stays unlocked and open for anyone to use. Do the police know about the door?" Amy's brain was whirling with this new information, giving her new ideas and making her forget why she had come into the backroom in the first place.

"Are you done cleaning that bottom tray in the freezer?" Shane's voice infiltrated Amy's thoughts.

"Um, yeah. I forgot what I needed. Wait! The mop and bucket. Where is it?" Amy looked around the back storage area but could not readily see it.

"Check the meat department. Empty it first and put clean water in it. It will be all gross with blood and meaty bits from their cleanup," Shane said, making a face.

"Ugh! Last time I emptied it, I almost puked," Amy said, covering her mouth and trying not to start gagging. She swallowed, clearing her throat.

"Yeah, I know. Try not to think about it," he said, taking the inventory clipboard into the big storage freezer to replenish the freezer in aisle three.

As the big heavy door sent a swirl of icy cold air around Amy's damp feet, she wondered why the killer didn't put Anna into the huge walk-in freezer. It would have been less effort on the killer's part. Was it some sort of cryptic statement? Why the aisle freezer under the vegetables? She made a mental note about the back door, to tell Officer Gerard or her uncle Randy. Determined to get her tasks completed today so she could leave early enough to get to the police station, Amy forced her feet to start moving.

Chapter 7

The tires of Randy's police cruiser crunched on the frozen snow as he pulled up to the station. He hoped that the forecast for two weeks of bitter cold would be wrong. No one in Saskatchewan wants the start of winter to begin in late September, but some years it does. Hopefully, the town of Glenmere would get a little warmer fall weather before winter closed down upon this sleepy town.

Randy didn't know what to expect when he arrived here after he finished his training in Regina, but his wife, Samantha, insisted that it would be great to be close to her parents while he adjusted to his new career. He was all geared up for high-speed chases and major crime scene investigations, like in the movies, not the lethargic policing of minor theft, arguments with neighbours and the odd domestic dispute typical of the Glenmere area.

Well, that's what he thought, anyway, until he assisted Staff Sergeant Micheal Gerard on the big fraud, murder and assault case last summer. Still, everything reverted back to these diminutive cases he was always handling. He tried not to be upset about getting kicked off the Anna Labrash case, but he was envious of the excitement of solving another big case.

Pushing through the front doors and past the front desk, Randy greeted the plain-clothes desk clerk, "Good afternoon, Gladys. Any messages for me?"

"Only about ten for you," Gladys reached over, taking a stack of pink slips from a pile labelled in front of her to give to Randy. "A few messages are from Officer Gerard. I think he will be busy with this new case and needs to let you know what you need to do for him. Also, I have flagged one as a top priority. I'm sure you will like that one." Gladys winked at Randy.

"Thanks, Gladys. I will be at my desk. If anything exciting happens, you will know where to find me." Randy groaned, looking at the message slips with the check mark beside his name, "Cst. Randy Doyle." Most were orders from his staff sergeant, Officer Gerard, just like Gladys had told him. He had a lot of desk work, follow-up calls and paperwork to complete. *Yahoo*.

Entering the roll call room, Randy made his way to the cramped cubicle designated as his desk. The desk was cluttered with yellow sticky notes, scraps of paper, and pink message slips that he had yet to address. He tossed the pink slips in his hand onto the pile of documents, removing his jacket and hanging it on the back of his chair. Who knew most of his police work would involve pushing paper around on his desk? The officer who encouraged him to join the police force didn't mention the paperwork.

After reorganizing his workspace, returning a few phone calls about missing cats and other uneventful things like filing reports, Gladys appeared beside him, "Officer Doyle, you have a visitor. It's your niece."

"What niece?" Randy shuffled his files distractedly.

"Amy Young, she's your wife's niece," she smiled. "The Petersen's new granddaughter."

"Oh, right. I will come up front. Amy will probably ask me for a ride home. I think I have done all the paperwork my brain can handle. Any excuse to stop sounds good to me!" Randy dropped a finished case report in Gerard's basket on his way out of the room. Randy looked at Amy, who was nervously twirling a strand of her brown hair. He noticed she was wearing her checkered blouse and vest with the Family Grocers' logo. Looking at his Timex watch, Randy asked, "Do you need a ride home? Or to work?"

"Um, no. It's not that. Is there someplace we can talk?" Amy said, biting her lip. "It's about the investigation at the store."

Raising his eyebrows, Randy turned to Gladys, knowing that Officer Gerard was out of the office. "Is the interview room available? I'm sure this won't take too long." He glanced back at Amy, thinking, *she looks like a nervous little fawn. She can't be more than five feet, if that.*

Picking up the phone, Gladys nodded in response to Randy's question about the interview room availability.

"Follow me," he indicated, walking down the short hallway, past crowded bulletin boards, to the interview room. "Have a seat in either chair. I don't suppose it matters which." Randy watched Amy look around the stark room before choosing the chair facing away from the two-way mirror. Usually, the interviewing officer sat there so that another officer or the video camera could witness the whole process. Still, Randy didn't think Amy had much to say since Gerard took her statement on Saturday. He didn't bother turning on the videotape recorder on the other side of the mirror. Didn't Gerard tell her to talk to him or Hanson if she had more to add to her statement? No, it's probably nothing, Randy assumed.

"Okay, I don't know much, but I was called into work today because Greg wasn't there," Amy fidgeted, playing with the buttons on her denim jacket.

Randy furrowed his brow and asked, "I'm sorry, but who is Greg?"

"Greg is one of the stock boys at the Family Grocers. He is the guy who dyes his hair with Kool-Aid, always different colours, so it changes all the time. I think the last time I saw him; it was... green, maybe blue?" she continued, twisting her hair. "I don't remember. We aren't friends."

"Okay, continue," Randy prompted, trying to get her to start telling the story.

Amy's eyes darted around the brightly lit room, never landing on his. "Anyway, Shane, the tall stock boy, had me help him clean the freezer in aisle three. You know, where Anna... well," she said, shrugging. "I don't know if this is important for your investigation, but today, Shane and I noticed that someone had jammed a piece of a cigarette package in the door jam that stopped the back door from latching."

Randy sat up straighter in his chair, leaning forward on his elbows, "Is this the first time that has happened?"

"Well, I noticed on Friday night that the door wouldn't shut, but I never looked to see why. I can only assume someone jammed the latch with the cigarette paper. Shane told me he thinks a few of the stock boys do it so they don't get locked out when they take the trash out to the bin," she said, putting her hands down on the table in front of her. "That's it. I haven't found anything else, but I'd like to find Leah. I still can't believe all of this happened. I feel so bad for her."

"Officers Gerard and Hanson are leading this case. Just let them figure this all out. It is not your job to get involved in helping solve anything. The police officers assigned to the death of Anna Labrash are both experienced in cases like these." Pulling a crumbled pink message slip out of his pocket, Randy wrote on the back of it, "Back door tampering: Gerard."

"Officer Gerard probably gets his notepads at Zellers," Amy softly commented, comparing Uncle Randy's organizational skills to Officer Gerard's.

Sighing, Randy rolled his eyes and tossed his pencil on the table. "Yes, yes, a pack of four for two bucks at Zellers, according to him. I've heard it a million times but I haven't gotten around to getting a pack yet." He shoved the wrinkled pink slip into his pocket and pointed at Amy. "Wait here. I will be right back to give you a ride home. It's a cold, frosty September day and I could use a break from all of my paperwork."

Randy left the interview room door open as he followed the hallway back to the front desk. He located the pink message slips and checked the box next to Gerard's name. He scribbled a note regarding the door being propped open, knowing the officers may have already noticed it during their investigation. Looking at Gladys, Randy said, "Please put this in Gerard's inbox."

Squinting at the message, Gladys asked, "Are you sure this is the important message your niece walked all the way over to tell you? Isn't there something else?"

"Well, I'm not sure Amy has any other information," Randy said, shrugging. He didn't know Amy well enough to understand why she would think the door being left unlocked was so important.

Gladys smiled, "She's a teenage girl. I'm sure she has lots to say. You need to ask a few questions and give her time to talk. She's not that much younger than you. She came here to talk to you instead of Officer Gerard because it feels more comfortable. You are family. That makes you less formal and intimidating than the other officers."

"What about Hanson? He's younger than Gerard."

"He's too intimidating for a young girl. Those cold blue eyes of his aren't exactly warm and inviting." Gladys paused as she reached for the ringing telephone, letting her hand rest on the receiver. "Go find out what else she has to say."

Randy returned to the interview room, stopping a few feet from the open doorway. Inhaling deeply and shaking his whole body, he mentally prepared to gently coax more information from Amy. He strolled into the room, trying to be friendly and casual, and he asked questions. "Is there anything else you can tell me about this case? Anything else you think might be important?"

"Like what?"

Randy shifted uncomfortably in the hard plastic grey chair, thinking about Gladys' comment about talkative teenage girls. "Like... how well did you know the Labrash family?"

"Well, I don't know the family, per se. They live out of town near Grandma Dorothy's farmhouse. I work with Leah at the diner and Anna at the grocery store. Neither one is in my class. I think they have a younger sibling."

"What grade would that be?" he prompted, realizing that he had never asked Amy about herself.

"I'm in grade eleven, and those two are in twelfth. I don't have much to do with Anna and Leah other than work-related. Both are nice girls, both hard-working. I don't know," she said, spreading out her hands. "I think Leah has a boyfriend, but I don't know who it is. He picks her up after her shift at the diner. Anna dates Liam."

"They are both in the same grade?"

"Twins, but not identical. I can tell them apart when I'm up close. Didn't you meet Leah? I suppose not; you were taken off the case because of me. Most of the Labrash family look alike, when I think about it. All of the Labrash families in town are related. Cousins, I guess."

"What else?"

"While cleaning the freezer, I couldn't help but wonder how Anna ended up there. There is not that much room: lots of shelves and products. Why didn't the killer use the gigantic walk-in freezer where the back stock is stored? The walk-in is super cold, but maybe that's a good thing. I don't know what a killer would be thinking," Amy rambled, leaning back in her chair and putting her hands in her pockets. "Like, why would someone put a dead person in the freezer? Icebox? My grandpa calls it an icebox, if you prefer it."

"The extreme cold of an icebox makes the autopsy more difficult," Randy said, tapping the pencil on the table and thinking aloud. "It is strange for the killer to put a body in the freezer in aisle three instead of the big freezer. I will ask Officer Gerard about it."

Suddenly, Amy's eyes widened, and she pulled something shiny out of her pocket. "I forgot about this," she whispered, holding a gold earring, the bright lights shimmering on its surface. "I was wiping the bottom of the freezer when this poked me. It was in my pocket," Amy said, sliding the gold hoop with the diamond across the table.

"What is so important about an earring in your pocket?" Randy asked, trying to follow Amy's thoughts. "Why was it in your pocket?"

"I just thought there was something funny about it. Like, what was it doing in the freezer aisle?"

"When did you find it? Today?"

As she explained, Amy's eyes remained focused on the earring. "I found it the day I found Anna in the freezer. I don't know why I did it, but I had to know."

"What did you have to know? Tell me," Randy whispered, trying not to distract Amy from whatever she remembered.

"I had to know who was in the freezer. A hand was sticking out of the door, holding it open. I don't know how I pulled myself across the floor, but I was on my knees. The floor was cold and wet. I remember that something poked me in the knee as I reached the door. It was this earring."

"What did you do with it?" Randy asked, leaning forward on his chair.

Amy shook her head, squeezing her eyes shut. "I put it in my pocket. I was going to put it into the lost and found bin, but I forgot."

"Did you just find the one?" Randy took a pencil out of his pocket, prodding the earring, being careful not to put his fingerprints on it. A million ideas crossed Randy's mind when he noticed the post of the earring, dark brown with dried blood. "Was there another one?"

"Just that one. Quite weird, right?"

Randy paused, looking down at the gold earring. "Who do you think this earring belongs to? Anna?"

"I'm not sure. It could be. I didn't remember the earrings when I gave my statement. Is that bad?"

"No, it's not bad, but not good. This could be important evidence for this case, or it could be nothing. What is most alarming about your statement is that you were the last person in the store. You were either alone or unaccounted for over several hours. A killer used your workplace to store a body." Randy became aware his voice was becoming more intense, but he couldn't control his frustration. "No one can verify where you were between nine o'clock Friday night and eight o'clock Saturday morning. It's a big window of time. You don't have an alibi and you were withholding evidence!"

"I didn't harm her in any way!" Amy quickly stood up, knocking her chair backwards.

Randy stood, faced her with his palms up, and yelled, "I didn't say you did!" He breathed deeply, trying to calm his frustration. "We have another suspect, but her time to be verified is only 8:47 pm to eleven o'clock Friday night."

"What? Who?"

"I'm sorry, but it's police business. I don't know why I told you. I'm not very good at this whole interviewing thing. I haven't had many opportunities to practice because I mostly observe. Hell, I'm not even working on this case!" Randy exclaimed. He paused, quieting his voice, "I better take you home. Your grandparents are probably wondering where you are."

Amy turned away, but her eyes found him in the mirror. Randy felt his heartbeat slowing as he regained control. He said, "I will have to make a report on the earring, stating that you found it before we began our investigation. Officer Gerard or Hanson may need to talk to you about it. I'm not working on this case." Randy scooped the earring off the table using his pencil and carried it out of the room, with Amy following.

Pausing at the front desk, Randy asked, "Gladys, can you give me an evidence bag, please?"

Gladys opened a drawer, rummaging around before producing a plastic bag and a black Sharpie. Uncapping the marker, Randy hastily wrote, "Labrash Case: gold diamond hoop earring."

Looking at what Randy scrawled on the bag, Gladys stated, "You know he is going to want more information on this earring. There is a form to fill out in regards to collecting evidence."

"I know. When I return, I will take evidence photos and enter the item into the evidence locker. I'm going out to drive Amy home. If I see Gerard before I can do it, then I will mention the earring. I won't be long," Randy replied. "I think he will want to see it before I do anything else with it. He may not want me to log it myself."

Gladys shook her head, frowning, "He's not going to be very happy."

"I'm not too thrilled myself," Randy said, turning and motioning for Amy to follow him out of the building.

On the way out of the main doors, Amy stopped to talk to a tall blonde girl with big hoop earrings. "Sarah! What are you doing here?" Amy exclaimed.

"I got a message to come here to talk to Officer Hanson," she swooned, smiling. "I will tell them Anna and her sister Leah left school Friday afternoon. They obviously had to be faking the family emergency because Anna entered the store that night. She looked perfectly fine to me... well, at the time."

"He is out of the office right now, but you can leave a message with Gladys at the front desk," Randy announced, pushing past Amy to start his cruiser. He waited five minutes for Amy before she emerged from the police station, but used that time to move paper and other items off the passenger seat. She climbed silently into the passenger seat, shivering and rubbing her arms.

"Maybe if you wore something warmer than a jean jacket, you wouldn't be so cold," Randy scolded, adjusting the heating vents to blow warm air on his cold passenger.

"I just figured out your other suspect is Sarah," she mumbled. "She is the other person who saw Anna last."

"Yes, you witnessed a fight between Sarah and Anna. Other staff collaborated with the story, but I wouldn't worry about it. It's all a part of investigating. We list suspects and then eliminate them individually as the evidence is collected. The truth always comes out in the end."

"How? You heard the officer say the security cameras were fake! It's my word against everyone's. Who do you believe? Your main suspects are just kids," Amy yelled, her voice shaking. She inhaled deeply, rubbing her face. Randy let her rant, thinking that there was nothing he could do right now, but he knew he would fight for justice. Amy rubbed her hands together over the heater, nodding to herself. "I think I need to talk to Leah, then I might feel better. I feel so bad for her and her family. I don't want her thinking that I had anything to do with Anna's death."

"Well, that sounds great!" Randy joked, unable to stop being sarcastic and immature. "Why don't you do that? It will make everything all better."

"It's not funny. I need to express my condolences to the family. I can imagine what Leah must be feeling. I have lost family members, too. Don't you know what that is like?"

"No, I'm sorry. It's been a long weekend of never-ending shifts and paperwork," Randy replied, feeling like an idiot. "Gerard and Hanson are running the lead on this case. I am handling traffic violations and stranded cats in trees under the supervision of Officer Trussell and Gilbertson. If I'm lucky, something interesting will come my way." Randy drove in silence, berating himself. How could he let his emotions interfere with his professionalism? He needed to get his act together so he would be ready when the next big case came along, if it ever did. This might be the case Randy has been waiting for. Unfortunately, it wasn't his.

Chapter 8

Sitting at the table to begin the supper meal, Amy inhaled the delicious aromas from the roast beef dinner. "Smells good! I'm starving."

"I thought you would have been home earlier today to try the fresh batch of oatmeal raisin cookies I made for you," Beatrice smiled. "I filled the cookie jar."

Amy looked at her grandparents, trying to form her thoughts into words. "On my way home from work, I stopped at the police station to talk to Officer Gerard, but the lady at the desk said he wasn't in. She suggested I talk to Officer Doyle... I mean Uncle Randy. Whatever," Amy said, waving her words away to dismiss her comments. "I wanted to tell the police about the store's back door. I also found an earring in the freezer aisle and forgot about it until I was cleaning it. I think it is important. Uncle Randy took it into evidence." She inhaled deeply, searching her grandparents' eyes for reassurance that she did the right thing.

George quietly set his fork down on his plate, wiping his mouth with his cloth napkin, "Dan made you clean that freezer?"

"It's okay. I mostly helped mark down all the stuff that we had to throw out. Shane O'Conner dug all of the spoiled food out of the freezer. What a mess that was! When I was wiping out the bottom tray with a rag, the earring poked me and reminded me it was in my pocket. Weird, huh?" Amy quickly shovelled creamy mashed potatoes into her mouth, talking around it. "I don't have much else to say about the earring. I don't even know if it was Anna's. I don't remember her wearing anything like it. Can we talk about something else?"

"We do need to talk to you about something very important. It can't wait any longer," Beatrice hedged, putting her hand on George's arm. "Every time we try to discuss this with you, you change the subject or tell us you are too tired to talk about it."

"Not this again," Amy complained, rolling her eyes.

"You need to listen," George stated, leaning his elbows on the table. "Our accountant has been reviewing all of the statements and bills past due for the house next door and the farmhouse you inherited last month. Although we were able to get renters next door, the rent will not cover all of the bills or the expenses I foresee coming soon. The furnace next door is patched together and needs to be replaced. We already cleaned out things you wanted saved from the farmhouse and put them into storage, now we need to look at paying the bills, taxes and repairs."

Reaching for a fresh roll, Amy said, "I remember all of the past due notices. I thought the estate was supposed to handle all the bills. Can you tell me what happened?"

"When Donald Tracker took over the law office and the estate after Dorothy's death, he was delayed in clearing up all of the paperwork. There were bills and property taxes due before he secured the funds in her bank accounts. Donald finally verified the accounts, but the money was fraudulently withdrawn. It was probably the guy that was impersonating your uncle, trying to inherit the estate. There is still money in the estate's investments, but that is inaccessible and can't be released to you until you are twenty-five. The estate has overdue payments to make on both properties. There is no way to cover the outstanding bills just by renting the two properties."

"So, what do I do? I'm already working at the Family Grocers and taking casual shifts at Frankie's Diner. I have committed to helping with a catering job with Frank too. I don't think that I can do anything else. I hoped to save for college, but this sounds more important." Amy said, frowning and dropping her fork on her plate. "I can't bear the thought of losing the farmhouse."

Her grandparents exchanged uncomfortable looks. "Just say it," Beatrice encouraged, nudging George.

"It's come down to this: you need to start selling the furniture and the tractor from the farmhouse, fix the furnace and clean out all personal items to get the farmhouse and its land for sale. The easiest and fastest way to do this is to have a farm auction," he said.

Amy sighed heavily. Looking down at her unfinished plate of food, she didn't feel hungry anymore. Her stomach felt a little queasy thinking about how she had once lived happily at the farmhouse with her Grandma Dorothy, until her unexpected death. It changed her life, but helped her find a family with the Petersens that she didn't know she had. "How much will be auctioned? Will I get to keep the farmhouse?"

"We need to auction almost everything, including the quarter sections of land surrounding the farmhouse. I already have the auction scheduled. We will have Edward Greene put the farmhouse up for sale as an acreage. I think it will be a tough sale with its recent history. I don't know if there will be any buyers wanting to pay what it is worth. If the land auction goes well, then we might be able to rent the house as an acreage instead of selling it." George said, leaning back in his chair. "I can't make any promises."

Amy's head started to whirl as her grandpa laid it all out for her. She knew that the bills were past due, but she assumed that Donald Tracker would take care of all the past-due notices and property taxes once he read the Last Will. She thought everything was in the clear and she had saved her beloved farmhouse, her childhood home, from being taken away.

Amy swallowed the lump in her throat, "Can I still have my grandma's car?"

"No, honey; it's already been sitting since April when she passed away. A new four-door Oldsmobile Ninety-eight is a pretty expensive, fancy car for a sixteen-year-old girl without a driver's licence. Your grandpa will help you trade it in for something more affordable," Beatrice said, reaching her hand across the table to cover Amy's. "We will find something practical for your needs."

Pulling her hand from under her granny's, Amy said, "I passed the test to get my learner's. Why can't I have the car?" She didn't like how her voice reached a high pitch, but she didn't try to control it either. "Isn't it mine? Why do I have to sell everything? This isn't fair!"

"Believe me, I have looked at all of the possibilities for you. Selling stuff is the best scenario. When you don't have the money to pay the bills, you need to sell your expensive things and live a smaller, less fancy life. You said you don't want to live at the farmhouse since the tragedy that happened there last month. It makes more sense to sell it and move forward. We will use the money from the sale to pay the outstanding bills, buy a reliable used car and invest the rest for college. Our boys never came back to live in Glenmere after they graduated; you will probably do the same thing."

Amy really couldn't argue; what he was saying made sense. She only wished she could let go of her emotional attachment to all the memories of the farmhouse and its contents. Sighing, she uttered, "What do I have to do?"

"When the highways are clear again, we will go to the farmhouse. We will bring stickers to mark what you will keep, prepare the clothes and personal items for donation, and make a big list of other considerations," Beatrice softly spoke, staring at the wall behind Amy like someone wrote her speech on the flowered wallpaper. "We will wait for good weather. It is supposed to clear up in a day or two if the weatherman has it right, but I heard it's supposed to get worse before it gets better."

"We don't have much time. The auction is on Friday," George commented, reminding Beatrice of the tight timeline.

Chapter 9

Monday, September 23, 1985

S lamming her school locker door, Amy hastily secured the lock, trying to ignore the whispers and cool stares she had been receiving from her classmates all day. It was obvious that many of the other students were talking about Amy finding Anna Labrash's body. Amy would have formed a united front with Sarah or Leah to clear up any misinformation and gossip if either of the two girls had bothered to attend school today.

Amy scooped up her messenger bag and, slinging it over her shoulder across her body, made her way to the main doors. She thought about using the student telephone near the office at lunch to call Sarah to find out why she wasn't at school, but the lineup was at least six students deep waiting to make a telephone call. "This school needs to put in another telephone for students," Amy muttered, rolling her eyes.

As she neared the main doors, she saw the trees outside swaying with the wind. Pushing the heavy glass doors open, Amy sarcastically exclaimed, "Ugh! Could the weather be any crappier? Honestly." The cold air stung her face, moistened with wet snowflakes sticking to it.

"Amy! Over here," a male voice called out.

Amy turned toward the sound of his voice, recognizing her grandpa, George Petersen's silhouette. "Oh, thank goodness! I thought I would have to walk home. Thank you!" she yelled, running through the crowds.

"Your boss, Dan, called. He needs you to come to work to cover Sarah's shift. I have your uniform in the car," he said, gesturing with his thumb and trying to put his back to the howling wind. "Let's get in the car and out of this nasty weather."

"Sarah wasn't at school today either. I couldn't call her at lunch. Did Dan say she was sick?"

"I didn't ask and he didn't say. You will have to ask Sarah yourself," he said, opening the passenger door of his black 1983 Buick Riviera to let Amy into the front seat. Closing the door firmly, he hurried to jump into the driver's seat. "It's slippery! I almost fell. Have you gone to the SGI office yet to book your driver's test?"

"No, I haven't gotten around to it, but I will. I've just been busy with stuff," Amy shrugged, not knowing why she didn't try to get her licence. She didn't need to have a driver's licence because she could easily get a ride from her family or friends. "What would I use for my driving test? This?"

"I haven't worked that out yet. I have been looking at the cars on the used car lot but haven't found anything suitable or affordable for you. I didn't know you were in a rush. I should have guessed that when you asked about Dorothy's blue Oldsmobile." He pulled into the Family Grocers' parking lot; parking close to the main doors. "I will pick you up tonight at closing. Maybe tomorrow you will wear something to school other than sneakers so you don't slip and fall on the ice. The weather will be changing. We will get freezing rain tonight."

"It's fine!" Amy emphasized, rolling her eyes. "The snow isn't even that deep yet. I'm sure I'll be good in my high-tops at least until November."

Amy made her way into the store, through the staff room to the ladies' room, where she would change into her blue checkered shirt, vest and blue uniform pants. She noticed the bathroom needed to be cleaned during her shift today. The garbage overflowed with discarded paper towels and the sink was dirty. When she emerged, other evening shift students were sitting in the staff room area waiting for the four o'clock shift to start.

She still wanted to call Sarah, but didn't want to use the phone in the staff room, so she left to use the telephone mounted near the last register. When she got there, Greg, who had now dyed his hair purple, was talking on the telephone with a customer placing a grocery delivery order for tomorrow. Wearily, Greg eyed Amy as he listened, writing down everything the person was instructing. "If that will be everything, I will have that delivered tomorrow. Bye." He hung up the receiver, disappearing around the corner of the cardboard box bin.

Looking at her watch, Amy noticed it was five minutes to four o'clock. If she hurried, she would have time for a quick telephone call to Sarah. Cradling the receiver and sticking her finger on the first number of Sarah's phone number on the dial plate, Amy began rotating the plate to the finger stopper. Releasing the dial plate, allowing it to reset while she listened to the clicking noises through the receiver, Amy waited for the call to be connected. Tapping her fingers on the shelf of the cigarette case, she waited while the telephone rang three times before Sarah finally answered.

"Hello?" Sarah answered.

"Hi. It's me, Amy. Are you sick today?" Amy asked, twirling the telephone cord around her fingers. "You weren't at school; Dan made me come in today to cover for you."

"No, I'm not sick. I just had a rough night, you know? I couldn't sleep. Every time I close my eyes, I have nightmares about Anna; I keep dreaming that she is chasing me! I was too tired to attend school, so my mom let me stay home. I told Dan I needed some time away because I'm *stressed out*," she complained. "I think with lack of sleep, I just couldn't face school or work. I should be better tomorrow."

"Sorry, but I didn't know. I'm the one who saw everything, but I don't have any trouble sleeping. Maybe I blocked it all out. I don't know what is wrong with me! The situation doesn't feel right," Amy said, nervously looking at the clock on the wall. "Do you want me to come by tomorrow morning and talk before school? I need you there at school with me. Everyone is whispering about me behind my back, but I can still hear them. It's so rude! Leah wasn't there either, so there was no one to help me stop the gossip. Sometimes I hate this little town." Glancing at the wall clock, Amy noticed it was already time to start her shift. "Look, we will talk tomorrow morning, okay? I have to work now. Thanks for that, by the way! I could have used a bit of a break myself," she added sarcastically before she could stop herself. The telephone receiver rang out noisily when she slammed the receiver into the cradle.

Signing into her register, Amy angrily pressed the lever for the turntable to bring the closed sign towards her to finish opening her lane. There weren't very many big grocery orders to pass through her register. Customer conversations circled the cold weather, whether or not this was the start of winter, and whether there would still be some warm fall days in October. It didn't matter to Amy what the conversation was, she just hoped no one asked about Anna, fearing that she would have to defend herself again. Amy hoped that the police would solve the case soon so she could continue with her boring life, as usual.

Eventually there was a lull of customers, allowing Amy to close her register to clean the staffroom washrooms. Customers also used the washrooms; there were no public washrooms available in the store, resulting in them getting dirty fast. It wasn't Amy's favourite job, but it gave her a break from running the register and a chance to move around a bit. Amy smiled, reminding herself that she preferred to clean the washrooms over cleaning out the freezers.

"Gloria, I am closing to go clean the washrooms," Amy said as she breezed behind the registers on her way to the staff room.

"Make sure you get the men's room. I heard Darryl complaining about it on my last coffee break. He said he's been using the ladies' room to avoid it," she called, watching Amy walk away.

Amy bent down to dig out the cleaning supplies and yellow rubber gloves from the bottom of the closet in the staff room. They hid under a pile of wet shoes and boots, which reminded Amy that she would probably have to mop the floors too. It wouldn't take long. Each washroom had the same setup: toilet, sink, vanity, paper towel dispenser and a small mirror.

Slowly pushing open the men's room door and flipping on the light, Amy turned her head, holding her breath. The odor emanating from the room was unbearable. She kicked the door to open it wide. Reaching her arm around the wall, she turned on the noisy fan. With a couple of long air freshener sprays from the aerosol can outside and inside the room, Amy held her breath while she quickly swept the floor. She swept discarded paper towels, a little plastic bag, and a whole lot of grime and muck, making a pile of rubbish just outside the door. She did the same with the ladies' room before using the dustpan to scoop both piles into the garbage can in the staff room. "Yuck! This job stinks!" Amy shook her head, reminding herself that she had already negotiated a raise for having to do this task. Now, she wondered if she should have held out for more as she sprayed the foam bathroom cleaner all over the sinks and toilets in both bathrooms.

She was sitting on one of the benches in the staff room, waiting for the foam to loosen all of the grime, when Shane rolled the mop and bucket into the room. "Oh, good. I'm going to need the mop after I finish the scrubbing," Amy stood, stretching to her full five-foot-nothing.

"I thought so. I noticed that the bathrooms were pretty gross. I don't think anyone else cleaned them today, so they are extra *rank*," Shane laughed, pushing his wire-rimmed glasses back up his nose.

"Thanks," Amy sighed, taking the mop. "I guess I better get started."

Chapter 10

Beatrice slid a plate of pancakes and a warm canter of syrup onto the table as Amy stumbled into the kitchen. "Thanks," Amy yawned, inhaling the enticing scents of the kitchen. "Are you baking cookies already?"

"Yes, double chocolate chip cookies this time!" she beamed, brushing flour from her apron.

"Isn't it kind of early for that?" Amy tried to run her fingers through her hair, but it was too tangled. "What time did you start this morning?"

Beatrice shook her head, turning the radio volume up to listen to the seven o'clock news. "...all buses for the Glenmere School District are not running. Repeat. All buses are not running! Last night's freezing rain resulted in icy road conditions. Schools are still open if students need a place to be. The police have issued a travel advisory, closing all highways within the area. Road conditions are extremely slippery in town! Glenmere's gravel trucks have started on the main street and will make their way around to all of the emergency routes first. If you must go anywhere, wear a pair of skates and head to work! If you wait long enough, the sun will melt everything by April!" The announcer laughed at his joke just before an ad jingle for Glenmere Hardware Store started advertising rock salt.

"Hmm. That doesn't sound very good. I'm sure Main Street will be driveable, but I'm unsure about the rest of town. We will probably have to wait for the fog to lift so the sun can melt the ice."

"The weather is still gross? I feel like I haven't seen the sun in days!" Amy muttered, slumping in her chair.

"It hasn't been that long," Beatrice turned her mix master back on to remix her cookie dough a little more before forming new dough balls for her empty cookie trays.

Leaving her empty dish in the sink, Amy looked out the window. "I can't even see across the street! I told Sarah I would pick her up on my way to school. She hasn't been feeling so great."

"What's wrong with her? Is she sick?"

"No, more like depressed or something. Sarah doesn't want to answer anybody's questions about Anna, but quite frankly, neither do I! It's a bit weird at school. Some people want the gossip and others avoid me like I might stuff them into a freezer if they get too close," Amy shrugged. "There's not much I can do, but at least if she would come to school, we could show everyone a united front, like we aren't going to take anyone's crap. Maybe I should go to the doctor and get an excuse note, too."

Beatrice inhaled deeply, turning and looking at Amy. "Come here and give me my morning hug." Drawing Amy into her arms and squeezing, she said, "I don't care what the town gossip is saying about you. We trust you! The truth will reveal itself. It always does. The lies people tell can hide the truth for a little while. Someone knows what happened to that poor Labrash girl, but the cold truth of it will have to wait until the police can find them."

Amy nodded, releasing herself from the safe, warm hug, "Sarah needs me. I will tell her not to worry. I better have a shower to get control of my hair unless I want to go out looking a bit punk-rock. I will call you when I get to Sarah's house."

After her shower, Amy pulled her damp brown hair into a high ponytail, securing it with a yellow scrunchie. Hastily applying some blue eyeshadow and pink lipstick, she grabbed her messenger bag and Sony Walkman, returning to the kitchen. "Okay, Granny, I'm going to leave now so I have time to pick up Sarah and talk to her before we go to school. She needs to pick up her homework. If no one is at school we will go back to her house." She pulled on a bomber jacket over her jean jacket for an added layer to protect her from the ice fog and freezing water droplets. "I don't work today so I will be home early to eat cookies!"

Beatrice kissed her granddaughter on the cheek, "Be careful crossing the street; drivers will be all over the place. Cars will not be able to stop."

Amy pressed 'play' on her yellow Sony Walkman to listen to her new Bryan Adams' *Cuts Like a Knife* cassette. She let the music fill her ears and skated her feet over the slippery sidewalks, wondering if ice skates might work on these ice-covered surfaces. She lost her footing a few times, grabbing onto nearby branches and releasing a shower of heavy, wet frost upon her head. The coldness of it sent shivers down her spine with an icy water trail as it melted. She noticed her hair was frozen stiff when she bent over to try to shake away some of the frost from her hair. "Brrr! I better not catch a cold."

Eventually, Amy reached the post office on Main Street. The road crews had not gravelled and salted Main Street like the radio announcer thought they would. The ice and snow continued to impede her walking. Amy's music became static and the play button popped out with an audible clunk and vibration on her hip. Turning to walk through the park beside the post office, Amy thought she heard someone behind her wipe out on the sidewalk, but she couldn't see anyone through the fog. She flipped her cassette over to the other side, pressing the play button. She was sure that she would have a few bruises on her backside by the time she got to Sarah's house too.

Suddenly, Amy felt her feet go out from under her and slip towards the low white branches of the trees overhanging the dark path through the park. Amy's arms flailed in mid-air, failing to grasp anything as she floated momentarily before crashing down onto her back. The world seemed to spin like a record player as Amy tried to take a breath but couldn't seem to inhale.

Amy looked up, confused, becoming vaguely aware of a warm wool blanket placed around her shoulders. People moving about had blurry faces reflecting flashing red and blue lights. The extra lighting glowed in halos, adding colour to the frosty trees in the park. Amy stared at the blurry lights, blinking.

A man leaned closer to her face. Rubbing her arms, he said something to her. Amy focused on the movement of his mouth, trying to understand what he was saying. "... hear me? Amy?... okay?" he asked.

Amy didn't answer, confusion clouding her senses. She couldn't figure out what she was doing. She looked around as voices struggled through her hazy mind.

"We need a coroner. This one is dead."

Amy struggled to focus her eyes, whispering, "I'm not dead." She tried looking around. She found herself sitting on the park bench. "Where am I?" A bright light flashed in and out of her eyes, preventing her from seeing what was happening around her in the park.

"...a concussion... and there's blood," a female voice said through the fog. "I will radio dispatch."

Turning her head, Amy focused on the person beside her on the cold park bench. At first, she thought the person was out of focus, but her brain eventually realized that the image of a man covered in frost was playing tricks on her mind. He was wearing several layers of clothing, unmoving, like a statue on the park bench.

A face leaned closer, eventually coming into focus. It was Officer Doyle, Amy's uncle. "Amy, are you okay? What happened? Why are you in the park?" he shook her slightly.

"I'm going to school. It's slippery," Amy mumbled, trying to clear her vision.

"Yes, it's very slippery. This park isn't on your way to school. What are you doing here? It would be best if you had stayed home. There is no reason to go to school today."

Amy paused, trying to push the fuzzy clouds out of her head, "Sarah. Sarah's house is over there." She pointed to the other end of the park with her mittened hand, almost touching the dead man beside her. She drew her extended hand back slowly. Is this happening again? She could hear the tinny sounds of music emanating from her earphones dangling between her knees.

"We are radioing dispatch to tell your grandparents to meet you at the hospital. It would be best if you had stitches," Randy's voice was quiet, softened with concern. "Who was with you? Who called the ambulance? Do you know? Who else was in the park?"

Amy tried to think of the answer to Randy's questions but only saw brief images: ice, post office, and red and white shoes. "Someone was here."

"Yes, who was here with you?"

"I don't know. I remember red and white shoes. Worn out high-top sneakers," Amy shook her head; realizing that it made her dizzy, she stopped. "I don't know the dead guy."

Clearing his throat to hide a laugh, Officer Doyle straightened himself to a standing position, "I don't imagine that you would."

"I found something on the ground," an officer said, using a pair of forceps to put evidence into a plastic bag.

"Hey, look at me," Randy said, squeezing Amy's shoulder and drawing her attention. "This nice lady is a paramedic. Her name is Ruby. She will help you into the ambulance to take you to the hospital for stitches on the back of your head. You hit your head on the sidewalk near the bench. Your grandparents will pick you up at the hospital. I will telephone them for you. Please don't leave the hospital until they come to drive you home. No school for you for a few days, I think."

Ruby, the paramedic, smiled, putting an arm around Amy, "Okay, we are going to stand up and walk over to the stretcher. It's just a few steps. Come on, you can do it! Get ready, one, two, three." Amy stood up, happy to be held in the stable arms of the paramedic because the world spun and almost sent her crashing back down to the sidewalk. She hoped that it was early enough to keep gossiping bystanders from witnessing what happened in the park and associating her with the death of another person.

Chapter 11

Back at the office, Randy sifted through the files that piled on top of his desk while he was gone. One file had a pink slip attached to it with the message: "Ronaldo Baysic, CI" and a mark in the box next to the words "top priority." According to the paperwork found in the file, Ronaldo Baysic was a homeless man who frequented the Community Church run by Pastor Bill for the Dollar Meal Program and Cold Nights Shelter. Ronaldo also found shelter in the jail cells of this very station, charged with drug possession, being under the influence of illegal substances, and loitering. At some point during his time in the cells, Officer Gerard convinced the man that he would feed him meals in exchange for information regarding drug deals in the town of Glenmere. Randy tried not to seem surprised that Gerard had found himself a confidential informant, but he wondered why his staff sergeant had put this file on the desk of one of his rookie officers. Not that Randy was complaining; the case promised to be more interesting than the cold case files, neighbour disputes, lost pets, traffic violations and petty theft that he usually handled.

He picked up the photo of the informant to study it, thinking about what he would have to do for this case. The file had mugshots and rap sheets going back two years before his enlistment as an informant. There were no arrests after Baysic's enlistment. Randy frowned, noticing the file was missing relevant information like next of kin, known associations and what he reported to the police. As Randy filed through the paperwork, the realization of who this was dawned on him: Ronaldo Baysic is the name of the frozen popsicle stick on the park bench. "Shit!" Randy realized that he had just been given the case file so that he could track down and inform the Baysic family of the man's death. So much for the excitement of bringing down a drug dealer in Glenmere with the town's only informant dead. All hope of taking down a drug dealing operation disappeared. Randy leaned back in his chair, closing his eyes and sighing.

"Is there something you need help with?" Officer Trussell asked, craning his neck to look over the cubicle divider.

Randy absently shook his head, sitting upright and leafing through his paperwork. "No. I got it." The informant was dead. Randy was sure the autopsy would come back with cause of death due to a drug overdose. "Open and shut case. It isn't anything I can't manage on my own. I just have to track down the next of kin on this case file."

Officers Gerard and Hanson strolled into the roll call room. Jeffrey Hanson sat at his desk to check his pink message slips as Micheal Gerard stopped to ask questions to a few other police officers in the room before stopping to talk to Randy. "Tell me more about the earring you collected, Doyle." He flipped open his little coil notebook, pondering what he had written. "Is this the earring?"

"Yup, that looks like the one I wrote about on the pink slip. I haven't written the report yet; I wanted to talk to you about it first."

"I want you to start talking about who gave it to you and when they gave it to you."

"Sure. Amy Young found it on Saturday morning at the Family Grocers on the floor near the victim. She pocketed it and forgot to produce it during her interview. When she was cleaning the aisle freezer, she remembered it was in her pocket and brought it in after her work shift ended. You and Jeffrey Hanson were out so I collected it for you. It probably belongs to the deceased, Anna Labrash. Did you find the match in the list of effects from the coroner?"

"No, but we will keep looking." Officer Gerard said, pausing to clear his throat. "It might turn up at the primary scene of the crime once we find out where the victim was killed. We are waiting for blood reports to determine the cause of death. The Medical Examiner says there are no signs of strangulation or foul play, except where the body was found. Someone put the girl in the icebox. The M.E. said the time of death is between seven-thirty Friday evening and three in the morning," Gerard read off his notes, flipping through the pages.

"That's a big window of time."

"Unfortunately, the cold temperature of the freezer lowered the body temperature too quickly to get a smaller window for the time of death. Did Miss Young mention anything about the sister, Leah Labrash? Did she see or talk to her?"

Randy frowned, turning in his chair to face Gerard directly. "No, she didn't say anything about the victim's sister, but she did say she plans to express her condolences to the family. Why? What did the sister say?"

"We have not been able to locate Leah Labrash. I find it strange that the family doesn't seem to know where she is, or they do and they aren't telling. It is definitely suspicious. We need some clarity on this case which I think only the sister can give us. She has to know something we don't know," Gerard said, shaking his head. "Can you go to the jewelry store to check whether this earring was recently purchased there or not? I checked with the family. They can't verify if the earring belongs to the victim."

"It could be the victim's or the killer's earring," Officer Trussell said. "There is blood evidence on it. I swabbed it for testing, hoping we can find a blood match."

Officer Gerard ignored Trussell's comment, waiting for Randy's answer. Pressing his lips together, Randy's thoughts seemed to go to all kinds of possibilities, "Do you want me to follow the earring to find a lead? I thought you didn't want me working this case."

"I don't have time to track down who this earring belongs to. Hanson and I are still talking to witnesses, family and friends to try to narrow down the timeline. I want you to find the match to this earring and then I will take it from there. Be on the lookout for the sister while you are poking around town. Tell me immediately if you find either one," Gerard folded his notebook closed, shoving it back into his breast pocket with his pencil.

"I could do that, but I also have to talk to Hank Vandercamp at the impound lot. I got a message saying he found something in a vehicle and needed an officer to check out. Gladys' note doesn't say what, but it might be related to the drug ring Hanson was working on before you gave me the case. Can I have the earring or a photo of it to take to the jewellers?"

Gerrard placed the evidence bag with the gold and diamond earring into Randy's palm. Randy turned it over in his hands, studying the neatly rewritten label on the bag and frowning. The writing on the evidence bag was not his. He would have to slow down and write more clearly the next time he wrote the description on an evidence bag. He didn't need someone wasting time by redoing his work. "Take it to the evidence locker, Doyle. Use the Polaroid on the desk to take a photo. Keep the photo on you at all times until you find its match. Ask Hanson or Trussell if you need help. They could both be helpful to you. Do you think you can manage?"

The Ice Box

"I think I can manage this small task." Pushing himself out of his plastic desk chair, Randy took the evidence bag to the evidence room, frustrated, thinking that Officer Gerard didn't trust him to do this small task without error. He scolded himself for not following all procedures when Amy brought it to him. He should have taken his time documenting the earring properly.

Locating the instant Polaroid camera sitting on a black velvet cloth and turning it on, Randy waited for it to come to full charge. As the camera powered up with a high-pitched buzz, he slid the earring out of the bag onto the black velvet. Looking through the viewfinder, he moved back and forth until he decided on the right angle before pressing the capture button.

When the photo paper shot out of the bottom of the camera, Randy waited patiently until the image was revealed before deciding that it was not clear enough for his purposes. He repeated the process until he was satisfied that two pictures were good enough to see clearly. Tossing the blurry photos immediately into the trash, Randy filed and locked the earring with one photo in the evidence locker. He tucked the other photo into his breast pocket as he walked back to his desk.

Chapter 12

Slowly pulling his police cruiser to a stop in front of the office of Hank Vandercamp's impound lot, Randy looked up and down the quiet street. The small structure served its purpose for the little town of Glenmere. Randy navigated the icy sidewalk, wondering why the owner didn't sprinkle some salt. He entered the office and found Hank eating a piece of pie behind the desk. Coveting the flaky crust with dark purple filling with interest, Randy decided to stop at Frankie's diner for pie later. "Good afternoon, Hank. I hope I'm not interrupting your lunch. I got your message that you wanted an officer to look at one of the vehicles on your lot. I'm Officer Doyle with the Glenmere Police. What is the problem?"

Hank wiped his mouth with his hand and said, "Yeah, I impounded a 1971 gold Lincoln Continental. The car's plates expired six months ago and were registered to Mrs. Edith Marshall. I called her and she told me that she transferred the ownership to her nephew. Mrs. Marshall said her nephew forgot to bring the paperwork into SGI to renew the registration."

"This doesn't sound like something that requires police help. Is there more to this story? Your message said that there was something you wanted me to see." Randy sighed, feeling like this was another big waste of his time when he could be out looking for the match to the gold earring.

"I asked Edith if I could have the keys to move the Lincoln to the back lot so it would be out of my way. After she gave me the keys, I moved it. There was a gas leak or something because when I moved it, I couldn't help but notice the strong smell. I opened the trunk to see if I knocked over a gas can when I moved it. After what I saw, I called the police station, leaving a message to have someone come out to look." Hank scooped the last of his pie into his mouth before he grabbed the keys from a drawer in his desk. "Just follow me."

Randy followed Hank across the icy impound lot to the back corner where the gold Lincoln was parked. One light cover was open and the other one closed. The front bumper was bent on the driver's side as if the driver had run into something. "Who is Edith's nephew? It doesn't look like he has been caring for her car."

"She didn't say his name, but let me know that it would probably be several days or weeks before he would pay the towing and impound fees to get it back.

That's why I asked her for a spare set of keys to move it out of my way," Hank explained, shrugging, like storing a vehicle until someone could pay was normal.

"Looks like he needs new tires, too. I doubt these bald tires would be useful after the freezing rain and ice fog we have been having lately." Randy knelt, inspecting the front tire. He inhaled the smell of gas and oil, wondering if this car was road-worthy. Randy studied the car's body, imagining the blue plume of a noisy engine roaring down the streets of Glenmere and knowing he had seen this car driving around town last week. "Where was the car towed from?"

"I got a call from Marcel, the pharmacist at the drugstore. He says this car keeps showing up behind his store where the pharmacist and staff park their vehicles. I towed it from there on Thursday."

"Did he mention if he knew who kept parking it there?" Randy questioned.

"No. I didn't ask. Marcel wanted it towed. I towed it," Hank jingled the keys, fitting them into the door lock. "Have a look inside. I will open the trunk for you, too."

Randy leaned in to look around the front seats. Covering his nose, he tried to block the aroma of stale cigarette smoke mixed with discarded food containers assaulting his nostrils. He noticed the glove compartment was open, candy wrappers and crumbled pieces of paper falling out. Randy carefully unwrinkled a piece of paper with the drugstore logo on the top. It was a note from the pharmacy owner in red scrawl threatening to have the car towed if the owner parked behind his store again. The story Hank has been telling him so far seems to check out. Nothing interesting. Randy flipped the glove box door to close it, but the broken latch let the door bounce open.

Leaving the car door open, he walked around to the trunk to look inside. The interior was littered with discarded clothing, empty bags of chips, candy bar wrappers and loose twenty-dollar bills. Randy leaned in to have a closer look. He laid his eyes on little baggies with granular crystals. Randy knew the candy bars would give drug addicts the sugar craving they needed. Pulling a pen out of his pocket, Randy moved a shirt to look underneath it. Prescription pill bottles rolled out from under the shirt: Percocet, Contin, Valium and a few others Randy didn't recognize. The bottles had Edith Marshall's name on them. Randy fished around with his pen to see what else he could find in the trunk. Besides a few white pills and traces of white powder lying on the carpet, Randy found little baggies with white capsules in them. One thing was for sure: he was confident that the driver of this car was using and possibly dealing drugs. *Finally, something a little interesting,* Randy thought, smiling to himself. "Hank, I'm going to take some evidence and fingerprints. Can you refuse to release this vehicle until I'm through with it? I am opening a full investigation and will have it towed to the police impound."

"Whatever you want. It makes no difference to me. I can file paperwork with the police to collect my fees from Mrs. Marshall if she refuses to pay me."

"I'm just going to radio in and grab a few evidence bags and my fingerprint kit. I would appreciate it if you wouldn't mind giving me a photocopy of your report. I will be out here working for a bit, but I don't think I will be on your lot for more than an hour. I guess it will depend on how many prints I can lift." Randy looked down at Hank's hands, gesturing at his work gloves. He asked, "Did you wear gloves when you drove this car?"

"Um, yes; I usually don't bother, but with this weather I wear gloves because my hands get so achy and stiff." Hank looked down, flexing his hands inside his work gloves. "I guess wearing gloves helped lessen your work, eh? You won't lift any of my prints."

Randy smiled, "Just one less fingerprint to identify."

It took Randy a little longer than expected to fingerprint the car, carefully dusting the black powder around the trunk lid, door handles and steering wheel. It was lucky for him that this car had not been cleaned in a while because there were unmistakable fingerprints almost everywhere. There were several different prints in the backseat, but Randy wasn't hopeful that he would match them to anyone other than the nephew who reportedly drove the vehicle. He bagged prescription bottles, loose white pills, money and packets of drugs, using block lettering to neatly label everything with its description and the car's year, make and model.

"Thanks, Hank! I will let the office know they should request the car from you. If someone comes before it can be processed, request proof of insurance and registration to be able to drive it off your lot. Get a photocopy of the driver's licence while you are at it, too." Randy opened his trunk, putting his bagged evidence and collecting kit inside.

"I always take a photocopy of the driver's licence. It saves me trouble later on if there's going to be any," Hank replied, waving and turning back into the little office of the impound lot.

Slowly driving his police cruiser down the back alleyway of the stores on Main Street, Randy looked at the tight parking spots for each business. The real estate office, drugstore, jewelry store and radio station had marked signage designated for staff parking behind their buildings. The Family Grocers designated their small alley space into two areas, one as an unloading zone for receiving freight and the other to house a commercial red dumpster. *No parking. Where did the grocery store staff park?* Randy wondered, checking his rearview mirror.

Satisfied that everything in the back alley appeared in order, Randy drove around to the front of the pharmacy building, angle parking in the nearest space available. The chimes above the door gaily jingled as he entered the drugstore. The aromatic scents of perfumes and soaps tickled Randy's nose as he walked to the pharmacy counter at the back of the store and waited, holding his evidence bags containing the pills, while the petite man spoke to one of the customers with a slight French accent.

"How can I help you today, officer?" the pharmacist asked, pulling a red pen from his white lab coat pocket.

"I am Officer Randy Doyle. Are you the store's pharmacist?"

"Yes, I'm Marcel Janvier. How can I help you today?" He clicked the end of his pen, preparing to write on a pad of white paper on the counter. Randy noticed the pad had the pharmacy logo emblazoned across the top, matching the wrinkled note he found in the gold Lincoln's glove box.

"I am investigating the gold Lincoln Continental towed from behind your store for possible drug trafficking. What can you tell me about these pills?" Randy asked, laying the evidence bag with Edith Marshall's prescriptions on the counter. "They were among the assortment of drugs found in the vehicle."

Marcel inspected the pill bottles, reading the labels. "Interesting. Mrs. Marshall was just in yesterday to replace her prescriptions. She needed an early renewal; she said she lost them when she went out of town to visit her sister. I guess she misplaced them."

Randy eyed the white paper pad on the counter, wishing he had a notebook. "Is it unusual for her to have to replace her prescriptions?" When the pharmacist turned away to get Edith's prescription record, Randy quickly tore several pages off of the pad of paper, swearing to himself for not bringing notebook paper for himself. Pulling a pen out of his pocket, he began his notes with the pharmacist's name.

"She's had a few prescriptions refilled early, but yesterday was the first time she requested all of them before she would have needed them," Marcel Janvier looked up from his file. "All of her medications were scripts from her doctor. That's all I can tell you."

"Can you identify these pills?" Randy placed his evidence bag containing a loose assortment of white and yellow pills on the counter.

Marcel pulled a magnifying glass out of his pocket to inspect the pills. "The yellow pills are Codeine Contin 100 mg and the white ones... hmmm." He flipped the bag over to see the other side of the pills. "The white ones are unmarked, most likely homemade."

Randy frantically scribbled the information down on his notepaper. "What makes you think that it's homemade?"

"It's slightly irregular with a diamond stamp on one side. That is not a manufactured drug. The person who made the pills used a mould to press the powder into it. The diamond is probably used to trademark it. It could be anything really: cocaine, fentanyl or anything that could be crushed and mixed in to form this pill."

"Like heroin?"

"Heroin is a brown powder, but it could be a component of these pills. You won't know until you send it to the lab for chemical testing," Marcel pushed the evidence bags toward the end of the counter for Randy to take away.

Picking up the bags, Randy asked, "Did you ever see the person parking in your staff parking area out back?"

"No, but I left notes under the wiper blade asking them not to park there. It happened frequently in the summer, but this last month it was mostly on the weekends. I thought the person had found somewhere else to park until it started reappearing. I needed my parking space, so I had it towed. Hopefully, I won't find it there again."

Turning to leave, Randy stopped when he spotted the jewelry rack at the end of one of the product aisles. "One more question, if you please," Randy fished the photo of the gold earring out of his pocket, sliding it across the counter toward Marcel. "Do you sell these earrings in your store?"

Marcel looked carefully at the photo. "Just one moment." He took the picture over to his assistant, who shook her head. "No, officer, I'm sorry. We do not carry anything like this."

"Thank you for the information. If you think of anything else about these pills or the gold car, contact me at the police station." Randy left the drugstore with unanswered questions, but felt he was onto something big. He was closing his trunk when he eyed the jewelry store between the drugstore and the radio station.

Next to the open sign for the jewelry store, Randy read a sign that said, *Low monthly payments on all layaway plans.* An electronic bell chimed twice as Randy entered the store and passed the sensor. A young woman cleaning the glass displays stopped what she was doing when he entered.

"Good afternoon, officer," she smiled, straightening one of the thick gold chains around her neck. "Are you looking for something for your wife? Depending on what you wanted, you could have something paid for by Valentine's Day on a layaway plan."

"I am looking for a particular pair of earrings," he pulled the photo out of his pocket, placing it on the glass in front of her. "Do you recognize this earring?" Randy unfolded the papers he had taken from the pharmacy to add to his notes.

"Yes, we do have similar earrings in stock. They range from forty-nine to seventy-nine dollars, depending on the hoop size and the diamond," she walked around to a display cabinet, pointing to the earrings.

Officer Doyle joined her beside the display case, attempting to compare the photo to each pair of earrings, but all the jewelry sparkled and glistened without looking unique to him. "Do you see what I am trying to find?"

"Right there. Are those the ones you mean? They are sixty-nine plus tax. Shall I ring them up for you, or do you want to match that purchase to a gold chain?"

Realizing he'd been unclear about his intentions, Randy clarified, "No, this has to do with a police investigation. I'm not here to make a purchase. Do you have a record of anyone who may have bought earrings like those recently, say, in the past couple of months?"

Her smile faltered slightly, knowing there wouldn't be a sale. "I'm sorry, but we only keep records of the layaway plans. Usually, I don't allow small items like these to be placed on layaway. When customers want to buy watches, rings and other more expensive items,

I will offer the layaway plan to help them to afford these beautiful things. If that is all, I have a lot of glass to clean."

Feeling like the conversation was over, Randy thanked her for her time and left the store with the information she provided him. The icy wind ruffled his hair, stealing away one of the loose pages that Randy was using to write his notes. He chased after it, stomping his boot down on top of the errant paper. Randy's wet boot print blurred some of the ink on the paper. "I really got to go to Zellers and get some little notebooks and pencils," he grumbled, deciding it was time to bring his evidence to the station and start his report.

Chapter 13

Amy briskly walked through the main doors of the Family Grocers, turning into the smoky staff room and noticing a weird chemical smell. It didn't take long to recognize that the scent was coming from a Jiffy permanent marker. Greg was sitting on the side bench concentrating on colouring his old sneakers with a black permanent marker. She tried not to shake her head, knowing it would make her dizzy. The last thing Amy needed was people in town gossiping about her fainting at work. Amy could only imagine what people must be thinking since she'd found another body. *Well, it's more like she happened to be sitting on the same bench as a dead guy when the police and ambulance arrived.* Amy frowned, thinking, *if only I could find out how I ended up on the park bench in the first place.*

Amy hung up her jacket in the closet, straightening her uniform vest. She moved toward the chairs across the staff room from Greg to wait for her shift to begin, but the permanent marker smell made her head hurt and her stomach roll. Amy straightened her vest, deciding to leave the staff room to start her shift early.

"What are you doing back at work?" Greg sneered, looking up from his task.

Crossing her arms, Amy sat down, "What's it to you?"

"I figured you would have quit your job in this hell hole and never looked back."

"I don't know what difference it makes to you, but I like my job. Dan is a good boss. I have never had any problems with him."

"Yes, but with everything that has happened, I'd think you would have left this behind you," he motioned with his black marker-stained fingers, pointing around the staff room. "I wouldn't be coming in here if I were you," Greg said, tossing the spent black marker into the large garbage bin. "If I kept getting associated with crime scenes, I would move away from this dinky little town and hit the big city as fast as possible. No one wants you here!"

"I don't know what you are trying to say, but just to be clear: I had nothing to do with Anna's death. I only found her!" Amy said, her voice straining against the fumes and smoke in the staffroom. Amy felt the wet cuffs on the polyester fabric of the uniform pants rub damp coldness against her bare ankles as she crossed her legs.

"How dare you suggest that I move away! What business is it of yours anyway?"

"I don't care what you do, princess," his purple hair fell over his eyes, making him flip it out of his way. "I just know I wouldn't stay here if I were you. This town is too dangerous for you! You will get yourself killed."

Amy didn't know what to retort to satisfy Greg's obnoxious comments, realizing he didn't usually bother to talk to her. *What is his problem, anyway?* Amy glanced at the staff washroom doors, wondering if she would have to clean them tonight. She didn't feel up to the extra task today. Her head was throbbing, but she didn't know what to blame: her mild concussion, the argument with Greg, or the fumes in the staffroom.

"By the way, you don't need to clean the bathrooms tonight. They are clean," pushing himself up off the bench, Greg strolled out of the room.

Chapter 14

Friday, September 27, 1985

The auctioneer's voice echoed out of the open overhead doors of the three-bay shop and over the heads of the people pushing into the cramped space. Pulling her hood strings tighter and making her way against the crowd of people, Amy burst out into the cold, biting sting of the northern wind, running across the yard and into the warmth of the farmhouse.

Slamming the door to dull the auction sounds, Amy scanned the room until she located a staticky radio squawking with the auctioneer's voice on the kitchen counter on the far side of the room. Inhaling a deep breath and noticing the room was filled with odours of burnt coffee, Amy frowned. She realized that her childhood home was no longer a place where she could escape the realities of the outside world. Amy eyed the furniture from all over the farmhouse, identified with lot number tags, pushed up against the perimeter of the spacious kitchen. It all looked strangely out of place: the dressing table from her grandmother's bedroom, the armoire from the attic, the sewing desk from the back bedroom, and the floor lamp from the family room. Pushing herself away from the door, Amy ran her fingertips along the large oak table as she walked around it, bumping into a large plastic garbage bin filled with Styrofoam cups, dirty napkins, auction flyers, and used coffee grounds. Two women stood over the telephone mounted on the kitchen wall in the corner. One woman was clicking the receiver, frowning and trying to get whoever was on the party line to get off so she could make a call. Walking through the living room, Amy noticed several people standing in line to use the only toilet in the house. Some people were sitting on the furniture pushed against the walls, bragging about their low winning bids and arguing whether the outbid items were worth the price.

Shaking her head in disgust and turning towards the hallway, Amy waited for a man and a woman to exit. She paused, thinking about her old bedroom, now emptied of personal possessions and filled with random furniture and boxed lots for the auction. Amy fished out a key from her pocket, reading the "private access" sign taped to the bedroom door that had belonged to her grandma Dorothy. The doorknob gave her some trouble, as it often did, but with a bit of jiggling the door popped open. Although Amy and the Petersens had removed her grandmother's possessions from this room, her presence was still strong. Amy closed her eyes, deeply inhaling the faint scent of her grandma Dorothy's lilac perfume. Shaking her head, Amy mused about how living here with her grandmother simultaneously seemed so long ago and like yesterday.

Closing the door, Amy approached one of the folding chairs set up for the family. During the estate auction, this room provided a private retreat to escape overwhelming and stressful emotions. Amy, the only living relative connected to this estate, considered this room her sanctuary. Her paternal grandfather, George Petersen, was somewhere around the farm today overseeing the auction, but Amy wasn't sure whereabouts. She last saw a glimpse of her grandpa about an hour ago, only to lose him again in the crowd.

Crying softly, Amy sat quietly in one of the folding chairs that faced the large window, reliving memories as they washed over her. Her grandma, Dorothy, told her that this bedroom was once the kitchen, but became the main bedroom when a contractor made the house larger to accommodate the growing family. As she stared out the window, Amy's eyes blurred, watching the people crowding in front of the open shop doors like ants on an anthill. The wind sent gusts of snow swirling across the yard, hitting against the window in icy bursts. Amy shivered, rubbing her hands on her pants for warmth.

She sat for a while, unmoving, before she noticed that someone had sat down in the chair beside her. Blinking, she turned her head slightly to see who it was. His long legs were sprawled out in front of him, one arm casually draping over the empty chair on the other side of him. "What are you doing here?" Amy reached up, pulling on a loose strand of her brown hair.

"I heard about the auction on the radio and decided to see what it would be like in person," Shane said, pushing up his glasses with his shoulder. "It's a public auction."

"Don't be a moron," Amy scolded, rolling her eyes. "I meant in this room. It is for family only."

Shrugging and dismissing her comment, Shane replied, "Mr. Petersen told me where to look for you. I thought you could use a friend."

"I have friends," she said, looking down at her fingernails.

"Yeah, I didn't see Sarah anywhere. Where is she? I don't see her here sitting next to you."

"Um, she's busy with... Matt," Amy whispered. It had been a while since she had talked to Sarah; she saw her best friend less frequently now that Sarah and Matt were dating. Anytime she tried to speak to her, she only got the latest on Sarah's boyfriend.

"Well, I'm here. We can pretend to be friends," he said, nudging her arm with his elbow. "Are you doing okay?"

Looking out the window, Amy quietly responded, "It feels like some kind of dream. I lived in this house with Grandma from when I was five until April when my world took a weird turn. My answers would be much different if you had asked me how I was doing in March. Now, I feel like that was a dream and this nightmare is my reality." Amy wiped the end of her nose with a well-used tissue, sniffing.

Shane shifted in his seat, trying to think of something to say. "How long is the auction?" he asked.

"I don't know. The auctioneer started with the tractors and items in the barn and outbuildings. I think they were doing the shop when I came inside. That is still in progress, but I could be wrong. The auctioneer will call for bids on the sections of land surrounding the farmyard from that location. The auctioneers will use a reserved minimum bid for the farmhouse. The real estate guy will take over the sale if the bids don't meet the minimum price. I want to leave before the auctioneers move on to the furniture," Amy sniffed, wiping a tear away. "I can't bear it."

"Are you crying?" asked Shane, shifting uncomfortably in his seat.

"No, I'm all done crying."

"You're done?"

"I'm done. I'm not a little kid," Amy announced, angrily throwing the wet tissue at the window. "I'm also done with feeling sorry for myself because of what others have done! I won't let people think they can bully me and take advantage. I'm just... done!"

"Don't you want to keep anything? Or are you going to buy new stuff?" he asked.

Amy laughed, "No, I can't buy new stuff. I have to pay the bills on this place and the house next to us in town. Renting the house in town will help pay for what needs repairing, but I have to sell the farmhouse to pay the back taxes and penalties. It will be tough because we aren't sure if anyone will buy it with its recent history."

Shane cleared his throat, "Um, didn't you inherit a whole pile of money this auction will add to?"

Shocked, Amy turned wide-eyed, unable to find her words. "What are you talking about?"

"What do you mean? You inherited all of your grandma's money and two houses!"

Realizing very few people know about the particulars of Dorothy Young's will, Amy knew that whatever Shane was talking about was from town gossip. "First of all, I don't know what business it is of yours or the whole town's, but I inherited a neglected house that needed many repairs and a new furnace, with outstanding taxes and utilities. And, yes, I inherited this property, too, which hadn't had any of the taxes or utilities paid since my grandmother passed. Her old lawyer retired and sold his practice, leaving Mr. Tracker to handle things, and he didn't!"

"Whoa! Calm down!" Shane motioned, raising both of his hands in surrender.

"Don't tell me to calm down!" Amy argued, trying to keep her voice controlled. She no longer wondered why deal-seekers were complaining about high bids. "The money my grandma had in the bank would have covered everything, but some guy impersonating my uncle made a large withdrawal. No one can get it back! We hired accountants and lawyers. It's gone! As for the rest of it, I don't get it until I'm an adult. So, no, I'm not rich." She sat upright in her chair, crossing her arms in front of her.

"If you are looking for a rich friend, you are looking in the wrong place."

Inhaling deeply, Shane said, "I didn't come here looking for money. I'm sorry you have gone through that; I'm really here to see what you need. A friend? A piece of pie? A punching bag?"

Amy kicked the floor with her toe, smiling. "Did you say pie? I didn't see any pie."

"I didn't either, but I'm always hungry," Shane smiled, pulling his car keys out of his plaid coat pocket, jingling them. "What do you want? Do you want to stay here or leave?"

Nodding, Amy replied, "Yes, let's get out of here. It's too depressing. I should have stayed home." Shane stood up to his impressive six feet in height. Frowning and swallowing her pride, Amy looked up and said, "I'm sorry for yelling. I'll have to remember that town gossip is why everyone is being so weird lately."

"What do you mean by weird?" Shane said, following Amy out of the room.

"Some people who normally never talk to me have been extra nice lately," Amy replied, fishing the key out of her jeans pocket. "Even Greg from the Family Grocers started a conversation with me the other day. He asked if I was quitting my job. The whole conversation was, well, weird and creepy."

"I wouldn't worry about him. Greg is a bit weird and creepy." Shane joked, watching Amy lock the bedroom door and pull up her hood. "I recommend you stay away from him."

The Ice Box

Amy led the way to the front door, zipping up her jacket, and asked, "Where are you parked?"

Grimacing, Shane replied, "Out on the road, a few cars to the left of the start to the driveway."

The wind was still gusting, cold snowflakes whipping around Amy's face as she and Shane raced across the yard and away from the crowd. Sheltered from the chilly breeze by the large pine trees lining the driveway, Amy slowed, knowing the wind would bite her cheeks at the driveway's opening. Bracing for the chilling blast, Amy asked, "Where is it?"

"Um, about fifty cars this way," Shane said, leading Amy to the left onto the road.

"Did you say fifty or fifteen? Maybe we should have just taken my grandma's car. Grandpa parked her Oldsmobile beside the farmhouse," Amy said, tightening the strings of her hood, crossing her arms and hugging her body for warmth. She shivered and her teeth started to chatter. Her eyes watered, blurring her vision as she followed behind Shane's tall silhouette. The gravel road was frozen and rutted, making walking in one of the tire tracks easier with her high-top sneakers. Ice formed where water had pooled when it rained a few days ago, crackling under her feet and making some areas hard to navigate. Amy kept her head down, watching where she stepped until she ran into what felt like a wall. "*Ooof,*" she craned her head back, realizing she had run into Shane. He stood facing her, reaching out to steady her. "Sorry, Shane. Are we there yet?"

"Yes, this is it," Shane proudly announced, opening the driver's door of his 1977 two-tone brown Chevrolet Chevette and climbing in. "Get in!"

Amy moved around the back of the hatchback, steadying herself on the ice-covered ruts by holding on to the vehicle until she could open the door. The door was much lighter than the Buick's doors and swung open quickly... too quickly. The howling wind pulled the door handle out of her cold, numb fingers, flinging the door wide. She had to use both hands to close the door against the wind. Letting out a deep breath, she slammed the door shut. "That's better."

Shane fiddled with his cassette tapes, looking for music to put into his tape deck. "What do you want to listen to? I've got Micheal Jackson, Aerosmith, Led Zeppelin, and a mixed tape."

Amy shook her head. "I don't know. Whatever, maybe the mixed tape."

Shoving the tape into the stereo, Shane steered the Chevette into the tire ruts of the gravel road as Aerosmith blasted from the rear speakers. The compact car bounced along on its thirteen-inch tires until they reached the highway pavement. The town of Glenmere was thirty-five kilometres to the East. As the heater finally started to blow warm air, Amy directed the air vents towards her face, holding her icy hands over the warmth. Her fingers felt stiff as she flexed them. "Can we make a stop at the Labrash's? I want to see how Leah is doing."

Turning down the music, Shane looked at Amy, "What?"

The Ice Box

"Can we stop at Labrash's to see how Leah is doing? She hasn't been around Frankie's since we found Anna. I want to check on her and express my condolences."

"Do you know where she lives? I'm not sure."

Amy scanned the intersections, reading the green rural route signs as they passed, "I think it's two more grid roads up on the left side of the highway. It's a grey home not far from the intersection."

"Okay, I know which one you mean. I went to a gravel pit party a few weeks ago in the area."

Raising her eyebrow, Amy responded with sarcasm, "Oh? A gravel pit party? What did you do there?"

Shane smiled and ignored her question, turning onto the gravel road, pulling into Labrash's yard and up to their two-story grey house. A few cats peeked out from under the wooden front steps, cautiously assessing them. Amy could hear meowing as she stepped up the stairs to knock on the door. She leaned forward, listening to children's voices on the other side. Turning to Shane standing at the bottom of the stairs, she whispered, "I can hear talking." A ten-year-old girl looking like a younger version of Anna and Leah opened the door. Amy smiled with relief, thinking this was the right place. "Is Leah here?"

The girl shook her head, pushing her black hair away from her face. "No." Nervously, the girl played with the door knob.

Trying to get more information, Amy continued, "Do you know where she is?" The girl shook her head, looking curiously past Amy at Shane.

"I'm Amy Young. I work with Leah at Frankie's. Do you know when she will be back?" Amy asked. The girl shrugged her tiny shoulders, releasing the doorknob.

Another child with the exact family resemblance came to the door, opening it wide. He looked to be a bit older than the girl. Pushing the dark-haired girl behind, he scolded, "We aren't supposed to talk to anyone." Frowning at Amy, he firmly shut the door. Amy turned, opening her mouth to say something, but not knowing what to say, closed it again.

Shane smiled, returning to his car, "I guess we go for pie now, maybe a burger."

Amy followed him, climbing into the passenger seat, "What do you suppose that means? Why can't they tell me where Leah is?"

"You are a stranger to them. The whole 'don't talk to strangers' thing. Have you heard the commercials? You can ask a waitress at the diner if they have seen Leah. Someone must know where she is."

Amy didn't know what to think. *Where would Leah be if she wasn't at home or work?* Amy tried to remember when Leah was last seen at school or around town; had she been seen since she and Shane found Anna's body in the freezer? She couldn't recall seeing her, but then again, Amy missed a few days at school after she slipped on the sidewalk and hit her head in the park. Amy's eyes widened, speculating that Leah must be in hiding. *Why? Who was she hiding from? Where could she be?*

Chapter 15

Smoothing out one of the note pages on his desk, Randy tried to decipher his handwriting to transfer the information he collected into the case files. What he thought would be a simple illegal park and tow ended up providing Randy with a possible drug traffic violation or illicit drug use case; he wasn't sure which one. Randy noted the known particulars: the impound lot call, the vehicle description, the prescription pill bottles, capsules, white powder and the baggies of pills. Balling the papers from his note-taking at the impound lot, he aimed and tossed each one in the air at the waste basket. The first paper ball landed on the floor near the basket; the second ball hit his target. "Yes! Two points!" Randy leaned back into his office chair, stretching his back. Officer Trussell looked up from his desk across the short barrier, smiling at Randy's playfulness.

Officer Hanson leaned over and picked up a crumpled note, smoothing it out. "Do you need notes on each cat you rescue from a tree? What's this? A parking violation? Did a neighbour get mad at someone for parking on the public street in front of their house? That happens in Glenmere."

"No, it isn't. The boring park and tow turned into a confiscation of drugs and money from the trunk of the towed vehicle. I'm checking into it. I think it has to do with the drug trafficking you were investigating with your informant," Randy replied, grinning with excitement.

Hanson leaned over, pushing little notes around on Randy's workstation, "Maybe you should get yourself a notebook like Gerard so you can write neater. How do you even read this?" picking up a few loose notes, Officer Hanson mocked, "Look, this one has mud on it! Water makes the ink run; use a pencil."

"I dropped these pages in front of the pharmacy," Randy grumbled, reaching for the paper. Randy tried to snatch the note from Hanson but only got away with half of the page, "Damn, look at what you made me do now."

"Yes, I noticed that the note pages had the pharmacy log across the top. Did you go there to steal paper, or were you there for something else?"

"I was there looking into some prescription pill bottles found in the impounded car. I wanted to prove that the owner of the car or her nephew is selling prescription drugs."

"...and?"

"Nothing I can say for certain. The pharmacist says everything is legit."

"Where are the pill bottles?" Officer Hanson said, lifting a few files on Randy's disorganized desk and accidentally letting a few pages fall to the floor. Officer Trussell looked up briefly at Hanson's comments, shaking his head.

"I already logged them into the evidence locker," Randy smiled, proud of himself for remembering to do that as soon as he arrived at the station. He didn't want to misplace evidence, just in case this led to a drug arrest.

"Well, I wouldn't get yourself all worked up about it. I'm sure it's nothing worth your time. You can go back to helping old ladies walk across the street and rescuing cats stuck in trees until Gerard needs you for more important things," Hanson said, crumpling up the notepaper in his hand and tossing it into the wastebasket like he was doing a jump shot on a basketball court. "Two points! I still got it."

Shaking his head, Randy leaned over his file folder to re-read what he had written. "Licence plate number?" he mumbled, looking for the paper with the vehicle description. Randy still had to run the plate to verify the vehicle's owner. He searched under the files piled at his desk but couldn't find what he was looking for. "Where is it?"

Pushing his chair back and looking under his desk, he retrieved a few balled up pieces of paper. Opening each sheet, he still didn't find the page he needed. He walked over to the waste basket and sorted the papers, finally finding what he sought. Hanson had balled up the page Randy used to record the vehicle description and licence plate with the other piece of torn paper. Randy fumed, picking up the pages and notes that had fallen to the floor. "First, Hanson teases me about fluff cases, and then he throws away my notes! Is he trying to make me look incompetent?"

"Don't let Hanson get to you. He is just trying to be a big shot in hopes of becoming a detective one day. Do what you must to keep your job, and don't worry about promotions; they will come when they come," Officer Trussell smirked, handing Randy more fallen sheets. "Ignore over-achieving assholes like Hanson. He's just trying to be the heavyweight who gets all of the promotions. I can help you whenever you want, but I prefer not to do any of your paperwork. Try to keep yourself more organized; it does make things easier. You know I am all for making things easier."

Rolling his eyes, Randy collected his file and moved to the shared telephone at a desk on the other side of the room. He needed to verify when the impound lot received the tow request. Dialling the telephone number, Randy waited for someone to answer the call. "Yes, hello, Hank. It's Officer Doyle, calling to verify information on the seventy's gold Lincoln. When did you say you towed the old gold car to the impound lot?"

"Let me check. Hang on," Hank said. Randy listened to the muffled sound of shuffling papers as he waited for Hank. After a few minutes, Hank returned to the line,

"It came on Wednesday. The owner picked it up early this morning."

"What? Who picked it up? I had requested to have the car towed to the police impound lot."

"I didn't get the transfer request. Edith Marshall, the owner, came in person. She didn't transfer the plates to someone else like she said. She had all of the paperwork showing insurance and registration. Mrs. Marshall also paid the impound fees. Without your request, I had no legal reason to withhold the car from her."

Randy scribbled the details on the yellow legal pad near the telephone, adding to what little he already knew. "Was she alone or with someone?"

"She came with her nephew. He drove it off the lot for her. I think the old gal is a bit crazy."

"Crazy?"

"She's a little high-strung. Mrs. Marshall tried to talk me into giving her a deal on the impound fees because she is a senior. I told her I didn't have a senior discount and that she could either pay the fees or leave. The nephew paid the fees, saying he didn't have time for arguments. It's good he came with her or we would still be arguing! The woman was determined to get her car back."

"So, just crazy-mad, not crazy-crazy. Did you get a copy of the driver's licence?" Randy asked, rolling his eyes. "Did she have picture identification?"

"I got a copy, but she didn't have the picture identification part, just the paper part you renew every year that fits into the pocket on the back of the picture ID. That's all I need, anyway."

Randy sighed heavily, rubbing his hand over his face. "Okay, that doesn't help me at all. Did you recognize her or her nephew?"

"No, I can't say that I have ever seen the two of them before. I don't know. Don't all old ladies look the same? Same hairdo, big sunglasses, weird red and purple hats?"

Randy thanked Hank for his time, returning the handset to its cradle. He thought he should run the plate to verify the current address for Mrs. Edith Marshall. If Randy was lucky, the older lady would open up to him about what she knows about the nephew's bad habits. Hoping he would make a discovery, Randy got to work on finding Mrs. Marshall.

Chapter 16

Turning onto Fifth Street West and parking his police vehicle across the street in front of the tiny house, Randy scanned the quiet neighbourhood around Edith Marshall's home. The place looked like a 1930s build from the Sears catalogue. The driveway was empty, but Randy took notice of the fresh oil stains darkening the packed sparse gravel. He followed the cracked cement blocks to the doorstep, looking for the doorbell and finding none. Randy knocked loudly on the screen door. A middle-aged woman with mousy brown hair opened the inside door. "Can I help you with something, Officer?" she asked.

"I am Police Officer Doyle. I want to talk to Edith Marshall. Are you her?" he asked, knowing that this woman was too young to be the person he sought.

The woman smiled slightly, "No, I'm Edith's caregiver, but I will get her if you want to talk with her." The woman walked to the back of the house, where Randy assumed the bedrooms were. He pulled slightly on the screen door, finding resistance against an inside latch.

The caregiver slowly escorted an elderly lady towards the door, shuffling forward with her walker. Her hands shook with each slide of the device. "Who is coming to visit today?" Edith asked her caregiver.

"It's a young police officer," the caregiver explained, smiling at her charge. "He came to talk to you."

"Is my boy in trouble again?"

"No, I'm sure everything is okay," the caregiver assured her, nudging the elderly woman closer to the screen door to make introductions. "Police Officer Doyle came to visit you. Say 'hello', Edith."

Pushing up her thick glasses with her frail hand, Edith parroted with a smile, "Hello, Edith!" The caregiver grinned at Edith's response, shaking her head.

"Hello, Mrs. Marshall. I'm a police officer. My name is Randy Doyle. How are you today?"

"I'm going to have a visitor today. My son is taking me on a holiday!" Edith said, proudly smiling.

Randy looked questioningly to the caregiver, who shook her head, mouthing the word *no*. "That sounds nice. Could you tell me about your car?"

Frowning with confusion, Edith asked, "Who are you? Where's my son? He's a good boy but gets into a little trouble now and then." The older woman tried to remove her glasses, but the caregiver gently slapped her hand away.

Releasing a deep breath, Randy thought he needed to redirect his questions to the caregiver. "I'm sorry, what is your name?"

"My name is Loretta," she replied. "The family visits occasionally, but it's rare. In her condition, she never leaves the house except when I take her to medical appointments."

Knowing that Hank had confirmed Edith Marshall as the person who picked up the car from the impound lot, Randy dismissed her statement. He continued with his questions and asked, "Does Mrs. Marshall own a 1971 gold Lincoln Continental?"

Looking at Edith, Loretta's smile faltered, "She owns it, but she doesn't drive, for obvious reasons."

"Where is the car now? The driveway is empty. Is it around back?"

"Um, it was stolen. I don't know where it is right now," Loretta shrugged, reaching and pulling Edith back away from the door. "If that is all, I need to get Edith down for a nap. Thanks for stopping by, officer."

"Just a couple of quick questions before I go," Randy called through the screen door. "When was it stolen? Why didn't you file a police report? Hank at the impound lot confirms that it was towed, impounded and picked up. Can you explain this?"

Loretta turned her head over her shoulder, urging Edith to the back of the house. "It went missing a few weeks ago, but it was not worth reporting. It was a piece of junk, anyway. I couldn't rely on it. I guess that's why someone had it towed."

"One last question: how have you been getting Mrs. Marshall to her medical appointments since the vehicle was stolen and impounded?"

Loretta stopped, turning her head slightly to speak. "Her nephew was driving her. I just bought a car but haven't had time to get plates. It's parked in the back. I think my car will serve my purposes much better. Have a good day, Officer Doyle."

Randy smiled, walking back toward his parked car. He knew that he was getting closer to finding his suspect. If Randy could find the car, he would find his drug dealer to make the arrest. As he was about to cross the street, Randy noticed a little old lady in a purple bathrobe waving to get his attention. Thinking she wanted him to rescue a cat, Randy rolled his eyes and changed his direction to see if he could help. As she started walking toward him, Randy noticed she wore fuzzy slippers matching her purple bathrobe. He increased his walking speed so the older woman would not have to walk too far in her bedroom slippers. Forcing a pleasant smile, Randy asked, "What can I help you with today?"

"Are you the new police officer? I haven't seen you in town," she said, patting the curlers on her head.

"I am police Officer Doyle. Do you have a crime to report?"

"I just wanted to tell you that the people in that house are drug dealers! It would be best if you arrested them! We have been having trouble on this street with cars coming and going all day and night. I think it's because of them. My long-time neighbours that lived in between our two houses moved away last spring to get away from them. I complained to another officer, but nothing seemed to come from it!"

"What is your name, please?" Randy smiled, reaching into his pocket for loose note paper and a pencil to write down details.

"Mrs. Agnes Wright, with a *w*, not an *r*," she replied, ensuring Randy spelled her name correctly.

"Yes, of course. Do you ever see a 1971 Lincoln Continental parked in the front driveway of that house, Mrs. Wright?"

"I don't know. What colour is it?" She patted her hair curlers as she talked. "There are all colours of cars: white, yellow, and green."

"It's a big gold car that is old and needs repair. Loud muffler, maybe. I noticed it had a broken headlight cover, too."

"Yes, that car comes around a lot! It's loud and blows a lot of smoke. Sometimes the young man who drives it has trouble starting it."

Randy looked at the empty driveway two houses down, thinking about the oil stains. "Have you seen that car recently?"

"I heard the young man starting it this morning."

Turning back to face her, Randy frowned, "You *heard* it, but you didn't *see* it? Is that right, Mrs. Wright?"

Frowning, Agnes pulled her fuzzy robe closer around her neck. "Yes, but it always sounds the same. My hearing is good."

Randy thanked her for her information, returned to his vehicle and wondered if he should put a warrant out for the old car's driver. After all, the caregiver said the vehicle was missing.

Chapter 17

Slamming her locker, Amy turned to Sarah, "All I'm saying is that I haven't seen you or talked to you outside of school. It's like we aren't even friends anymore."

"No, it's not that. I have been going to school and then straight home. Honest," Sarah protested, crossing her heart. "It's no big deal! I'm just sitting around."

"More like talking on the phone with Matt, you mean. You start dating someone and suddenly, your best friend doesn't exist anymore. Did you forget that we have been best friends since first grade?"

"But, I-"

"Why would you ditch me just because you are dating someone? I don't care who you date, but don't pretend I don't matter to you anymore."

Sarah's eyes widened, "First of all, I'm not dating Matt. Where did you get that idea?"

"What do you mean? Everyone is talking about how you and Matt are always together after school," Amy replied, nervously twirling a strand of hair and juggling her books in one arm.

"Well, there's more to this than meets the eye. Everyone can gossip, but you never even asked me for the truth. You could have called me, asked me to my face, and found out what is happening with me. That's what best friends do! We ask if we want to know something."

"Okay! I'm asking you now. What is going on with you? You aren't coming to work anymore. You don't phone me. When I phoned you, your mom said you were not home. I can only assume you are out on a date with Matt since I have no information other than the rumours spreading around the school."

"He's just walking me home," Sarah whispered, looking over her shoulder. "I haven't been going out anywhere. I'm not even taking calls from anyone!"

"Why aren't you taking anyone's calls?"

"You never know who is stalking you until you end up dead in a freezer in aisle three," Sarah said, referencing Anna Labrash's murder.

"Stalking? Who said someone was stalking Anna?"

"Um, no one," Sarah looked away, pulling her binder out of her locker. "But I'm sure that's why Leah and the rest of her family have avoided everyone in town. Leah still hasn't returned to school. I heard no one in town has seen anyone in the family anywhere. Isn't that odd?

Shouldn't someone see a family member getting groceries or picking up the mail?"

"It is odd," Amy agreed. "Shane and I stopped at the Labrash place on the day of the farm auction."

"How did the auction turn out?" Sarah asked, pulling her books out of her locker.

"It went better than Grandpa expected. He said the auctioneers sold the land at a fair price. As long as we can get the farmhouse rented before the end of October, we won't have to sell it."

"That's great news!" Sarah exclaimed. "Tell me what you talked about with Leah. Did you find out anything?"

"It didn't look like there was anyone around except two kids. The boy slammed the door in my face before I could talk to Leah or a parent," Amy shrugged. "I keep looking for Leah but haven't found her yet. I have a feeling that if I could find Leah, we'd solve this whole mystery of who would want to harm Anna and stuff her in a freezer. I haven't even heard of a date for the funeral! It seems so weird."

"You need to be careful. This little town of ours is more dangerous than it seems. It is giving me the chills!" Sarah warned, hugging her binder closer to her chest.

"It's just that I'm trying to find answers. I can't help thinking I have seen something, but my brain isn't cooperating," Amy replied, thinking about the morning she found Anna's body. "Was Anna wearing earrings when you saw her at the grocery store, the night before she died?"

Sarah stared blankly at Amy, blinking rapidly. "I don't know. Why?"

"I found an earring on the floor near the freezer while helping Shane clean it. I think it was either hers or the person who put her body there. I want to ask Leah, but I can't find her. It could be a clue!"

Shaking her head incredulously, Sarah said, "You shouldn't go around chasing after clues to solve the case just because you have a family friend and an uncle on the police force. Let the police do their jobs! If whoever did this finds out you are digging into things, you could make yourself a target."

"I don't know why I'd be a target! Only one person has been threatening me lately," Amy said, tightening the scrunchie holding her ponytail.

"Threats? From who? Is someone stalking you?" Sarah asked, raising her eyebrows.

"Well, when I think about it, maybe that guy, Greg Holman. He seems to be everywhere I go lately. It's creepy. He keeps telling me to quit my job and stay home before I get hurt. He has some nerve! He thinks that I don't need to work because of my inheritance. I don't see why it is of any concern to him. It's not like he can cover my shifts and do what I do."

Smirking, Sarah rolled her eyes, "The gossip isn't always on the mark. I know you aren't a millionaire."

Amy was at a loss for words as she watched Sarah walk away from the lockers. *A millionaire, me? Who would think that? That must be what Greg heard and why he keeps telling me to quit my job*, Amy thought. The warning bell buzzed, indicating that the break was over and her class was about to begin. Pivoting on her toes, Amy rounded the corner, almost running into someone tossing a disposable cup with remnants of blue slushie into the open trash can. Some of the blue liquid splashed back, landing on Amy's pants. "Great! Just great," she mumbled, trying to shake off the mess. "Can my day get any better than this?" She hurried down the long hallway and ducked into her health class, sliding into her desk and preparing for another lecture on nutritional snacks and healthy eating.

Chapter 18

Officer Randy Doyle pushed on the main doors, strolled into the station, and stopped at the main reception desk. "Hi, Gladys. Is Gerard in the station?" he asked.

"Yes, Gerard and Hanson just brought in a suspect in the big case," she said, smiling and handing him pink message slips with the name *Officer Doyle* written on the top.

Randy absently accepted the messages, looking down the hallway toward the interview rooms. "Are they down in interrogation now?"

"No. Gerard just brought the guy into holding and is processing the arrest." The phone on the desk started ringing. Gladys held up her finger to pause the conversation as she answered it. "Glenmere Police Department, what is your emergency?"

Randy was curious about the suspect in the Labrash case. He hadn't even finished looking for information on the earring that Amy found. He wondered if he still needed to find more information or if he could focus his time tracking down the driver of the gold Lincoln. Randy wished the suspect was in the interview room. He was interested in watching and listening from the observation room, but being in the holding area with the suspect was a whole other story. Deciding to ask Gerard later about investigating the earrings, Randy proceeded to the roll call room to sort through his pink messages and loose note pages at his desk.

"Are you still using the scraps of paper?" Hanson said, smoothing out a crumpled note on the drug store paper pad. "Did you go back for more pages, or is this the same batch from when you talked to the pharmacist the first time?"

Randy grabbed the piece of paper, tearing it in half. "Let it alone. I just needed to write a few things down about the drugs I confiscated from the trunk of the car in my report," he snarled.

"Why are you wasting your time investigating some guy who is probably just another drug user?"

"Something is just not adding up. I started out investigating a parking violation, but I found prescription pills and other drugs. I haven't had a chance to talk about it with Gerard. I need more information before I read him into what I have found."

"I wouldn't worry about it. It's probably someone stealing prescriptions. I'm sure it's no big deal. You will be back to helping old ladies with cats in no time," Hanson replied, grinning and firmly punching Randy in the arm.

"I heard you apprehended a guy on the Labrash murder case," Randy said, resisting the urge to rub his arm where Hanson's punch landed. He didn't want to give him the satisfaction of knowing that the jab hurt.

"Yes. We are taking our time filling out the paperwork, crossing all the *t*'s and dotting all the *i*'s sort of thing. Let the scum bag sit on ice for a bit before the suspect can call his lawyer. I can't wait to be in that interview. I think Gerard will let me take the lead in this one. It's about time he recognized my detective skills! I expect a promotion after this case."

"Did the suspect confess?" Randy asked, wanting to know if Amy was off the suspect list.

"No, not yet, but the guy is pretty mad. He took a few swings at me. I'm adding resisting arrest to the charges. We will have to wait for him to cool off before we interview him to get his statement. I bet he will lie about his involvement, but I am ready. I will write down some questions while I wait for the interrogation." Hanson puffed out his chest in pride, pretending to buff his nails on his shirt. "I will be using toxicology reports as evidence for his crime."

"Was it drugs?"

"No, the girl was poisoned with a drink laced with Thallium. It takes about eight hours to kill you once ingested," Hanson stated. "I found the poison in the janitor's closet at the high school."

"You arrested the janitor?" Randy asked, raising his eyebrows.

"Yes! It is Ralph Norman." Hanson rubbed his hands together, smirking. "It was awesome! Mr. Norman had the poison on one of the shelves with the cleaning supplies. I will have this case wrapped up in record time, ready for a reporter to interview me for next week's paper."

"Sounds like you have a good case. Has the toxicology report come back for the homeless guy yet?"

Shaking his head, Hanson replied, "I don't know. You are just going to have to go through the reports that came in yesterday and look for it yourself. I wouldn't worry about it because the homeless guy was a known drug user. The report will indicate a high level of illicit drugs. I think the medical examiner listed the cause of death as hypothermia or exposure leading to death."

"Well, drug overdose is the likely scenario. I don't think it was cold enough for hypothermia. Baysic has survived colder nights on the streets." Randy said, tossing his pen down onto the piled-up paperwork. "I think I would like to watch you interrogate the janitor."

"Why are you interested in my guy? It's obvious that the two cases aren't connected."

"Well, I must seek out those learning opportunities every chance I get. Gerard wants me to increase my skills by observing other officers at work," Randy tried to look earnest, thinking that he had to stroke Hanson's ego a bit to get in on witnessing the interview.

"Gerard doesn't want you involved in this case since your niece found the victim and is still on the suspect list. I can't have you tainting my evidence against this guy. It's my collar on this big case," Hanson stressed, pounding on his chest. "I'm taking all of the credit."

Hanson's boastfulness didn't settle well with Randy. Running his fingers through his hair and inhaling slowly, Randy didn't want to knock Hanson off his pedestal unless he felt justice was not prevailing. He was confident Amy was an unlikely suspect, but he didn't like to bring that up. Not now, anyway. "I want to watch you interrogate from the other side of the glass. How would that taint your case? You just said the two cases aren't connected: one poisoned, the other overdosed." Randy argued, confident that Hanson's ego would want to have an audience. "What are you worried about? I thought you had this case all wrapped up already."

Officer Hanson stared directly at Randy, finally making his decision; he smiled condescendingly. "Sure, rookie. You can watch my skills in action. Just be sure to stay behind the glass. It will not taint the case if you don't come into the room or talk to my suspect."

"That sounds great," Randy said, trying to keep his voice neutral. "I can't wait."

"Maybe later I can look at your drug user and solve that case for you, and then you can move on to other fun cases," Hanson jabbed, leaving the area.

"Yes, like rescuing cats. I know." Randy exchanged glances with Officer Trussell, who had listened to the exchange.

Chapter 19

Saturday, October 05, 1985

Juggling the heavy grey tub full of dirty dishes in her arms, Amy used her foot to push open the swinging door of the community hall's kitchen. Blowing her hair out of her eyes, she dropped the container on the counter beside the others waiting for the industrial dishwasher. Slipping one of her jelly bean shoes off, Amy rubbed her toes and regretted two decisions: agreeing to work this catering job and wearing these plastic shoes. She should have changed into high-top sneakers but needed to rush to get to the hall after school to help prepare for the catering event. Looking at the angry red marks on her foot, Amy briefly considered going barefoot like some of the wedding guests walking around the hall. Sighing and putting her plastic shoe back on her foot, Amy decided she didn't want to ask Frank if she could go barefoot. She knew he was already concerned with worker shortage because Leah still hadn't returned.

Busying herself with throwing out the trash and scraping food from plates, Amy got into a rhythm, forgetting about her sore feet and squished toes. The music started blaring just as the dinner staff finished cleaning the kitchen.

"It's time to start prepping for dessert and midnight lunch!" Frank hollered. "Amy, go check and see if they have finished the ceremonial cutting of the cake. We will bring it in here, cut it and plate it."

Wiping her wet hands on the oversized apron she wore; Amy left the steamy kitchen to find the cake table nestled in a darkened corner of the hall. She smiled at the bride and groom, two-stepping to twangy country music around the master of ceremonies, who was trying to get them ready to play a game to entertain the guests. Looking around at the smiling guests, Amy blinked against the camera flashes, recognizing several familiar faces in the crowd waiting for the spectacle.

Turning toward the cake table, she noticed Greg staring at her. Amy paused, glaring at him. She mouthed, "What are you doing here? You better stay away from me." She stood still, unmoving, and watched him shake his head in disapproval. Frowning, Amy continued walking toward the table to confirm the happy couple had performed the ceremonial cutting of the cake. Amy removed the decorative top tier of the cake with the bride and groom figurines and set it on the table. Licking the icing off her fingers, Amy rolled the trolly away from the wall, transferring the edible slab of cake onto it.

Once Amy returned to the kitchen, Frank carefully removed the slab cake with its pillars onto the clean stainless-steel counter, instructing his staff, "Cut the cake into one-inch squares and plate it. If people ask for it, we will add ice cream to their plate. Who wants to dish out the ice cream?"

"Where is the ice cream?" Bob Crookedneck, one of the cooks, asked. "We didn't bring over any ice cream."

"What?" Frank said, wiping the sweat from his brow with a handkerchief and looking around. "Okay, Amy and Kimberley, go get the ice cream! Here are the keys to the van," he said, holding a set of keys in his chubby fingers and looking at Kimberley.

"I baked and decorated this cake. I am not leaving someone else in charge of it to get the ice cream," Kimberley said, wiping the icing off her fingers onto her orange and blue frilly apron. "Get someone else to do it."

Turning to Amy, Frank asked, "Have you got your driver's licence yet?"

"No," Amy blushed, tucking a strand of brown hair behind her ear and wondering why everyone thought it was so important.

"I do! I want to drive," Carly piped up, smiling and pulling off her white kitchen apron, reaching for Frank's keys. "I will go!"

Reluctantly, Frank gave his van keys to the young waitress. "Carly, be careful driving," Frank cautioned. "The roads might have been wet when we came, but they are probably icing over again. Park the van in the back and use the backdoor. The back door key is this one with the blue rubber ring."

"I got it, but can I also swing by my house for a different pair of shoes?" Carly asked, sweetly batting her eyelashes at Frank.

"Sure, but take Amy and drop her off at the diner first. She can get the ice cream out of the walk-in freezer and stack it at the back door while you get your shoes. You must hurry; we can all go home once we serve the cake!"

Amy quickly pulled off her apron, following Carly out the back door, "When did you get your licence?"

Grinning, Carly pulled open the driver's door of the cube van, "Last week! I've taken the driving test before, but this time, I finally passed."

Amy's eyes grew wide. Faking a smile, she said, "That's great. Good for you." Climbing into the van's passenger side, Amy noticed the lingering smell of the meal they had served earlier that evening. The steam from the hot food had cooled, frosting up the inside of the van's windows and windshield. Amy shivered, wishing she had grabbed her sweater on the way out of the hall.

Carly scraped at the frost with her press-on fingernails as she drove haphazardly toward the diner. The seatbelt jerked against Amy's chest as Carly came to a jarring stop in the staff parking area behind Frankie's Diner. Pulling the keys out of the ignition, Carly said, "I'll get the door unlocked and head over to my place. Get everything by the backdoor and be ready to roll when I return. I won't

The Ice Box

be long. I live two blocks away. If we are lucky, we will all have cake and ice cream, too."

Amy followed Carly to the backdoor of the diner, watching her insert the key into the doorknob. "Someone left it unlocked. Small towns; am I right?" Carly rolled her eyes, turning back to open the van door. "I'll only be fifteen minutes!" She slammed the door, starting the van.

"No problem," Amy said, pushing the door open further and feeling for the light switch. The fluorescent lights hummed with electricity as the kitchen lit up, making Amy blink against the harsh lights. Amy noticed that the kitchen was clean, except for a box of crackers that someone had knocked over on the counter. Ignoring the small mess and the eerie silence of the dark seating area, Amy shook her head. She reached for the large handle on the walk-in freezer, reminding herself the sooner she finished this task, the sooner she could go home. A noise from the sitting area, sounding like feet shuffling, startled Amy. She gasped, looking nervously into the darkened sitting area. "Carly?" She called nervously, trying to see into the shadows cast around the tables; she saw no one. Forcing a deep breath and trying to calm the quickened beating of her heart, Amy shivered. "Oh, my God. I'm losing it! There is no one here."

Amy yanked on the industrial handle and pulled open the door, stepping into the darkened walk-in freezer, surprised to find it shrouded in icy darkness. "Lights?" Amy looked up, expecting to see a string, but found none. "Where's the light switch?" She wondered, looking down around the floor, spotting milk crates with tubs of vanilla ice cream in them. She released a deep breath. Dragging the first crate across the floor and into the kitchen area, Amy noticed the light switch on the wall next to the open freezer door.

"Oh, good, I hate the dark." Flipping on the switch, Amy walked back into the freezer. She barely registered the sound of the door slamming shut behind her. Amy couldn't breathe. She was staring into the cold, dead eyes of a body stuffed into the corner against the shelving. Releasing a piercing scream and turning to flee the horror, Amy crashed into the closed door. "Open the door! Get me out of here!" She yelled, pounding the frosty door with her fists.

Amy banged on the door for what felt like an eternity until the door finally opened, sending her sprawling onto the warmth of the kitchen's orange ceramic tiles. Swallowing hard and glaring up at her rescuer, Amy took a deep breath. "Carly, it's about time! Where the hell were you?"

"What's your fucking problem? I went home to change my shoes," she said, pointing to her blue Reebok sneakers with pink laces. "What have you been doing while I was gone? You are supposed to get the ice cream ready to load."

Picking herself off the floor, Amy rushed to the wall-mounted telephone, searching the bulletin board beside it for the police emergency telephone number. "Forget the ice cream! I've got to call the police!"

"Why?"

"There's a dead body in the freezer!" Amy yelled, lifting the receiver and dialling the number she needed to connect to the police station. As she waited for the call to be connected, she pulled the tangled cord as far as she could, peering into the open freezer, "Who is it?"

Cautiously moving closer to the dead body, Carly quietly said, "It's Anna's boyfriend, Liam Hildebrandt! That's sad."

A female voice floated through the telephone handset, "Hello? Is anyone there? What's your emergency?"

Shaking her head, Amy shuddered, "Yes, yes! I am in the kitchen at Frankie's Diner. We have just found a dead body in the freezer!"

"Leave me out of this!" Carly hissed, backing out of the freezer and holding her hands up in mock surrender. "This is all you, bitch! People seem to drop dead all around you. I'm not going to be next!"

Amy frowned at Carly, continuing to talk on the phone, "Yes, I'm still here. Please send Officer Gerard and Officer Doyle immediately!" She hung up the receiver, chewing on her lip.

"Now what? Do we have to wait for the police?" Carly asked, jingling the van keys in her hands.

"Yes, we do," Amy answered, crossing her arms defensively.

"Oh, no. I'm getting out of here! While you wait, I will deliver the ice cream as promised," Carly reached for the crate on the floor. "The last thing I want is for Frank to fire me over melted ice cream."

"You can't just leave! The police will want to talk to you," Amy pleaded.

Carly paused, hoisting up a crate onto her hip, "I have an idea: you wait for the police, and I will deliver the ice cream and tell Frank about the body in his freezer. I'm sure the police will want to talk to him, too. I will send him over here. If we can avoid having the police disrupt the wedding, everyone will be happy. If the police need me, I'm sure you will give them my name, just like you turned the police onto your friend Sarah."

Ignoring Carly's sneer, Amy had to admit having Frank come here, instead of the police tracking him down during a wedding celebration, did sound like a good idea. "Okay," Amy hesitated, avoiding discussing her recent involvement in criminal investigations. "But you will need to talk to the police, too. I am going to tell them about you and me being here tonight. They must know where I was today and who saw me."

Carly rolled her eyes, "You would know! That's fine with me."

"Fine!" Amy cursed, wishing Frank would fire her.

While waiting by the open backdoor, Amy pulled someone's sweater off one of the hooks by the backdoor to cover her cold arms. Ignoring the jingle from the pockets, she welcomed the warmth the too-big-for-her-frame sweater provided.

Chapter 20

Amy stood in the open doorway, pulling the sweater tighter to ward off the frosty air while she waited. Her wait seemed endless as she stood still, watching two police cruisers ablaze with flashing lights and blaring sirens skid to a stop behind Frankie's Diner. Officer Gerard and Officer Trussell, the first police officers to arrive, rushed toward the open door and pushed Amy aside. Shaking his head and raising his eyebrows, Officer Gerard said, "I'm not happy to see you here, Amy. This call will be the third dead body you've found. Wait here while we search and secure the scene."

Amy nodded, feeling her stomach plummet to her toes as she watched Randy and another officer exit the second cruiser. She held onto the door frame to steady herself, fighting the lump in her throat. Amy knew this didn't look good. "I know," she sighed, shrugging her shoulders. Amy fought tears, threatening to overspill onto her cheeks. "I'm not doing it on purpose. I don't know why this keeps happening to me! I don't want more gossip flying around town than there is already."

Turning to Randy, Gerard instructed, "Give Miss Young a blanket from your trunk and wait here. Trussell and I will have the first look and process the scene."

"All clear!" Officer Trussell called, returning to the bright kitchen.

Randy absently nodded, watching the other officers survey the scene. "Are you alright, Amy?"

"Yes," Amy answered, letting the words drop unspoken between them, pulling the sweater tighter around her body to fight off her chills. He had already lectured her about staying out of trouble and away from people who might be involved with the murder of her fellow employee. She didn't need to hear the same lecture again.

Officer Gerard returned, holding his notebook and pencil in his hand. "Doyle, take Amy down to the police station. We will question her there to avoid contamination of the crime scene. I will call the station for another officer. Call George Petersen to go to the station to wait with Amy. I am certain we will find evidence confirming a connection to the Labrash case," Gerard announced, flexing his authority. "Don't talk to anyone at the station about this case. Don't take Amy's statement until I can witness it. It would be best if you stayed away from this case, Doyle. Do you hear me?"

"Yes, I know," Randy sighed, shaking his head.

The Ice Box

Amy looked down at her cold and numb feet, tapping the plastic shoe up and down and realizing she was the reason her uncle couldn't work this case either. She followed him to his police car, squeezing into the passenger seat and pushing papers and parking violation booklets onto the floor as she sat. Randy eyed her but didn't say anything. Thankfully, the vehicle was still running and spewing warm blasts of air. Amy closed her eyes, allowing the warm air to blow into her face while she tried to block out finding another dead body.

Despite the warmth of the sweater and wool blanket, Amy sat in the waiting area at the police station in front of the main desk, still shivering. Her teeth chattered.

"Can I get you another wool blanket while you wait?" the desk attendant asked, showing concern.

Jerking her eyes toward the voice, Amy slowly responded, "No, thank you. I don't think that will help me. Could I have a pad of paper and a pen? I want to write my statement and leave as soon as possible."

Wrapped in the itchy wool blanket, Amy crossed her legs, tucking her feet under her for added warmth while she let the words pour onto the yellow legal pad. She started with her concerns for Leah and her unsuccessful search, looking for her without any success, ending with the moment the police arrived at the diner. When she looked up from the pages she had written, she was surprised to find her grandpa, sitting quietly beside her, reading a Western, or at least pretending to read.

"When did you get here?"

"Oh, I don't know. Several chapters ago, I guess. Randy called me to sit with you while he waited for Officer Gerard to return to the police station."

"Did he say how long it's going to be? I feel like I have been here forever," Amy said, rolling her eyes.

"Well, you have certainly been busy, judging from all the pages you used on that pad of paper," he smiled, crinkling the corners of his eyes. He reached over, putting his arms around Amy.

"They are on their way back now," Randy breezed into the waiting area, sitting across from Amy. "I'm sure this won't take long. Officer Gerard or Hanson will take your statement and ask a few questions. Because you have already gotten started, it should be quick," he shrugged, hoping that Gerard wouldn't be upset that she had already written out her statement. He stayed in the roll call room, away from Amy, while she wrote her statement. He didn't want to influence the case.

The heavy metal doors opened, blowing Officers Gerard, Trussell and Hanson in with a cold breeze that sent icy chills around Amy's shoulders where the blanket had slid down.

Officer Gerard approached George, reaching to shake his outstretched hand, "George, I wish I could say..."

"There she is!" Officer Jeffrey Hanson declared, reaching for Amy's shoulder and forcing her out of her chair. "Amy Young, please stand. I am placing you under arrest for interference with a crime scene, obstruction of justice, conspiracy to commit murder and indignity to human remains."

"Hanson!" Randy yelled, jumping up and stepping in front of Amy. "What the hell are you doing? What kind of shit police work is this?"

"Back off, Doyle!" Officer Hanson yelled, pushing Randy away with the hand holding his cuffs. "This is my job! Don't be an asshole!"

Amy looked at Officer Gerard, wide-eyed, "What's going on?"

"Back down! Both of you!" Gerard roared, grabbing each officer by the cuffs of their collars, trying to hold them apart.

"What is going on out here?" Officer Trussell asked, trying to push between the officers.

Amy yelped, Hanson's fingers digging into her shoulder with the tugging and pulling among the three men. The yellow legal pad she was holding crashed to the floor. Her eyes watered. Turning to her grandpa, she cried out, "Help me!"

"Doyle, go to your desk and stay there! You are assigned to desk duties while you learn protocols."

"But, I-" Randy paused, realizing that he couldn't risk messing with this case or the real murderer could get off on technicalities, but this was ridiculous. "I know Amy is not involved in this case. Why would Hanson waltz in here and arrest the kid?"

"We are not pressing charges at this very moment," Officer Gerard stated, glaring at Officer Hanson. "We will get Amy's statement first, then decide whether or not someone will press criminal charges, or did you forget procedures, too? Hanson, you aren't a rookie anymore! What has gotten into you? Release Miss Young and calmly receive her statement!"

Reluctantly, Officer Hanson released his grip on Amy's shoulder. After a brief pause, Amy felt everyone slowly release their hold on her as her grandpa rolled her into his arms for a warm, protective hug. The itchy blanket had fallen to the floor in the commotion. Amy filled her lungs with air, inhaling the warm scent of her grandfather and feeling the security his embrace provided.

"I think we are making a mistake," Hanson argued, pointing his finger at Amy. "These two cases are connected. Miss Young has been at *both* scenes! How do you explain it?"

"She's just a kid in the wrong place at the wrong time! You've read her statement from the first case. You are the one who arrested the school janitor, Ralph Norman! Release Mr. Norman from lock up. He can't be the suspect if they are connected and Amy did it as you claim," Randy argued, poking his finger into Officer Hanson's chest.

Hanson's face reddened with anger. He grabbed Randy's hand and pushed him away, "Just back off my case, Doyle! Ralph Norman and Miss Young were both at the school when someone administered poison to the first ice box victim! It is quite possible, rookie, that they worked together on this! I will prove it."

"Worked together?" Randy said incredulously. "What's the motive? Why would a teenage girl help the janitor poison other students? Come on, teach me! What is going on in that idiotic head of yours?"

"You son of a bitch, Doyle!" Officer Hanson yelled, advancing on Randy and shoving him backwards. "I have more experience than you with criminal investigations. It is a process!"

"Enough! This office is not a playground! Doyle, go to my office to wait for me! Cool your jets until I talk to you," Officer Gerard roared with authority. "Hanson, escort Miss Young and Mr. Petersen to the interview room to receive her statement - calmly! She has already written out her statement. Please pick it up off the floor, Hanson, and start reading it! I will be there in a moment to assist in questioning."

The officers all looked at each other, unmoving from their defensive positions. "Move it!" Gerard ordered, realizing that no one was following his orders.

Hitting his shoulder into Hanson when brushing by, Randy mumbled, "This is *not* over."

"Are you alright, Amy?" Officer Gerard asked, glaring at Officer Hanson. "Please forgive these two officers for their misconduct. I will see that it never happens again."

Amy nodded her head against her grandpa's chest, sniffing and mumbling, "I'm okay. I'm safe right here."

Officer Hanson leaned down, picking up the yellow paper pad with Amy's statement, "If you follow me right this way, we will get started."

Pulling away from her grandpa's embrace, Amy nodded and quietly replied, "Sure."

"Here, you can use my handkerchief, girlie," George said, raising his eyebrows.

Amy felt dread deep down in her chest, knowing it would be a long night. She followed Officer Hanson and her grandpa into the interview room, sitting at the metal table and wrapping the wool blanket around her shoulders. "I didn't do it," she stated matter-of-factly, hoping to get this over quickly.

"I will read your statement and ask questions to clarify," Hanson replied.

"Okay." Amy waited patiently, watching Officer Hanson begin to read.

Occasionally, Officer Hanson frowned or squinted at the words Amy had written. He leaned back in his chair, flipping through each page of her statement. Throwing the legal pad onto the table at last and standing up across from her, he said, "Please stand up and remove all items from your pockets, placing them on the table in front of you."

Frowning, Amy asked, "Why? What do I need to do that for?"

"It's okay, Amy, just do as Officer Hanson asks. I'm sure it will be fine. As soon as Officer Gerard verifies your statement, we will go home for freshly baked cookies and milk," George advised his granddaughter.

Amy unfolded her legs to stand, letting the blanket fall in a puddle around her feet. She emptied the pockets of her dress pants: a gum wrapper, five quarters, a rainbow hair scrunchie, a plastic fork, and a used napkin she had blown her nose into earlier this evening. "That's all of it."

Officer Hanson studied the contents on the table before looking her up and down. Amy felt violated under his scrutiny. Pointing, Hanson demanded, "Empty the other pockets, too."

Amy looked down at the oversized grey sweater she had taken from the coat rack at the diner. "What other pockets?" she asked.

"The two front pockets. Empty them and remove the sweater. I want to see if you have any other pockets or are concealing something."

Amy looked at her grandpa for reassurance. He nodded wearily. Thrusting her hands into both pockets simultaneously, Amy scooped up everything from the sweater pockets, placing the items on the table with her items. She removed the sweater, slowly turning around with her arms out at her sides until she faced the police officer.

"This is interesting," Officer Hanson said, grinning like the Cheshire Cat. "This is all the evidence I need to press those charges I was interrupted from doing in the foyer. I knew I was right to suspect you."

Confused, Amy stared at the item he was holding on the end of his pen, "I don't get it. What do you mean?" She scanned the items she had placed on the table, looking back at him.

"This, Miss Young, is the matching earring to the one found at the scene of the first ice box victim," Officer Hanson stated triumphantly. "You are under arrest! Mr. Petersen, you might want to hire a lawyer."

"How could this be happening?" Amy asked, struggling to find the right words.

George slowly stood, putting his arm around Amy, "We will not answer your questions until we have legal counsel present. Lead me to the nearest telephone to make some calls."

Turning to her grandpa, Amy cried, "But it's not mine! You have to believe me!"

"Shush, don't say anything," George said, patting her shoulder.

"But, Grandpa! It's..."

"Don't say anything! We will work this out with a lawyer," George reassured her. "When my lawyer presents himself, we will answer Officer Gerard's questions," George smirked, implying Officer Hanson wouldn't be the one to question Amy.

"You are going to need a good lawyer. I just caught your granddaughter red-handed!" Officer Hanson replied, plastering a fake smile on his face. "The school janitor would have needed one of the students to help poison the first victim during class. The second victim is also a classmate. I will find proof that she slipped poison into a drink the second time, too. I believe the charges against Ralph Norman will hold with Amy as his accomplice. You'll see!"

Chapter 21

Defeated and emotionally drained, Amy pushed open the door of George Petersen's black 1983 Buick with her foot. She absently studied the fresh frost on the white picket fence, sparkling with the pink hue of the rising sun. "I feel... I don't know, tired or whatever. I'm not sure."

"Don't worry, we will eat a big breakfast and go to bed," George said, guiding her up the slippery sidewalk. "I doubt your granny slept last night. I'm one hundred percent convinced she has been baking all night. That's what she does when she is worried. I didn't want to repeatedly telephone her while we were at the station in case she managed to get some sleep. The last time I called her was around one-thirty when the lawyer arrived." He reached for the door, opening it for Amy.

Warm, delicious smells surrounded Amy like a welcomed embrace, pulling her into the kitchen and allowing her to forget her weariness. "I am starving! Your kitchen has the best smells ever!"

"Thank goodness! I thought you two would never get here! Come in, come in. Close the door! You are letting the heat out," Beatrice instructed, setting another plate on the overfilled table. "I just called the station to see what was happening. Gladys was coming on shift. She told me you two were driving home. I asked her to pass a message to Randy to come to breakfast. Did he follow you over?" she asked, looking out the steamy kitchen window.

"No, I don't think so. I didn't even know Randy was still at the station. He should have been off work last night right after I arrived there. I thought Gerard sent him home," George said, frowning and sitting at his place at the table. "I'm afraid we haven't seen him since Randy and Officer Hanson fought over Amy's arrest. Gerrard threatened him with a suspension if he got involved in this case. I hope Randy isn't still in trouble; I'd hate to think he would lose his job over this."

A brief knock on the kitchen door announced Randy's arrival. "Good morning," he said, entering the home. "Strong coffee, please. I should have been home several hours ago, but something tells me my day is just starting." Randy sat at the table, accepting a hot mug of black coffee and a cream pitcher. Randy added a splash of cream to his mug, sipping quietly and wearily looking at George. "What did the lawyer tell you?"

"We are not supposed to talk about it," George replied, squirming in his seat. "But if Hanson had half a brain, even he would know that whatever piece of evidence he thinks he got from Amy's pockets, he shouldn't be jumping to the conclusion that Amy is involved in this case... this one or the last ice box murder. It's all a series of unfortunate coincidences."

"The *ice box murders*? Where did you hear that phrase?" Randy sat up straighter, almost spilling his hot coffee.

"At the station," George said slowly, leaning his forearm onto the table. "Hanson used that term. Hanson connected the girl in the freezer at the grocery store to the kid at the diner in what he called the ice box murders. Why?"

Slowly, Randy relaxed, leaning back on his chair. "Is that what you heard him say?"

Amy chewed and swallowed hard, giving her a moment to gather her thoughts. "I did. He also said I had evidence in my pockets confirming my connection to both cases."

"What was in your pockets that he was so interested in?"

"A gold earring."

"Was it your earring?" Randy said, trying to see if Amy had pierced ears or not. She did, but she wasn't wearing any at the moment.

"It wasn't even from my own pockets!"

"Did it look like this?" Randy said, pulling a few bits of paper and a grainy Polaroid from his uniform pocket.

"Is this the earring?" Amy pulled the photo towards her, studying it thoughtfully. "Yes, I think it is the one.

"I thought you said it wasn't from your own pockets?" Randy queried.

Amy hugged herself, fighting off the chills running down her back and trying to remember last night's events. "I was wearing a sweater that I got from a hook at the diner. The earring was in the sweater pocket. I don't know who the sweater belongs to, but I put it on because I had the door open waiting for the police to arrive; I was cold."

Randy held his small pencil, ready to write, "Did it fit you?"

"The sweater? No, it was too big for me."

"What colour was it?"

"It was grey. It's still at the police station!" Amy exclaimed, rolling her eyes. "I didn't take it home with me."

Randy wrote down what Amy had just told him; clarifying her statement, he asked, "Have you ever seen that sweater before? Where did you find it?"

Amy blew her limp bangs out of her eyes, telling this part of her story for the millionth time. "Like I told Officer Gerard, I don't know who it belongs to, where it has been, or how the earring got into the pocket; it was hanging by the back door and I put it on. I didn't know the earring was in the pocket!" Pushing her plate away, Amy stood up at the table. "Why is everyone trying to pin this on me? I didn't do anything!"

Clearing his throat, Randy said, "This is my photo of the earring you found near the freezer at the grocery store. If the one you found in the sweater pocket is the same, then you have found both earrings at two different crime scenes. It's tough to explain the circumstantial evidence. I understand why Hanson wants to charge you as a prime suspect."

Amy slowly sat back onto her chair, realization dawning on her for the first time. "I found the set! I know why Officer Hanson accused me of tampering with evidence and crime scene interference, but that still doesn't answer the questions: who really did it, and what's so special about an earring? I've seen those earrings at the drugstore. They aren't expensive or anything! I'm sure half of the women in town own that pair."

"The drugstore? I was there asking questions about another case involving a parking violation. I couldn't verify where those earrings came from. I didn't find them at the drugstore. I thought the earrings you found were from the jewellers. The lady told me they were from her store," Randy said, scribbling another note on a wrinkled paper scrap. "Do you think Anna Labrash bought those earrings at the drugstore?"

Amy looked up at the ceiling, slapping herself on the forehead. "That's it! That's what was so weird. I just figured it out!"

George stopped eating and moved to the edge of his seat, "What did you figure out?"

"The earrings! They weren't Anna's. She wore clip-ons. She had to slide them off to answer the phone at the grocery store. Sometimes, she would leave one on the ledge by the phone, forgetting that she was walking around with only one earring. I had to return her forgotten earrings to her more than once during a shift."

Randy's brain kicked into high gear with the new information, mumbling as he wrote, "Earrings, not Anna's, possibly the killer's. Check the drugstore." Shoving the papers into his slightly wrinkled uniform shirt, he stood up to leave, "Thanks for the coffee, Beatrice. It looks like it will have to keep me awake a little longer. I have to follow this lead on the earrings! Finding the source for the earrings is the only part of this case assigned to me. Gerard can't yell at me for doing what he told me!"

Beatrice Petersen quickly wrapped up an egg salad sandwich, shoving it into a paper sack with freshly baked double chocolate cookies. "Here, Randy; take this for your breakfast. I know you will be out longer than you expect, dear."

Randy reached for the lunch bag, kissing Beatrice on the cheek. "Thanks. Please do me another big favour and call Samantha. Tell her I'm still working!"

Beatrice moved the cookie jar out of the way, dragging the telephone on the kitchen counter to dial her daughter's number. Turning to Amy and George, she said, "Finish your breakfast and crawl into bed! Hurry it up! I feel this will be another long day for us, too."

Chapter 22

"Amy! Wait for me!"

Amy turned, watching her friend rush to her. "Sarah! What's going on?"

"Damn!" Sarah gasped for air, swallowing hard. "I was calling you, but you didn't hear me. Are you ignoring me, or have you lost your hearing since I talked to you last time?"

Amy continued walking up the steps into the post office. "I just didn't hear you, okay? I have a lot on my mind lately. You must have heard by now that Liam was found dead at Frankie's Diner, and with my bad luck, I was there to find him. Your favourite police officer thinks that I am walking around poisoning people and shoving them into deep freezers." Rolling her eyes and shoving her key into the lock to open her mailbox, Amy whispered, "I wouldn't blame you if you don't want to be around me. Hanging out with Glenmere's Most Wanted will ruin your reputation. What will people say?"

"That's not what everyone is saying," Sarah insisted, shaking her head. Her gold hoop earrings jingled against her neck with the movement.

"I'm sure everyone is talking about how I have found two, no, wait, three dead bodies. I almost forgot about the guy in the park. Why is it that I'm finding them? What is it about me?" Amy stressed, twisting a strand of her hair between her fingers. "I'm not doing anything on purpose. I just don't get it."

"I heard that someone is trying to frame you for Anna and Liam's murders. It's rather weird that you haven't figured it out yet. Someone who knows you and where you will be is trying to frame you. Come on, think about it! Everyone knows you work at the Family Grocers and Frankie's Diner. Someone stashed both bodies at the places where you work."

Amy could think of only one person who knew where she would be last Tuesday in the early morning fog, but why would Greg want to frame her for murder? It didn't make any sense. Shaking her head, Amy growled, "I don't know why he is doing it, but when I get my hands on that blue-haired freak, I am going to be a murderer! He must have overheard me at the store when I called you to say I would walk to your house to talk to you. He knows where we both live; it wouldn't be hard to guess that I would take a shortcut through the park to put me into another crime scene."

"What? Who are you talking about?" Sarah asked, raising her eyebrows and grabbing Amy's jean jacket sleeve. "You mean Greg, right? I don't think it's him, and I think his hair is a different Kool-Aid colour this week."

"Who else could it be? Lately, I seem to find him watching me wherever I go. Think about it! It makes sense to me. I see him everywhere," Amy excitedly explained.

"Oh, I think you are getting ahead of yourself. Greg might be weird, but he isn't a killer. It is hard to avoid anyone in this small town. I see lots of the same people walking around every day!"

Counting on her fingers as she listed off her reasons, Amy explained, "He works at the Family Grocers where the schedule is posted in the staff room for anyone to see. I saw him at Frankie's Diner when someone sent me a threatening note. It must have been him!"

"He threatened you? Like, what did he say?" Sarah asked, frowning.

"He keeps telling me to go home and live off of my millions like a good girl," Amy said, putting her mail in a bag as they left the post office. "I saw him again at the community hall the night I found Liam's body!"

"The wedding? Lots of people were in the hall. I could have been there too, but I decided to stay home," Sarah said. "Besides, I have been getting threatening messages, too."

"See? He's giving you the gears. Watch out!" Amy warned, grabbing onto Sarah's sleeve. "Officer Hanson said that someone poisoned Anna while she was at school that Friday, but she died several hours later.

He said that the janitor, Mr. Norman, was locked up at the police station and needed a student accomplice to poison Liam. It all fits! Greg is the accomplice, helping Mr. Norman poison the students."

"What kind of poison takes hours to kill you? I thought that was like instant death or something?"

Frowning, Amy tried to remember what Officer Hanson told her in the interview room. "Um, some poison that can be slipped into food or drink without tasting funny. I can't remember what it was. It started with the letter *t*. I'm sure I would remember it again if I heard it. Still, I remember Officer Gerard explaining to my lawyer that it would have made Anna very sick for several hours before she died. They have to check Liam's blood for the poison to be sure it is the same thing, but the police are confident."

Sarah grabbed Amy's arm, stopping them both from walking, "That's so strange. I remember hearing Leah and Anna both left school early on Friday afternoon. I didn't think anything of it at the time. Anna wanted me to cover her shift for a family emergency. What if the emergency was that she was sick from the poison? Maybe I shouldn't have yelled at her!"

"Did you see them both leave school?"

"No, I didn't."

Amy took a deep breath and grabbed Sarah's arms, "This is very important: who did you hear was sick? Both of them or just Anna?"

"What do you mean? Why would Leah be sick?"

The Ice Box

"No one has seen Leah since her sister was found dead. Is it possible someone poisoned Leah, too? Will her body be found somewhere next?" Amy asked. "I don't want to be the person who finds it!"

Sarah looked at Amy with confusion, shaking her head, and said, "Didn't I tell you that I saw Leah?"

"What?" Amy said, shaking Sarah. "When? Why didn't you tell me? Where did you see her?"

"Yesterday," Sarah said, pushing away from Amy's firm grip. "I was just coming out of the pharmacy. She was across the street from me. I called out and waved, but she didn't hear me."

"So, you didn't get to talk to her. Who was she with? Did you tell the police?"

"I'm sure lots of people saw her. She was with a tall boy wearing a bunnyhug, you know, a black hooded sweatshirt with a front pocket. They turned around the corner, heading to the East side of town. I didn't think anything of it. Should I have?"

"I don't know what to think, but I will mention it the next time I see Uncle Randy or Officer Gerard. In case they ask you, you should think about what you remember. Any details you can remember will help." Amy lost herself in thought, trying to figure out why someone hiding out from everyone suddenly appeared on Glenmere's main street. "Next time you see Leah, follow her! I need to talk to her. She knows who poisoned Anna, but I think she is too scared to tell anyone!"

Chapter 23

Walking into the small brick building that served as Glenmere's medical office, Randy approached one of the three receptionists at the desk. Putting his lips together into a grim expression, Randy waited for the woman to finish her telephone conversation. "Good morning, I am Officer Randy Doyle. I need to speak to Dr. Michaels about a police investigation. Is he available for a quick discussion?"

Looking over the counter and scanning the room, the receptionist stated, "I'm not sure he can see you today unless you make an appointment. He is already running behind with a full schedule of patients waiting to be seen. It's already the cold and flu season."

"This really can't wait. I won't take up more than five minutes of the doctor's time," Randy said, promising something he didn't know he could deliver. "It is important to police business as part of a criminal investigation."

The receptionist stood, leaving her ringing telephone unanswered. "Hang on a minute. I will be right back."

Randy tracked her movements with his eyes until she disappeared down the long hallway leading to the exam rooms and offices. He looked around the waiting room. Patients had stopped reading the wrinkled, outdated fashion and National Geographic magazines, glaring at him for delaying their appointments more than necessary.

The receptionist finally returned, motioning at Randy to follow her. He quickly followed her down the long green-carpeted hallway, amused with the woman's hurried strides and determination to get him to a door at the far end. "Five minutes," she warned. "He's already over an hour behind today."

"Thank you. I will be precise and get to the point," Randy said to her retreating backside, knocking softly on the door.

The door was opened almost immediately by the man Randy recognized as Dr. Michaels. "Officer, come in and shut the door," he said, sitting back in front of his desk littered with folders and medical reports.

"Thank you for meeting with me. I am investigating a prescription drug dealer and I want to ask a few questions."

"Maybe this is something you need to discuss with the pharmacy," he said, pulling a chart before him. "I only issue prescriptions to my patients who make an appointment to come and see me. I give out samples for the drugs I prescribe, but everyone I see has an appointment with medical needs."

"What about senile patients? People living with dementia? Do they have to book an appointment to renew their prescriptions, or do you do it automatically? How does it work for them?" Randy wondered, deciding he wouldn't need to write anything down for this interview.

"Most dementia patients are living at the nursing home on Second Street. Those people don't come in for appointments. As doctors, we take turns going to the infirm once a week to renew prescriptions and care for their medical needs. Occasionally, the nursing staff call for a special on-call doctor's appointment."

"What about the rest of the patients? Are any of your dementia patients living at home with family?" Randy hinted, fishing for more information on Mrs. Marshall's mental state.

Dr. Michaels tossed the pen he was holding on top of his files, showing annoyance at this line of questioning. "A few patients are cared for at home by their families, but it is difficult. Family members must bring their loved ones in for an appointment. It's not easy, depending on the patient and progression of the disease."

"What if the family can't bring the patient in for an appointment? How does the family member request prescription refills?"

Dr. Michaels shrugged, saying, "It would be a rare occurrence. I can't recall anything like it happening. Sometimes the pharmacy phones or faxes a request to our office to renew an existing prescription. I will fax the

The Ice Box

renewal back to them but issue a few days to a week of pills. A partial renewal gives a person a week to come in for an appointment for a full script."

"What about when the office is closed? What does the person do?"

"Hopefully, people are organized enough to arrange a prescription renewal before it runs out on the weekend. Either they wait until our clinic is open again on Monday, or they waste time in the emergency room at the hospital. If I'm the on-call doctor, I get a telephone call at home stating the request for the prescription. I keep a few prescription pads at home to fax to the pharmacy in case of an emergency. I don't always have to go to the hospital to see the patient for minor things like that."

"Have any of your prescription pads gone missing?"

Startled, the doctor turned in his chair and looked up at Randy. "No, I don't think so, but I wasn't aware that I needed to check my inventory. How recently are you suggesting this may have happened?"

Randy shook his head, thinking, *Maybe I got this all wrong. But then again, if he was helping deal drugs by writing extra prescriptions, he isn't about to tell me now, is he? A doctor would have his licence to practice suspended.* Rubbing the stubble on his chin, Randy said, "Well, I'm not sure, but the pharmacist, Marcel Janvier, seems to be getting a few extra prescriptions filled at the pharmacy by a patient named Edith Marshall. She keeps losing her pills and getting new refills. Mrs. Marshall would be one of your dementia patients still living at home with relatives. Do you know anything about her family losing her pills?"

"Well, the name doesn't ring a bell; I have too many patients to remember everyone and I can't discuss a patient's medical records without their consent or a warrant," Dr. Micheals smiled, clearly trying to end any further questioning regarding Edith Marshall.

"What can you tell me?" Randy eyed the doctor suspiciously, wondering what the good doctor might be hiding.

"I can tell you the following: to my knowledge, I am not missing any prescription pads, but that is hard to inventory. It's common for patients with dementia to have a family member bring them to appointments since they can't do it themselves. Occasionally, we will renew prescriptions for long-time patients without seeing them. As far as I know, I have not written any extra prescriptions. Also, I doubt Marcel would be handing out extra pills. The pharmacy regularly does an inventory of street-sellable prescription drugs. Does that answer your questions? I have a hell of a lot of sick people to attend to before lunch."

Standing and taking his cue to leave, Randy said, "Thank you for your time, Dr. Michaels. I will let you know if we need anything further for our investigations."

Feeling that something was wrong after leaving the medical clinic, Randy thought, *Why wouldn't he know his patient? A dementia patient living at home is a bit unusual. He said most of them live at the nursing home. Wouldn't anyone who wasn't in nursing care stand out to him? Maybe I should ask the pharmacy when they last did inventory.*

Chapter 24

Officer Lloyd Trussell ambled into the roll call room at the station and sat down at his desk across from Randy. Tossing some pink message papers over the short divider, Trussell said, "Doyle, can you check into some of these complaints? I have to take care of this other call that is fifteen miles out of town. It will take most of my shift to get out and back."

Randy picked up the pink message slips with Trussell's name written across the top. "I'm sure I can find the time to answer one or two, but I won't make any promises."

"No need to get your panties in a twist. It doesn't matter when you handle them. I don't have the time to do extra calls this week."

Stretching and grabbing his empty mug, Randy stood. "I'm going to need more coffee to motivate me to push papers around and follow up on all these messages." Walking over to the coffee station, he wondered why Trussell had even gone into policing; indeed, he would have been a better night watchman or gate security.

"Doyle, in my office!" Gerard demanded, breezing through the room into his office.

Randy finished pouring coffee into his mug before entering Gerard's office. Sitting down, he blew across the top of his mug, trying to cool the hot liquid. Randy's first sip was bitter and burned his tongue. "What's up, Boss?"

"I need the earring from the Labrash case back in evidence to compare it to the one found on the Hildebrandt kid. Did you take it out of evidence to discover which store stocks it?"

The hair on the back of Randy's neck stood on end, knowing he didn't want to get in trouble for messing around with an investigation involving his niece as a prime suspect. Randy shifted in his chair, balancing the hot mug in his hands. "The one Amy found? It's been in evidence since I logged it in the book."

"You didn't take it to the stores to locate the supplier like I asked? Did you leave it someplace?"

"No," Randy swallowed. "I took one of the photos to a few places around town, but I couldn't match it to anything in the displays."

"How many photos did you take?" Gerard said, removing the notebook he kept in his uniform pocket.

"I remember using the Polaroid to take three photographs. Because the first one was quite blurry, I threw it in the trash bin. The second and third exposures were better than the first. I used one photo to question the jeweller and the pharmacy staff. I didn't take it anywhere else. I attached the last photo to the case file."

"Which case file?" Officer Gerard asked, frowning and throwing down the open evidence log. "I have not seen any photos and you didn't log anything in the book."

Randy leaned forward, skimming the page, looking for his handwriting. "I know I logged the evidence. I am positive I followed the procedures! I created a file with Amy's statement when she found the earring near where she discovered the first victim."

"I have gone through last week's entries. You didn't log the evidence! It is missing along with your file with Amy's statement. Do I need to remind you how important it is to log the evidence and avoid cases involving your family? Where would we be if we had another suspect in custody with a big-shot lawyer asking for release based on circumstantial evidence? We would not be able to make the charges stick! You have disrupted the chain of evidence. I was hoping you could give me the photo you still have in your possession. I have looked through the case files and I can't find your reports or the photos inside of any of them. I need to compare the earrings in these cases."

Randy reached for his breast pocket but only found his crumpled loose notes with the pharmacy letterhead. Patting his pant pockets, he still came up empty. "I guess I don't have the photo," Randy said, clearing his dry throat and wondering where he left it.

"So not only did you fail to log and store evidence, but you have lost the photos that you took of the evidence? Doyle! You need to get your shit together! Be more organized. Your lack of organization could have lost the key evidence tying these murder cases together!"

Gerard's voice struck Randy deep in the pit of his stomach. "Wait! I left a photo on the table at George and Beatrice's house. I was still following up with a lead I have on the earrings and carrying it around in my pocket," Randy continued, taking a deep breath with relief. "I will check my work area under all of my paperwork for the missing reports and the missing evidence. I had stapled a photo into a case file; maybe it's just in the wrong one?"

Gerard breathed deeply, exhaling through his nose and trying to control his temper. "I am frustrated. Randy, you need to find me those photos and that evidence or your job is on the line! I have already broken up a fight between you and Jeffrey Hanson this week. You are on probation! Pull up your socks, get a decent notebook and stop fighting with other police officers trying to do their jobs! I was hoping you would stay away from these murder cases. Do you want to keep rescuing cats out of trees or do you want to help put criminals behind bars?"

Randy swallowed, trying to remain calm and professional. "I am interested in handling more investigative cases. I am trying to stay out of the murder cases, but things keep landing in my lap. I am starting to think my parking violation case and the murder cases are connected!"

"Your parking case and the murder cases are connected? I am not jumping to the same conclusion.

Where is your proof?" Gerard shook his head, looking unimpressed with the rookie cop in his office. "Is it lost with the rest of your paperwork?"

"I have been trying to work out the connection but haven't found it yet. The parking violation case seems wrapped up with the dealing of prescription drugs. I think someone at the pharmacy is dealing pills, and that person is also involved in the two murders."

"It doesn't seem to have a connection. I need the missing evidence for my murder cases. Get the photo from the Petersens and find the missing evidence! I will be writing you up for tampering with evidence if you don't come through for me! Your ass is on the line. If you screw up again, you will receive a suspension."

"I will do better. I started writing stuff down like you said," Randy pleaded, hoping to stay in his boss' good graces. "I will get you that evidence."

"While you are at the Petersens picking up the photo, ask them if they know Amy's blood type. The blood type found on the earring doesn't match the victim. I want to know if I need to ask for a blood sample from Amy."

Randy nodded and left Gerard's office, feeling that he had nothing left to say. Dumping the rest of his coffee into the sink and kicking himself for being so disorganized, Randy wondered, *Are these cases related? I'm seeing connections where there aren't any. Did I log it in the wrong book? I remember bagging and sealing it into the pouch. Did I leave the photos at my desk? I remember which locker it went into in the evidence room. It's too bad this little detachment doesn't have someone in charge of evidence. It's ridiculous!*

Chapter 25

The weather was warming to seasonal autumn trends, melting the ice and snow. Amy exited the main doors of the Family Grocers, glad to be finished with the short work shift. Her stomach rumbled with hunger. Amy unwrapped the lock from her orange ten-speed bike secured to the bicycle stand, squinting at the dark clouds intermittently blocking the sun. She dug out her gloves, judging the road conditions. The streets were wet from the melting ice and snow, but the area down the middle of Main Street was dry, promising a better place to ride to keep the spray from the back tire from soaking her backside. Amy knew she must wash and dry her blue uniform tonight before tomorrow's shift.

"Hey!" Sarah said, applying her bike brakes and coming to a squealing stop beside Amy. "I'm glad I caught you before you left work."

The Ice Box

Smiling, Amy replied, "Hey! What are you doing here?"

"I was hoping to catch you to tell you the good news."

"I could use some good news. Lay it on me!"

"I talked to our boss today," Sarah said, dismounting her bicycle. "I will be coming back starting tomorrow after school."

"Awesome! We are short-staffed with losing Anna and you being gone. We will be working tomorrow's close shift together. What are you doing tonight? Wanna come over for supper?"

"Sure! I will phone my mom from your place. I'm sure it'll be fine," Sarah shrugged, rotating her bike around to get ready to leave the parking lot. "Do you think your grandpa will offer me a ride home later? Are you listening to me?"

Amy wasn't listening. She was focused on looking across the street, watching Leah exit the pawn shop and climb into someone's car. "Look! It's Leah!" She pointed, opening her eyes wide in surprise. "I've been looking everywhere for her!"

"Hurry! Let's go after her!" Sarah called over her shoulder, pushing off with her foot and pedalling out of the parking lot.

At the sidewalk dividing the parking lot and the street, Amy and Sarah braked, skidding to a complete stop and watching the driver of the old car back up to maneuver a wide U-turn in front of oncoming traffic to go in the opposite direction.

Pushing off with her foot, Amy glanced over her shoulder for oncoming traffic as she exited the parking lot. "Oh, no, you don't!" Amy started pedalling as fast as she could, chasing after the vehicle with the loud exhaust. Amy shifted down through her gears, listening to the bicycle chain click on the spool as she increased her speed. "Hurry, Sarah, we can't lose her!" She pumped the pedals hard, moving to a standing position for more leverage and ignoring the spray of muddy water. Amy carefully watched the vehicle pull farther away from them, waiting to see if it would go straight or turn in the distance. Sucking in the cold air and trying to work up some moisture in her mouth, Amy felt her heart hammering in her chest. She thought they could eventually catch up to the car if they could keep track of where it had gone. "If only I hadn't been getting rides everywhere lately, then I could pedal faster," she yelled into the wind. Amy watched the light-coloured car make a left turn in the distance, keeping their eyes on the dispersing blast of black exhaust smoke where the vehicle turned. Amy blinked, focusing on pushing her tired legs to pedal harder. Her lungs burned with each gasp of cool autumn air.

Licking her dry lips, Amy sharply turned the corner, swerving around a parked car, almost losing control of her ten-speed on the wet asphalt. Gasping for air, Amy allowed herself to sit back on the seat to try and catch her breath. She grinned at Sarah with relief, pointing to the car that they were chasing parked ahead on the next block. Amy inhaled sharply, watching a tall person in a black bunnyhug, cross the street and enter the driver's side.

"There's the car!" Sarah managed to pant out. "It looks like they are leaving again."

Amy swallowed hard, calling out, "Wait! Stop! Stop! Don't leave!"

The black hooded figure turned slightly, checking over his shoulder before closing the driver's door. He started the engine. It roared to life, blowing noisy exhaust smoke before speeding off again.

"Come back! Leah!" Amy yelled, feeling defeated. She allowed her bike to coast to a slow stop alongside Sarah. Unsure of what to do next, Amy inspected the houses on this street, noticing the curtains swaying in the front window. "I think I know which house they visited. Do you see the curtains moving?" Amy said, pointing to the small home across the street. "That house is either the house the driver came from or someone who might know who the driver is or which house he briefly visited. We need to knock on the door to find out who was driving that car! It's the best we can do. I need to find Leah and talk to her."

Sarah shrugged, setting her bicycle in the long grass of an unkempt yard mixed with melting patches of snow. "I think I recognize that car. Did you think it was familiar?"

Taking a few deep breaths to calm herself, Amy dismounted from her bicycle and pushed it to a tree, leaning her bike against it. "I don't know. Maybe. My best guess is a family member or a friend is driving her around. She has been avoiding everyone in town."

Feeling defeated, Amy slowly crossed the quiet street to approach the house. Knocking on the front door, they waited patiently until a middle-aged woman appeared behind the screen door.

Opening the door a few inches, the woman wearily spoke, "Unless you are selling Girl Guide cookies, I'm not interested."

"Sorry, no cookies. Did you see a guy in a black bunnyhug either come to this house or next door? He had my friend in the car and I'm trying to find her."

"Maybe. Who is the girl you are looking for?"

"Um, her name is Leah. Her sister died recently and I haven't been able to..."

Smiling and opening the door wider, the woman leaned towards Amy, "Are you sure it was your friend? Maybe the boy was your boyfriend taking out another girl behind your back?"

"No, I don't know him," Amy answered, frowning and shaking her head. "I didn't even recognize him. We couldn't see his face with his hood pulled up. Did you see him or the car? I saw you looking out the window a minute ago."

Amy and Sarah waited awkwardly while the woman seemed to think about her answer, looking over her shoulder. "Yes, I saw him."

"And?"

The woman grinned, "I think I can help you out."

"So, you'll tell me who he is?"

The woman crossed her arms and said, "I have a better idea. I will take you to his house. Come on in! I will grab my keys and take you for a little ride."

"I'll just wait out here. I think I have a leg cramp," Sarah said, limping around in a small circle and rubbing her leg.

Amy nodded, crossed the threshold and stepped into the cluttered kitchen to awkwardly stand near the kitchen table. Alarm bells sounded in her head, but Amy ignored the warning. She knew she should not enter a stranger's home, but she was determined to find Leah. Amy distractedly followed little white tablets scattered across the kitchen table with her eyes, spilling out from an overturned orange pill bottle. Her eyes stopped on the name on the label; all of the hairs stood up on Amy's neck. She knew the identity of the black-bunnyhug-wearing driver with Leah! Lost in a turmoil of thoughts, the sudden bang of the door slamming shut behind her jolted Amy, unaware of her surroundings, just before her knees buckled under the weight of something hard hitting the top of her head. Amy crashed into the table, her vision fading to black until she lost all consciousness.

Chapter 26

Almost running into Officer Lloyd Trussell and spilling his coffee onto the orange carpet on his way back to his desk area, Randy shifted his mug into his other hand. "Ow! That's hot! Sorry, Trussell. Did I spill on you?" Randy inhaled deeply, trying to control his frustration.

"Nope, I'm good. Watch where you are going next time," Trussell said, smiling as he walked away.

"Yeah, no problem," Randy said, quietly distracted. "Why is Hanson sitting at my workstation?" Randy looked around at the other officers in the room; they were quick to duck their heads down, busy with their paperwork. Idle chit-chat seemed to cease to a sudden halt. Randy soundlessly walked up behind Hanson; using a firm and loud voice, he asked, "Is there something I can help you find, Jeffrey? You are messing up my paperwork."

Hanson jumped up from the desk, knocking the chair onto the floor and the mug out of Randy's hand. The mug tumbled down, smashing on the floor and sending hot coffee all over the bottoms of the two officer's uniform pants. "Shit! Why are you sneaking up on me like that?"

Shaking coffee from his hand onto Hanson's uniform shirt, Randy sneered, "I don't know. What are you doing messing up the files on my desk?"

Hanson puffed up his chest, taking a step closer toward Randy. "I need the statements you collected from your niece when she brought you the earrings into evidence. Where are you hiding them in your mess, rookie?"

Randy parted his legs into a wider stance, not wanting to let a know-it-all officer like Jeffrey Hanson intimidate him. His nostrils flared and he clenched his teeth as he blew hot air out of his nose. "You don't have that much more experience than I do! What brings you here to our small town anyway? Is the big city too much for you to handle?"

A burst of mocking laughter came out of his mouth. Grinning, Hanson argued, "You think I came here because I couldn't handle police business in Saskatoon? No, you little prick. I'm here because with last August's crime wave and murder case, Glenmere needed another experienced cop."

"What did you call me?" Randy snarled, pushing Hanson into the desk behind him. Officer Hanson quickly drew his fist back, ready to strike, but Randy was fueled by anger and quicker to release a right hook, landing close to the officer's nose. Several officers in the roll call room rushed the two officers, pulling them apart. "I'm the one who helped Gerard with those cases! I can handle the investigative work!" Randy growled through his clenched teeth, fighting against the officer holding him back. "You weren't here, cowboy!"

"What the hell is going on in here!" Officer Gerard bellowed from across the room. All officers, except officers Hanson and Doyle, turned at Gerard's voice.

Hanson slowly stood, keeping his cold blue eyes on Randy and shaking free of the officer holding his arms. Wiping the blood from his nose with the back of his other hand, he quietly whispered, "We will see what you can handle and what you can't. We all have our responsibilities around here."

Randy squinted at Hanson, quietly threatening, "I will have your job. You will see." His anger was still boiling, but Randy managed to contain it below the surface.

Stalking further into the roll call room and growling with disapproval, Officer Gerard inspected the commotion. "Everyone get back to work," Gerard barked. "What the hell is going on here?"

Unable to control his anger, Randy jumped at the chance and yelled, "Hanson was messing up my files and paperwork!"

"I was looking for stuff connected to my case, but the rookie is so disorganized that I couldn't find what I was looking for!"

"You spilled my coffee on me!" Randy shouted back.

"That was an accident!" Hanson protested, holding his hands up.

Gerard tried to calm the officers down by raising his hands in front of him. "Lower your voices! We are professionals here on the same team. We all must accept that we need each other's help to solve cases."

"I don't need his help!" Hanson and Doyle both shouted at the same time.

Gerard shook his head with disgust. "We are a team at the Glenmere Police Department. Together, we keep this town safe. Now, who threw the first punch?" He sternly asked, scowling.

"Doyle," Hanson muttered, using a tissue to wipe his nose.

"Yes, but he was about to hit me first."

"Did he strike you?" Officer Gerard asked, crossing his arms.

"No," Randy replied.

"Push you?"

"Um, no," Randy said, frowning. He knew this would not help him avoid working the parking violation and cat rescue cases. He would be lucky to be demoted to the file maintenance clerk position. "He didn't touch me other than when he stood up and knocked my mug out of my hand." Randy gently kicked broken shards of the mug with the toe of his work boots.

"Is this a fact, Hanson?"

Jeffrey Hanson cleared his throat, taking his time to answer. "Yes, sir."

"Officer Doyle," Gerard said, shaking his head slowly. "You are on suspension. I warned you about this."

"But I need to read Amy's statements. I think I just found a clue linking these cases!" Randy insisted.

"I asked you to stay out of the murder cases. I've already talked to you about your conduct as a police officer. You are putting me in a difficult position, Doyle."

"Yes, but-"

Sighing, Officer Gerard reached for his breast pocket to retrieve his notebook. "You are on suspension for your recent behaviour and conduct. Go home, Randy! We will talk about it after you have had a chance to cool off. Jeffrey, in my office. Now!"

Randy's jaw dropped. He was stunned and couldn't believe he had just been suspended right in the middle of solving the case of prescription drug trafficking and murder. *What the hell just happened? What was Hanson really up to going through my papers? He acted like he was up to something. He must have been stealing the evidence. No one jumps that high unless they are sneaking around. Hanson did this to me on purpose! He gets all the glory while I am under suspension and might lose my career?* Randy thought, kicking the trash can and turning to leave the detachment. His mind clouded with shattered dreams of becoming a big city detective, solving exciting action-packed cases. *Oh, shit! What am I going to tell my wife?*

Chapter 27

Blinking slowly, Amy tried to shake off the dizziness and confusion in the suffering darkness of the confined space. She fought hard against the nausea from the stench of oil and the metallic copper taste of blood. Amy struggled to find her focus. The last thing she remembered was the unexpected tackle to the floor leading her into darkness. Swallowing and licking her dry, swollen lips, Amy moaned, "Hello?" She struggled to open her eyes, blinking away dust and grit but still unable to see. "Oh, my head hurts." Amy felt her heart fill with fear, quickening its pace and hammering in her chest.

Amy cursed, finding herself bound in the trunk of a moving vehicle. She inhaled deeply, coughing from the fumes burning her eyes and nostrils. She retched and coughed, hot tears cleansing her eyes. The vehicle's movements, navigating the streets, shifted her body. Amy's mind raced with unanswered questions and impossible scenarios. She listened carefully for clues that might reveal the vehicle's destination. Laying still, Amy heard the hum of the tires, the rumble of exhaust, the blare of a siren and the squawk of music as other vehicles passed nearby. "I need help! Please help me! I'm here!" She yelled, hoping to be heard over the noisy rumble drowning her cries. Rolling onto her back and lifting her bound legs, Amy kicked the metal sides of her enclosure. "Somebody help me! Can you hear me?" she screamed. Amy lay quiet, listening for the sound of other vehicles nearby.

Her stomach rolled with the vehicle's sudden change in direction. She inhaled deeply, coughing from the oil and gas fumes assaulting her nostrils. She retched, choking on bile rising in her throat. "I need help! Help me!" she yelled into the darkness of her confined space. The rumble of the vehicle tires drowned out her cries. Attempting to signal for help, Amy repeatedly kicked the trunk lid. The small space limited her movements, but Amy continued to scream for help.

Amy lay still and listened to the hum of the wind mixed with the loud muffler. She lay quiet and defeated, realizing no one would answer her calls. "This is useless! Who's going to hear me?" she sobbed, squeezing her eyes closed.

Amy struggled to move against the pain in her shoulder to roll onto her side, flexing her bound hands behind her to return circulation. The scratchy rope cut into the tender flesh of her wrists, but Amy, determined to fight for her survival, ignored the burning pain. If only she could reach the box cutter in her pocket she could slice through the binding rope. The vehicle came to a quick and sudden stop, inertia rolling Amy's body into the trunk's corner. Amy winced against the pain, her head banging against the inside of the trunk, landing her against something soft. "Sarah? Sarah, is that you? Answer me! Are you okay?" No answer came from the body, lying unmoving across one end of the trunk.

"Sarah?" Amy called again, wondering if the darkness within the trunk was playing tricks on her perception or if the fumes were making her high. The shadows morphed into unnatural faces, laughing with every groan and creak of the moving vehicle. Amy shook her head, regaining control of her imagination and pushing the horrifying scenarios into the far corners of her mind.

Noticing a change in the noise outside the trunk and feeling the temperature drop significantly, Amy was alerted to the familiar noise of whooshing air, high-speed traffic and the hum of tires across highway pavement. Time seemed to stop as Amy's thoughts returned to dread, knowing that her captor had left the town of Glenmere.

Straining against the coarse ropes biting into her skin and waging war against her looming fate, Amy thought of her life outside of her confinement. Imagining the smell and taste of freshly baked cookies in her granny's warm, bright kitchen, Amy struggled to hold onto hope within the confines of the trunk. Her cherished memories were tainted with the bitterness of her current nightmare as her heart ached for a chance to regain her newfound life again. Amy heard a passing vehicle's whoosh, quickly returning her to her harsh reality. She swallowed, trying to gain control of her thoughts. Using her shoulder to brush hair stuck to the dampness on her face, Amy trembled with fear. She knew she needed to find warmth, cautiously rolling closer to where the other person lay. The movement put her back against the soft fabric of clothing. A light whisper of breath tickled the back of her neck. Amy tried to reassure the person lying behind her, confidently saying, "Don't worry, we will be okay."

"I'm cold," Sarah whispered back. "Where are we going?"

"I don't know where we are or where we're going, but we are on the highway," Amy answered. "I'm tied up. Are you?"

Moving slightly, Sarah sighed, "Yup, I'm tied up too. I can barely move. The spare tire is digging into my back."

"Do you want me to roll away to give you more room?"

"Don't bother. I am in too much pain to move," she answered.

Amy sensed the highway speed and terrain change as the girls bounced around in the trunk. "It feels like a gravel road. We might be close to our final destination. What are we going to do?"

"Nothing comes to mind. We should do what the kidnapper says and hope for rescue."

The Ice Box

"I think we need to escape once we get to wherever we are going. I still have my box cutter in my pocket. If you can help me get it out, we can cut the ropes," Amy said, trying to calm them both. "If these guys have anything to do with Anna and Liam's death, I am not going to eat or drink anything, no matter how hungry I get. Officer Hanson told us that the killer slipped poison into their drinks."

"How long can a person live without food or water?" Sarah asked, trying to raise her voice over the rumble of the vehicle.

"I'm sure we won't have to find out! Let's wait until we figure out another plan or someone comes to save us."

"I hope it doesn't take long."

After a few turns and a seemingly endless drive over rutted gravel roads, the vehicle holding them captive finally stopped. The sudden silence heightened Amy's fears and reanimated her wild imagination. She inhaled deeply, straining to hear muffled talking and finding it challenging to comprehend the situation. The motion of a door slamming rocked the vehicle. Someone cracked open the other door but left it open. Amy's eyes widened as she heard the metal jingle of keys opening the trunk. The trunk opened, blinding Amy with bright light. She squinted as the shadowy figure reached in and dragged her into the daylight.

Chapter 28

Randy paused, his hand almost touching the brass doorknob, listening closely for any noise coming from the other side. He looked around the quiet neighbourhood, noticing how the orange glow from the sunset cast strange hues. Inhaling deeply, Randy scolded himself for his cowardice, "Get it together, man!" He grabbed a hold of the doorknob, pushing the door open with a bit of force. It rubbed on its casing, making a creaking noise and reminding Randy that he'd never adjusted the frame. The smell of coffee filled his nostrils, propelling him into the quaint kitchen and over to the worn kitchen counter. Taking a mug from the drain board beside the sink, Randy shook out the excess water before helping himself to a hot mug of coffee.

"Just what do you think you are doing?"

Jumping slightly at her voice, Randy spilled hot coffee on his hand and all over the counter. "Shit!" he cursed, wiping his hand on his uniform pants.

"Stop, I've got it," she insisted, her blue eyes glaring at him. Randy stood up straighter, backing away from the mess he had just made on the counter.

"I think you made me burn myself," he snarled, watching her wipe up his mess. T-Bone let out a protective bark, which annoyed Randy further. "Go lay down, T-Bone!"

Her eyes searched him questioningly while she finished pouring his coffee. "Serves you right. I should train T-Bone to bite your leg when you walk through the door. What are you doing at home, anyway? Shouldn't you be at work?" Samantha asked. "You don't usually come home at this time. Is everything okay? You look like hell."

Looking down at the mug of coffee, Randy thought he would need something more robust for this kind of conversation. He reached around his wife, pulling a bottle of rum from the top cupboard. "I think I will need a little more than coffee! It's been a rough shift."

"Your shift isn't over. Are you sick?" Samantha asked, looking at her wristwatch.

Randy poured the amber liquid into a plastic cup, wondering what to say to Samantha. "No, just tired. Gerard sent me home early." He raised the cup to his mouth and poured its contents down his throat, feeling the rum burn into the pit of his stomach, and hoping it would soothe his injured pride.

Crossing her arms, Samantha frowned with concern, "No, I think there is more to this. What's bothering you?"

Randy looked out the small kitchen window, studying the light from the streetlights filtering through the yellowed leaves clinging to the birch tree branches in the front yard. "I don't feel like talking about it just yet," he replied, pouring another good shot of rum into his plastic cup.

Slowly sitting down at the table, she continued questioning, absently stroking the German Shepherd at her elbow. "Did something happen at work today?"

Randy eyed her wearily, wondering how much he could share with her, what he should leave out of the conversation and where to start. He'd wanted to have this conversation after he talked to Gerard tomorrow. If Randy could settle everything with Gerard, then he could return to his job without having this difficult conversation with Samantha. Putting the bottle of rum on the table, he sat next to her.

"What is it?" she reached for Randy's hand, stopping the cup from reaching his lips and searching his face for answers.

Randy stared into her pleading eyes and pulled his hand away, sipping on the rum. "I'm not sure where to begin or end."

"What happened?"

Sighing, Randy rubbed his hands over his face. He knew he couldn't avoid discussing it with her, especially if his suspension lasted longer than a day. He never could keep secrets from Samantha. She seemed to have some power over him. "I got into a fight with Jeffrey Hanson. That prick has been giving me a hard time at work! I'm not sure, but I think he has been messing around with my cases to get me into trouble with Gerard," Randy exclaimed defensively.

"A fight? Like, an argument, or a fight?" she mimed, playfully punching the air in front of Randy's face.

"Both," he sighed, releasing a deep breath. He let the mellowing effect of the rum relax him before he continued. "He has been on my back ever since he arrived in Glenmere. The guy is an arrogant dick. He seems to think that because he's worked in Saskatoon, he is a better police officer than me. I am good at what I do. I need the opportunity to show my stuff to Gerard so I can get off fluff duty." He slammed the plastic cup on the table, some of the amber liquid splashing out. Randy shook the excess rum off his hand before bringing the cup up and swallowing its contents in one gulp. "Hanson has been messing around with my notes, files, and case evidence. I couldn't take it anymore! I know he's screwing with me! He's trying to ruin my career," he cursed, pouring another three ounces into the plastic cup, wondering how much rum he would have to drink before he didn't care anymore.

Crossing her arms, Samantha eyed him warily, "I'm sure it's not as bad as it seems. Did you talk to Officer Gerard? After the big case you worked on with him this summer, I'm sure he knows you are good at what you do. You are good at your job."

"I don't know anymore. I should just quit my job, but then I don't know what I should do."

Samantha's eyebrows shot up, alarmed. "You don't know? I tell you why you don't know! Your dream is to be a police detective. It has been since the day I met you, way back when I was living in Regina. You can't quit now! We need your income just as much as we need mine. We talked about owning a home with real furniture and starting a family. I still want that, don't you?"

"Yes, of course I want that. I'm just frustrated." Tipping the cup to his lips, he held the burning liquid in his mouth for a moment before swallowing it. Randy picked up the bottle of rum, looking at its contents and wondering how much he had drank since he got home twenty minutes ago. He slid the bottle across the table with disgust.

"Go to bed. You have work tomorrow. We have rent and student loans to pay," she said, kicking back her chair. T-Bone barked with her sudden movements.

Randy gulped down the last of his rum. "I got suspended."

"What?"

"What did you expect? I got into a boxing match with Hanson in the office!"

"You will sleep in the other room tonight!" Samantha yelled over her shoulder, leaving the kitchen. "Tomorrow, you will get your ass back into the detachment to beg your boss for your job back!"

Randy winced when he heard the bedroom door slam. T-Bone started to whine, pacing from the hallway and back into the kitchen. "It's okay. She's not mad at you. It looks like we are sharing the dog house tonight." T-Bone wagged his tail, nudging Randy with his nose and sitting, looking at him expectantly. Randy paused, looking at Samantha's dog. He poured another ounce or two into his cup. "What? Do you have to go outside?"

T-Bone barked twice, wagging his tail.

Sighing, Randy drank his rum and stood. The room swayed, leaving him questioning what time he last ate. "Whoa! Okay, maybe the fresh air will clear my head a bit. Go get your leash."

Randy pulled his jacket tightly around him, finally managing to zip it up on the third try. T-Bone pulled Randy, staggering towards the open space of a schoolyard a few blocks from home. Watching the dog run around the playground equipment, Randy felt the warmth of the rum dissipating in the cool night air. "Let's go, T-Bone!" Randy said, rubbing his hands to warm them. He clicked the leash to T-Bone's collar, pulling him to the nearest sidewalk. He looked down the darkened street, trying to focus on directions as he tugged on the leash, crossing to the other side. Headlights from a slow-moving vehicle turning onto the street blinded Randy. Still unsteady with his footing, Randy stumbled and raised his hand to shade his eyes. T-Bone let out a warning bark.

"Geeze, give me a minute to cross," Randy muttered, talking to himself.

The driver unrolled the window, calling out, "Randy! What the hell are you doing? I've been looking for you, too."

"Well, you found us. Is that you, George?" Randy called, frowning. He didn't think Samantha would call her parents to go out to search for him, unless he had been gone longer than he thought.

"Yeah, it's me. Get in the car!" George replied, motioning for Randy to join him.

Randy walked around to the rear passenger side of the black car and put T-Bone into the back seat. The dog recognized the vehicle and didn't hesitate to jump inside. Randy's eyes roamed over the wet and muddy dog in the glare of the interior lights. "Sorry, George. T-Bone is quite dirty. I guess we were roaming the park longer than I thought. I can clean your backseat tomorrow afternoon," Randy said, chuckling and slamming the heavy rear car door closed. Stumbling slightly, he managed to get a grip on the passenger door and open it. He bumped his head on the door frame as he crawled into the warmth of the car. Rubbing his head, Randy said, "Thanks for coming out to look for us. You didn't need to do all that! We would have made it home soon enough for Sam to yell at me again."

"What makes you think I am out here looking for you?"

"You're the one who said you were looking for us," Randy hiccupped, covering his mouth with his hand.

"I am looking for Amy. She didn't come home after her shift. I phoned Sarah's house, thinking she might have gone there, but Mrs. Tyler said Sarah was meeting Amy. Bea and I weren't worried at first, but neither one has shown up anywhere and no one has seen them! We have been searching for the two girls for hours. I was looking for you to help me find them!"

"Jesus! I thought Samantha sent you out to look for me and T-Bone. I didn't know that Amy was missing!"

"I found her bike lock on the ground near the bike rack at the Family Grocers. The girls didn't show up at Frankie's either. I have given up hope that they have stopped somewhere to visit a friend, and I've started searching in a grid down every street."

"It's a good strategy to search for their bikes. If we can find their bikes, then we can find the girls!" Randy said, trying to think through the fog that settled in his brain. "Did you call the police?" He suppressed a burp, clearing his throat.

"I phoned Gerard. He mentioned that you were at home. Samantha said you were out walking the dog. She didn't sound pleased with you. Now that I've found you, I can see why," George eyed him up, making Randy feel sheepish. "Any chance you got in trouble for drinking on the job?"

"Hell, no! I didn't have anything to drink until I got home." Randy eyed his father-in-law, willing him to believe him. "I had a bad shift; I punched Hanson and got sent home. I thought I was on to a vital clue, but it was nothing. I drank a shot or two of rum before I left to walk the dog. I don't know when I left the house."

"My guess is two hours ago," George hesitated, moving the gear shift into drive. "We should get you out of uniform first, then get some coffee and a sandwich into you before we continue the search. Bea made me a thermos of strong black coffee."

"This is not exactly my shining moment. At least I'm not wearing my police jacket." Looking down at his pants, Randy was shocked to see that he was still wearing his police uniform. "I think I should tell you I have had more than just a shot or two to drink, George," Randy said, hoping the neighbours didn't notice that he was intoxicated while in uniform as he inspected the wet, muddy hems.

"I know," George replied, shaking his head and grinning. "You might want to keep your mouth shut around Samantha unless it's an apology. She had nothing good to say when I telephoned your house looking for you. Samantha told me you drank half a bottle of rum. I recommend apologizing and promising to have a real conversation after we find Amy. Mark my words: I'm confident she will be more concerned about Amy than how much you had to drink or whatever your fight was about."

"Noted," Randy said, shaking his head and trying to clear his thoughts. "What's the rest of your search plan?"

"It's not a complicated plan. Bea is making some sandwiches and snacks for us. I will drop you off to get changed into street clothes while I pick up the food and another thermos. Because you have been drinking, I will drive and you will direct."

"Is Gerard going to put officers on the search?"

George glanced at Randy; frowning, he said, "They have to wait a few hours before she is considered missing.

There is nothing they can do tonight. It's just our family and Sarah Tyler's family searching for the girls. It's too late at night to rally the neighbours."

"Because I'm off the force, I can help track her down as a civilian."

"Did you get fired? Gerard didn't tell me."

"I wasn't fired! Gerard told me to leave after I punched Hanson!" Randy yelled, angrily punching the dashboard. "I was suspended."

"Easy, son. You don't have to get in a fight with me or my car. I'm sure you can sort this out. I would start by sobering up and then put your pride aside and start apologizing to everyone: Samantha, Gerard, and Hanson."

Randy growled, flaring his nostrils. He inhaled deeply to relieve his tension, realizing George was right. How could he not be? George turned the corner, parking at Randy's house. The rum sloshed around in his empty stomach, making him a little queasy. He knew that he had to face Gerard, for Amy's sake and his own. Randy needed to go to the detachment to own his mistakes and make amends. "I will go into Officer Gerard's office tomorrow and plead for police help to find the girls. I will be even more useful if I can get off suspension. We will rally the family and the police to help search for Amy and her friend. We will search all night if we have to!"

"And Hanson? What about him? Will you apologize to him?"

Randy tried curbing his anger, thinking about what Hanson was doing to him and to his career. "I can't talk to that guy! I don't trust him not to make me look incompetent! We don't need him."

George sighed, signalling for Randy to get out of the vehicle. "I will come back to get you in about fifteen minutes."

"Okay," Randy agreed, slipping out and opening the passenger door for T-Bone. "I will be ready."

After a quick change into some dry clothes and an apology to his wife, Randy got to work on helping George find the missing girls. He groaned, biting into another mouthful of the lunch Bea provided. "These double chocolate chip cookies are still warm from the oven; when did she have time to bake?"

George grinned, wiping his mouth with a cloth napkin. "Bea has been busy in the kitchen for the last few hours, ever since realizing that Amy is missing. Baking and cooking are what she does when she is worried. She should have enough food to feed an army by morning if we need it."

Washing down the cookies with more hot coffee, Randy swallowed hard. "That's what we need."

"What? More food?"

"An army or, more precisely, a squad of police. Let's go to the station to round up some officers to help us search. We shouldn't wait. Something doesn't feel right; I can feel it in my gut. I will gather search and rescue teams; you call Beatrice from the station to find out if either Amy or Sarah have contacted home." Randy said, biting another cookie.

"What's that?" George exclaimed, slamming the brakes.

Randy coughed, choking on a mouthful of his cookie. "What do you see?"

"It's Amy's bike in the ditch near the tree."

Randy pushed open the car door, leaving it hanging open as he rushed out. Amy's bright orange ten-speed bike was sparkling with frost as their headlights lit up the scene. Clicking on his flashlight and scanning the grassy ditch, Randy said, "There's a blue or black bike over there, it's hard to make out the color in this light. It must be Sarah's."

"What street is this? Sixth? Seventh?"

Randy looked around at the darkened houses lining the street, recognizing one of the houses and trying to ward off chills running up his spine. "It's Fifth Street. I was on this street recently looking for the owner of a vehicle involved in parking violations and possible drug charges. This scenario doesn't look good. Let's load up the bicycles into the trunk! We need to go to the station right now; this private investigation just got upgraded to urgent police business. Drop me off at the station, then get Beatrice to round up the neighbours and Sarah's family." Randy looked at his watch, noting the early hour. "I'm sure just about everyone will be up soon. We already know Beatrice is awake, busying herself in the kitchen. Tell her to start phoning everyone as soon as the clock rings seven. I should have a plan in motion by the time you get back to me."

George slammed the trunk of the car, securing Amy and Sarah's bikes inside. "Did you forget that Gerard suspended you?"

Randy paused, inhaling deeply, and said, "I will do what I can to be put back on the force! But job or no job, I will get the help you need from the police."

"I will drop you off and go home to talk to Bea; that will give you the time you need to apologize to Gerard and rally police support to search for the girls," George said.

"If I am lucky, Gerard hasn't filled in any paperwork regarding my suspension. I am hoping we can pretend like it never happened. The whole mess could just disappear," Randy smiled, hoping for the best results. "As a police officer, I will have more resources at my disposal for a search and rescue."

"I know everything will work out the way it needs to in the end, but if he doesn't give you your job back, then at least demand that the detachment help us find Amy and Sarah," George said, turning his vehicle into the parking lot. "The girls have been missing for almost twelve hours now."

Chapter 29

Tuesday, October 08, 1985

Pushing open the heavy doors into the police station, Randy paused awkwardly at the front desk. "Good morning, Gladys. What's new since last night?"

Gladys shuffled around the papers on her desk, glancing at him. "I don't know yet. I'm just starting my shift. It doesn't look like I have any messages waiting for you. Are you in today?" She frowned, looking at Randy's civilian clothes and worn appearance.

"No, I'm here to talk to Officer Gerard about my niece, Amy Young. She has been missing since yesterday. Have you heard anything?" Randy asked, popping a mint from the candy dish into his mouth.

"I haven't heard anything yet, but I will let you know if I get any calls."

Thanking Gladys, Randy walked around the counter into the roll call room. The casual banter among the police officers abruptly stopped as Randy walked purposely toward Gerard's closed office door. Randy focused on keeping his eyes straight ahead, ignoring the curious stares. Knocking on the door, Randy inhaled and barged in.

Gerard looked at Randy and quickly ended his telephone conversation, pointing to a chair in front of the desk with his pencil. He scribbled a few things in his notebook and tossed his pencil on his desk. Looking up, Gerard commented, "Well, you look like shit this morning. Maybe you should go home and get more sleep! We will talk later."

"No, I can't," Randy said, clearing his throat and lowering his voice. He ran his fingers through his hair. "I'm sorry. It has been a rough night. Amy and her friend, Sarah, have been missing since six o'clock last night! George and I have been driving all over the place looking for her. We've only found their abandoned bicycles."

The door burst open and Officer Hanson barged in, announcing, "Swift Current Police detachment heard about our homicide investigations. They found two bodies and want to know if-"

"Two? Are they teenage girls?" Randy asked, panicking and bolting up out of his chair.

"Are you back to work, or just here to grovel?" Hanson smirked, taunting Randy.

"I'm looking for two missing girls!" Randy exclaimed, looking from Officer Gerard to Officer Hanson and forcing his fingers through his hair. "We have been looking all night for them!"

"In which case? I thought you left your shift early last night," Hanson frowned, crossing his arms. "You look like hell!"

"George Petersen and I have been up all night looking for his granddaughter, Amy Young and her friend, Sarah Tyler. They have been missing since yesterday. What did the Swift Current detachment say about their investigation?"

"I didn't know we were looking for two girls. You don't think they would be in Swift Current, do you? The fax doesn't give much information other than a brief scene description."

Randy let out a heavy sigh, not knowing what to say. He didn't want to tell the Petersens anything before he could confirm that the Swift Current case did not involve the death of their granddaughter. He stood and started pacing in a small circle within the confines of the crowded office, deciding he would drive to Swift Current to verify the identification of the bodies if he had to.

"Doyle, take some deep breaths, sit down and try not to jump to conclusions. I'm sure everything is okay. Hanson will phone the detachment in Swift Current to get a clear description of what they've found," Officer Gerard instructed. "Tell them we are looking for two teenagers. A short one with brown hair, the other, taller, closer to average height and blonde."

"I will do that right away!"

"Hey, thanks," Randy said apologetically, raising his eyebrows and trying to make amends to get the help he needed. "I will confirm with Sarah's family what she was wearing, but I know Amy was working. She was wearing a Family Grocers' uniform with a denim jacket and sneakers."

"That is enough description to confirm against Swift Current's findings. I'll let you know what I can verify," Officer Hanson said, leaving the office. Randy noticed Hanson's face was grim and severe, he nodded his thanks for Hanson's help.

"Now, sit down. We need to talk about your suspension, but first we will talk about the two missing girls. George called me last night looking for you. He said Amy had only been missing for a few hours then. He didn't call me back and I assumed she had come home. No wonder you have dark circles under your eyes! Start telling me everything George told you about the last known location of the girls and continue until this morning," Officer Gerard said, flipping to a new page in his notebook. He made careful notes, frowning as Randy described what he knew. Randy watched Gerard's face turn from concern to worry. "Okay, we will put an alert out to all police officers on duty today."

"Sounds good," Randy smiled, standing up. "I will go get changed into uniform and report back here ASAP."

"Not so fast!" Officer Gerard pointed to the chair, waiting for Randy to return to it before he continued. "You are not on the schedule for today."

"But-"

"But, nothing. You lost evidence and punched another officer. I suspended you."

"I'm sorry about that mess. I'm just frustrated with the razzing that Hanson has been giving me. I didn't lose that evidence. I swear!" Randy protested. "I know where I left one of the photos you asked me about."

"Where is it?"

"I had a photo in the pocket of my uniform. George confirmed I left it on his kitchen table yesterday. I will add it to the file when I return for my next shift."

Officer Gerard hesitated, "Give it to me directly. I want you to straighten out your desk and your case files. I can't find anything in your disorganized mess!"

"No problem, I'm on it," Randy said, getting up from his chair again.

"Wait! I'm not finished with you yet."

Randy hovered, sitting on the edge of the chair. "Sorry, I've had a lot of coffee and just want to help George and Beatrice find Amy. Let me come back on duty right away to use department resources to help them find the girls," Randy pleaded, running his hands through his messy hair.

"I'm not sure that is a good idea. It would be best if you avoided cases that are too personal. I will put Officer Hanson on the missing person case since he might already have a lead."

"You don't mean the bodies found in Swift Current, do you?" Randy said, raising his eyebrows.

Shoving his notebook and pencil into his breast pocket, Gerard leaned forward. "Hopefully, that lead doesn't get him anywhere. Hanson is experienced and did a great job following our leads on the ice box murders. He has made the charges against the school janitor, Ralph Norman. He will be available to help the Petersens look for the two missing girls while we wait for arraignment."

"But I can help with that. Put me back on the roster! I want officers that I can trust working this case."

"You can trust me. I'm also putting myself on the case as a favour to George. We have been friends for a very long time; I wouldn't want anything to happen to those young ladies."

"I think the more eyes on this case, the faster we can bring those two girls home. Can I come back on duty?" Randy pleaded, knowing nothing would keep him from searching for his niece.

"Technically, I haven't filed the suspension paperwork yet; I still have it on my desk. If you promise to go home, sleep, and have a hot shower, I will think about you returning to duty without filing the suspension," Officer Gerard said, winking at Randy. "You were on the night shift last night. If you return to work prepared to act professionally, you can report to the night shift tonight. You must stay out of fights with your fellow officers, or I'll damn well file this report! I doubt I can get you to stop looking for Amy Young and her friend, but I want you to keep things from getting too personal. It's hard to do; it will cloud your judgement and prevent you from making rational decisions. Let Hanson and I make all of the decisions."

Randy stood, agreeing with the terms and reaching across the desk to shake hands with his commanding officer. "I am sorry about the mess. I will do better." Exiting the office, Randy made a beeline for his cubicle to sort the files on his desk. Noticing Officer Trussell was absent from his desk and calling out to no one in particular, Randy asked, "Has Trussell finished his shift?"

"I'm sure he clocked out already. I think he's on your rotation - night shifts," an officer replied.

"Thank you. I will wait to talk to Trussell at the beginning of the next shift," Randy said, disappointed he couldn't ask Trussell to help look for Amy. Randy quickly finished stacking his paperwork and stopped at the front desk to ask Gladys for a radio, letting her know Hanson was to contact him on it immediately after his phone call with the Swift Current detachment.

Chapter 30

Amy awoke with a start when one of their captors opened the door to the basement, shoving someone down the wooden steps to tumble and land on the dirt floor. The heavy wooden door slammed shut with a resounding bang. Amy listened to a key turning the mechanism to relock the door. Brushing the damp earth from her torn uniform pants, Amy approached the crumpled form lying in a heap at the bottom of the steps and whispered, "Are you okay?"

Silence.

Amy looked to the floorboards above, following the sound of footsteps leaving the building out the front door and over a wooden porch. She exchanged a look with Sarah across the dirt basement, shrugging. Amy hesitated, waiting for the sound of vehicle doors slamming and an engine roaring to life. She bent over the crumbled heap to inspect the bound hands more clearly. "Sarah, bring me the box cutter so we can untie her," Amy ordered.

"Who is it?" Sarah whispered, struggling to stand, holding her injured arm close to her body.

Gingerly, Amy sliced through the ropes, discarding them in the dirt. She nudged the arm of the person lying on their face at the bottom of the steps. "Are you okay?" Amy asked. "They've left. It's okay to talk. Hello? Are you hurt? Say something!"

The new captive moaned, slowly rolling over onto her back and rubbing her hands over her face, smearing blood and dirt. "Ouch! That hurts," she complained.

"Stop! You are smearing dirt into your cuts." Amy reached, pulling her fellow captive's hands back. Amy stared with bewilderment at the familiar face. "Oh, my God! Leah? I've been looking for you!"

"Leah!" Sarah excitedly exclaimed. "We were following the car you were riding in! We would have called the police if we knew someone was kidnapping you!"

Slowly blinking her eyes, the girl squinted at Amy and Sarah, "I'm not Leah, I'm her sister. Would you help me sit up, please?"

"What is going on?" Amy asked, slowly pulling her into a sitting position and searching her dark brown eyes. "Is it you, Anna? I must be dreaming."

"More like a nightmare! Officer Gerard realized that my life was in danger after my parents confirmed Leah's death. He said that confusing the two of us was an easy mistake to make and decided to use the misidentification to protect me. He thinks the killer made the same mistake," Anna said, explaining her situation. "I have been trying to stay hidden ever since, especially after they found Liam dead, too. That freaked me out!"

"How did you end up here?" Sarah asked, brushing dust away from Anna's sleeves.

"I wanted to help my family prepare for a funeral, but I got careless and they found me. I'm sure I got here the same way you did: in the trunk of the old white car. I rolled around in the trunk until I ended up here."

"Us, too," Sarah said, rolling her eyes.

"But I only saw one woman at the house, the one who forced us out of the trunk and down into this basement. Who is the other kidnapper? Is it a man or a woman?" Amy asked, frowning. She had too many questions assaulting her at once and didn't know what to ask Anna first.

"I don't know. I didn't see his face or hear him say anything because I was fighting for my life! The other person held me while she punched me in the face, knocking me out. I woke up in the stinking trunk!" Anna cried, tears spilling down her face.

"I was unconscious before I was put in the trunk, but I woke up before I was dragged out and thrown down these stairs. I think I broke my arm," Sarah explained, cradling it.

"What about all the other stuff? Where have you been all this time? Can you start at the beginning and explain everything you know?" Amy asked, continuing her questioning.

"Well, it started about a month ago," Anna recounted, pushing her dark hair out of her eyes.

Amy stood, pacing back and forth and listening to every word of her incredible story. Finally, when she had heard it all, she ran her hands through her tangled brown hair. "We have to get out of here! These people are dangerous. The police will need to hear your story before it's too late. There is so much going on the police don't know about." Hesitating, Amy cautioned her, "But don't talk to Officer Hanson. He keeps trying to arrest me for murder or other made-up charges. You need to talk to Officer Gerard."

"Can you stop pacing? You are kicking up a lot of dust," Sarah complained.

Suppressing a cough, Anna declared, "I don't want to talk to the police. I want to go home to see my family and attend my sister's funeral. My family is trying to keep me safe; they don't know who to trust. It's not their fault that I got trapped by that woman. She tricked me!"

Amy stopped pacing and turned around, staring into the girl's brown eyes. "I'm sorry, but you have to talk to the police. Your testimony might be the only clue to crack this case wide open. Something is going on in our sleepy little town that the police are unaware of. We have to go to the police, then you can go home." Amy pointed to the little window and said, "We have to get out of here first. I couldn't reach the little window myself, and Sarah couldn't lift me with her injured arm, but together, you could push me up through the window."

"That is a tiny window. I can't fit through it," Anna said, squinting at the dirty window, pushing stray black hair out of her eyes. "How will we get Sarah through it?"

Amy walked over to the window, studying it. "I doubt you two will fit, but I might be small enough to go through if I take off my jacket and vest. If you can push me up there, I can get out and walk around to the front door and open the basement door. We will figure out where we are and run to the next house to telephone my uncle. It will be easy!" Amy raised her eyebrows, waiting for a response. Nodding, both girls agreed to the simple escape plan.

"I feel like we need road snacks for this," commented Sarah. "I didn't realize we would be without food and water."

Amy looked up at the dirty little window, trying to see what might be on the other side. "I think we need to make our move now. I don't know what time it is, but whoever put us here just left. We don't want to be here when they return." Amy studied the window, wondering if the swivel action fastener was painted shut. She hoped she could open the window when the other girls hoisted her up to it. She shook her head, willing away the fear creeping into the back of her mind.

"I will help you balance Amy on your shoulders and do what I can to help with my good arm. I don't think I can do much; it's up to you guys to get us out of here," Sarah said, making Amy aware of her presence next to her.

Amy shook her head and replied, "Sorry, I was just thinking about how to open the window once you two hoist me up."

"One step at a time. We will break it if that's what it takes," Sarah said. "Kick it out if that's the only way."

The two girls managed to get Amy high enough to reach the window. Amy tried to maintain her balance as the girls held her off the ground, but it wasn't easy. She grunted, gripping the metal clasp with both hands and trying to turn it. "Hold still. It's a little hard to open, but I think it's coming. I almost got it!"

"Hurry!" Both girls groaned in unison.

Finally, Amy felt the metal clasp spin open, releasing the dirty window. She blew out an exasperated sigh. "I got it! Try to push me up higher!" As her companions struggled to hoist Amy closer to the window, Amy used one hand to open it and the other to grab onto the dusty window sill. With a final surge of strength, Amy found herself partway through. Her hands clawed at the cold, damp earth, pulling the lower half of her body through the tiny window. It slammed shut when she pulled her feet through. Crawling back over, she pulled the window open, calling to her companions, "Go to the top of the stairs; I'll open the door in a minute."

Running through the tall weeds to the front of the dilapidated building, Amy tried to focus on her task. She was worried; there were too many unanswered questions: who locked them in the basement, who would rescue them, and what kind of lock was on the door? "One thing at a time," she reminded herself, tripping on a loose board on the front steps. Amy stumbled onto the wooden porch, noticing the cracked and peeling door paint. Before grabbing the doorknob, Amy quietly prayed, "Please don't be locked."

The doorknob creaked as it turned, but would not release the wooden door. "What the hell?" The door refused to open. Pushing her shoulder into the door, Amy turned the knob and kicked the door with her foot several times, trying to knock it off its frame. "Come on, you piece of shit!" She screamed, kicking with every ounce of her strength. "You are not keeping us here! You can't do this!" The porch groaned, startling Amy just as she felt something heavy hit her on the back of her head, the force of the blow blurring her vision. She was vaguely aware of the door opening in front of her and the wooden floorboards rushing towards her as she crashed into it. She tried to breathe, choking on thick plumes of dust.

The ringing in Amy's ears mixed with Sarah's muffled cries, "Do you hear me? Amy! Are you alright?"

Amy slowly blinked and clued in to the thumping noises coming from the basement door. "I'm coming," she croaked.

Chapter 31

After a few hours of restless sleep, Randy dressed in his uniform and pulled on his standard police-issued jacket to continue his search for Amy. Randy figured no one would know he wasn't back on the duty roster; he was counting on the uniform to give him the authority to do what he needed. He wanted to ask Edith Marshall's caregiver a few questions about the two abandoned bicycles found across the street from her house. His casual line of questioning would give him the excuse to look around the premises for any clues concerning Amy. From what he knew about missing person cases, Randy didn't want to dismiss any coincidences.

Randy was anxious to start his night shift, hoping Gerard wouldn't mind letting him return to duty a few hours earlier. He planned to stop at the police station to pick up a police cruiser and ask for any information Hanson had about the Swift Current detachment's case.

A few blocks from home, Randy slowed his red and white 1981 Ford Bronco to a yield at an uncontrolled intersection, allowing a familiar gold Lincoln Continental to zoom through. "Well, that's perfect timing! I can make an arrest and question the driver about Amy and Sarah at the station." Randy turned left onto Fifth Street, pressing his turn signal to follow the gold-coloured car. The vehicle stopped on the street in front of Edith Marshall's home. Pulling up to park two houses down, Randy watched someone wearing a black bunnyhug slam the rusted door and walk across the grass.

Holding his hand over his weapon and jumping out of his vehicle to intercept the hooded figure, Randy yelled, "Police! Stop and put your hands above your head!"

The teenager stopped, slowly turning around with his hands raised. "I didn't do anything. Why are you harassing me?"

"I'm Police Officer Doyle. Don't move! Are you carrying any weapons?" Randy squinted, trying to identify the driver hidden under the hood.

"No."

"What's your name?" Randy asked, placing his hand over his weapon.

"Greg," he replied.

As he advanced closer to have a better look at the driver, he realized that this wasn't who he was expecting and changed to a less aggressive tone. "Do you live here, Greg?"

"I rent a room."

"Does the Lincoln Continental belong to you or someone you know?"

"Yes, but-"

"Slowly remove your hood so I can see your face," Randy ordered. Cautiously, the young man pulled back on his black hood, revealing a shocking display of purple and green hair and a busted lip. Yes, he recognized this kid. "What's your last name?"

"Holman, Greg Holman," the teenage boy said, licking the corner of his bloody lip.

"Today doesn't seem like it's going too well for you. Have you been in a fight? Getting yourself into trouble?"

"I can't talk about it. It's just too embarrassing," Greg muttered, looking down at his feet.

Randy hesitated; he wanted to serve the warrant, but his plan wasn't to arrest this kid, even though he was the one driving around in the vehicle with a trunk filled with prescription and illicit drugs. Under Officer Gerard's direction, Randy had already filed a warrant for the driver of this vehicle after Hank told him the car had been picked up from the impound lot. He was expecting to catch Edith Marshall or her caregiver, Loretta. Moving in position to make the arrest anyway, Randy decided he could figure it out at the police station. "I have a warrant out for your arrest. Place your hands on your head." Randy guided Greg's hands down behind his back, placing his cuffs around each wrist. "Greg Holman, you are charged with failing to pay parking violations, driving an uninsured vehicle, possession of drugs with intent to sell, and uttering threats."

The front door burst open and Edith Marshall stormed out, yelling, "What are you doing here? Get away from my house! Leave my boy alone!"

Recognizing the older woman from his last visit, Randy spoke calmly. "Mrs. Marshall, I'm a police officer. Officer Doyle, do you remember me? I am arresting your nephew."

Edith gasped, shaking her head and looking around, "Where's my nephew? Did you arrest him?"

"Mrs. Marshall, where is your caregiver? Loretta? Is she in the house?" Randy asked, thinking either her dementia confused the situation or she played the part well during their last conversation. "Everything is fine. I'm taking your nephew to the police station with me. He is under arrest. Go in the house to get Loretta so I can speak to her."

"My nephew has one of those," Edith said, pointing at Randy's shoulder.

Randy looked down, trying to figure out what she was pointing to. "My name tag? Your nephew has a name tag, too. I'm sure most employees at the grocery store have name tags." He looked at Greg, verifying that he remembered where the teenager worked.

"She's not my auntie," Greg growled, shaking his head. "You are arresting the wrong person!"

"I take good care of you," the older woman scolded, smiling at Greg. "Mind your manners. Be polite and come back home. Everything will be fine."

Randy caught the sideways glances Greg was giving him, wondering what had gone on. Was Greg trying to communicate with his eyes? Did this older woman know what had happened? Hoping for more clues, Randy was determined to get more information from Greg while he was in custody. Randy cleared his throat, calmly explaining, "I am taking Greg to the police station. He is under arrest."

"You don't make the rules," Edith smirked. "You can't arrest him."

"It's okay," Loretta said, calling from behind the screen door. "He is under-aged and untouchable. There's nothing the police can do to him. The twerp will be back here soon begging for more money from Edith. He isn't paying rent; the kid's a freeloader! I wouldn't believe anything he says, officer. What are the charges?"

"I am arresting him for unpaid traffic violations, possession with intent to traffic and uttering threats. His caregiver can meet him at the station or I will have a court-appointed guardian supervise. Your choice."

"What drugs? I didn't see you search him or his vehicle," Loretta said, opening the screen door and stepping onto the front step. "You have no business coming here to arrest anyone. I saw you drive up in your vehicle. It's not a police issue. Are you sure you are a cop?"

"I have a warrant for the driver of this Lincoln Continental," Randy said, ignoring her comment about his lack of qualifications. "I watched him drive it. It is the same vehicle I searched through while it was on the impound lot. Mrs. Marshall picked it up before the police could move it to our compound. I have already seized the drugs. As the vehicle's driver, I am arresting Greg under suspicion of these charges."

"You can't arrest him; you aren't a cop," Loretta smirked, crossing her arms, smiling and leaning against the door frame. "What are you doing in a police uniform? I should have you arrested for impersonating a police officer."

Randy's stomach moved into his throat, reminding him that the town's gossip mill worked faster than lightning. It's too bad that good news travels slower than bad news. She may have heard Gerard suspended him, but she hadn't heard that Gerard didn't file the paperwork - a technicality, but it worked in Randy's favour right now. "I have every right to make an arrest. At our detachment, we work as a team to get the job done and keep the streets of Glenmere safe. I'm just doing my job. I will tow the car to the police compound. If you want to claim yourself as the driver, I can arrest you instead."

"You can threaten me all you want. I'm not worried. I have a car," Loretta said, smiling and pointing to a white 1964 Chrysler Newport sitting crooked across the driveway. "I have this magnificent beast to drive. The other day, I put a whole patio set in the trunk and brought it home. I plan to set it up in the backyard."

Randy looked at the car, shaking his head. Her oversized vehicle with the large trunk had rusted fenders and a rope holding the front bumper together. Randy grinned, imagining that that car didn't run any better than the Lincoln Continental. "You can direct all your questions to Officer Gerard, my supervisor. Have a nice day, Miss Flatiron."

Randy escorted Greg to where he left his Bronco, almost walking into his suspect when Greg stopped abruptly. His eyes widened, looking alarmed. "Are you a police officer?" Greg asked. "Loretta wasn't kidding! This truck isn't a police vehicle."

"Yes, I am a police officer. I interviewed you at the Family Grocers when your co-workers discovered a victim in the freezer section."

"Where's your police car?"

Clearing his throat, Randy explained, "I was actually on my way into the station when I saw your vehicle cross the intersection. I followed you for eight blocks until you stopped in front of Edith Marshall's house. There was a warrant for the arrest of the vehicle's driver. I was expecting Edith Marshall, Loretta Flatiron or Edith's nephew; I was surprised to see you. We are going to the police station where you will tell me about the drugs in your trunk. I will also be asking you about the threats you uttered toward Amy Young and Sarah Tyler. Depending on how your story plays out, I might have to charge you with kidnapping or aiding an abduction."

"Get out of town! Are you for real?"

"Yes, I'm the real deal," Randy deadpanned, mocking his suspect. He needed to keep his cool if he wanted to get information about Edith Marshall. Did the woman have dementia? Was she the drug dealer? Why did he find Amy's bike across the street from the house?

"Don't take me in and I promise to tell you what I know about the drugs, but I wasn't threatening anyone!"

Randy opened the door of his red and white 1981 Ford Bronco. "Get in! You'll sit in the passenger seat. This vehicle only has two bucket seats."

Flicking his colourful hair back with his head, Greg asked, "Can you drive around a bit and we can talk?" He angled his wrists, motioning for Randy to remove the cuffs. "Casual like?"

"No, the cuffs stay on. You are the only person who admitted to driving the vehicle. You can talk now or at the station, it's up to you. The prosecutor will use anything you say or do against you in court. I will appoint a guardian unless you have one to call. Your aunt? A parent, grandparent? Do you understand what I am saying to you?"

"I'm not Edith Marshall's nephew. Take the cuffs off and I will tell you all kinds of stuff, things you didn't even know you needed to know," Greg pleaded, shaking his colourful hair around. "I don't know who is all in on this mess and it's hard to know who to trust! If you take me to the station, I won't tell you everything."

Randy nudged Greg forward, putting his hand on the teenager's head and guiding him into the passenger seat. "You're kind of cocky, but I will ignore it. Talk as I drive or wait until we get to the station. It's your choice." Randy closed the passenger door, running around to the driver's side. He hoped that he could get Officer Gerard or Trussell to file these charges while he rallied others to help him search for Amy and Sarah.

As Randy pulled his vehicle onto the street, Greg said, "I can tell that you have no clue what's happening, but I'm going to trust you. You have to hear me out, okay? I'm trying to protect Anna! She's alive."

"Alive? Who else knows she is alive?" Randy asked, slowly driving to the police station, making unnecessary turns and delaying his arrival while he listened to Greg reveal details that could solve the open investigations. "How could she have been misidentified?"

"The Labrash family identified Leah in the morgue in the presence of a couple of police officers. It's hard to tell Anna and Leah apart from a distance; they are almost identical," Greg explained, rushing to defend himself. "Amy is the one who said it was Anna who she found. The police took her word for it until the family could confirm her identity. It was one of the officers who came up with the hair-brained plan at the morgue to let the whole town think Anna died instead of Leah. The officer thought it would protect Anna from danger while they investigated. Anna and her family were getting restless, waiting for the police to allow them to have a funeral. They started planning it anyway."

"Why is Anna's life in danger?"

"Anna witnessed something in the back alley behind the grocery store. She told a police officer, but he didn't do anything about it. Now, she is missing!"

Exhaling, Randy wondered which parts of Greg's story he could use to leverage the confession they needed to convict. Randy knew he needed to keep Greg safe because if he was telling the truth, the killer would end Greg's life, too. Randy devised a plan, knowing the only person he could trust to help execute it was Officer Gerard. Hopefully, it won't be too late!

Chapter 32

Pulling his Ford Bronco around the building and into the docking garage at the back of the station, Randy radioed for the single-car garage and waited for the door to open. He planned to deliver his informant to the station under the guise of serving a warrant, hoping Greg would stay on script. Randy knew he must follow police procedures while keeping Greg away from other officers until justice could be served.

Randy clenched his fists on the steering wheel, watching the garage door open. He started questioning his plan to go directly to Officer Gerard, the only person he could trust. Randy inhaled, rehearsing his plan to march into Gerard's office and confront him about Greg's secret reveal. He would explain that he is taking advantage of the arrest warrant on the gold Lincoln as an excuse to protect Greg while they determine which police officer is covering for a killer.

According to dispatch, the Lincoln's plates were expired. Randy assumed Edith Marshall produced a forged registration at the impound lot when she picked up the vehicle. Greg said he could not provide a valid driver's licence, proof of ownership, insurance or registration and freely admitted to all traffic violations. Randy didn't want to arrest the kid after listening to his pleas, but a warrant was out for the driver of the vehicle because of the drugs and money confiscated from the impound lot. He had no choice: he had to file charges. Any other officer would have acted on the warrant and pressed the charges, but luckily for this kid, it was Randy with him in custody. Randy had his sights on a more significant and critical culprit, using Greg as his informant and making the charges against Greg disappear with a plea deal in exchange for his testimony. Hopefully, Officer Gerard would provide him with support to fry the bigger fish. Gerard had to know which officers were present during the identification of the Labrash girl. It would narrow the suspect list before he starts investigating his fellow officers.

Opening the passenger door and reminding Greg to follow his lead, Randy firmly said, "Okay, Greg, please step out of the vehicle. Don't forget to smile at the security camera over my left shoulder. I will take you through to the processing desk; once you are processed, we will get you some first aid, and then you will be detained in a holding cell."

Greg flipped his purple and green hair out of his eyes, scowling, "I wasn't lying to you! This situation is not right! Why am I still getting arrested? I was trusting you!"

"Listen to me! It would be best if you kept your mouth shut. I already explained your legal rights. You are a minor. We cannot question you without a guardian present, but if you freely want to blab your story, officers will be happy to soak up every word and file charges. Think about what will happen if you do! Everything has consequences. Who is going to pay those consequences? You? Anna?" Randy looked hard into Greg's fierce eyes. "Remember, you talk to me or Officer Gerard. No one else!" Randy led his handcuffed suspect into the station's booking area to start processing, hoping for a goddamn miracle. *The kid has balls! I have to give him that. I don't know if this was a good idea, but I'm sure Officer Gerard will either back me up on this or fire me,* Randy thought, pressing the button and waiting for the buzzing sound of an unlocked door.

Officer Brandy Gates looked up from the papers she was shuffling around on her desk. "Officer Doyle, what happened to him? The kid's lip is bleeding! You don't have to cuff a kid for stealing."

"He was like that when I found him. He isn't here on theft charges. I am serving a warrant for the arrest of the driver of a vehicle that is suspected of being used for drug trafficking. I will also add a few traffic violations to the charges. Start processing him, take photos, and call for first aid. At the same time, I will telephone social services asking for a public guardian to be sent to the station so I can legally question him," Randy said, trying to keep things professional. Still, he couldn't help but wonder how this scenario would all play out. "Don't let anyone interview him before I get him a guardian. I need to talk to Officer Gerard before I process the arrest."

"I assume you got the message that the bodies found in Swift Current were both male, not female," Officer Gates stated, raising her eyebrows. "Are you working that case with Hanson? He was looking for you."

"I didn't check my messages, but I appreciate the news. I asked Hanson to keep me informed, but he still needs to update me. Did he say anything else about my missing persons case?"

"No, he didn't. Does the kid know something? Maybe he goes to school with the girls. How old are they?"

"Nah, he wouldn't know them. I'm charging him with traffic violations and a drug charge," Randy responded, glaring at Greg to keep him silenced. "It's unrelated."

"Hey, and do I get a lawyer? That's part of my rights too, right?" Greg scowled, licking at the corner of his mouth with his tongue where the blood was drying. "I'm not talking without legal representation."

Randy looked at Officer Gates, raising his eyebrows and grabbing a pen to sign the intake forms. Throwing down the pen on the paperwork, Randy commented, "Get the kid some Band-Aids before he calls a lawyer. Call me when he is ready to be questioned! I will talk to Gerard about helping me close this case. Buzz me out, please. I don't have my keys." Randy walked over to the buzzing door, taking him out of the station's secure area.

Randy walked quickly through the corridor, patting the Polaroid in his pocket and rounding the front desk. Scooping up his pink message slips, he headed to the roll call room to collect his files from his workstation. Hastily, he shoved loose papers into the files to keep everything together. "I really got to start being more organized. I thought I organized these files," he mumbled to himself, reminded of his promise as part of the condition of his return to work. With the files stacked in his arms, he headed for Officer Gerard's office. The door to the office was closed. Randy leaned slightly toward the door, listening for voices. Hearing nothing, he knocked and waited for the door to open.

"Officer Doyle, how nice to see you back in uniform," Officer Hanson smirked with sarcasm, making a sweeping bow gesture and opening the door. "Won't you come on in!"

Randy nodded, wondering what he should do. He couldn't risk getting into another argument with Hanson; Gerard would fire him for sure, and then he would lose the backing of the detachment. Looking at Gerard sitting at the desk, he ignored Hanson's theatrics. "Gerard, I need to talk to you about a suspect I have in booking."

"What's going on?" Gerard said, neatly closing a case file and reaching for his notebook in his breast pocket to prepare for new information. "I wasn't expecting you so soon."

Clearing his throat, Randy pushed ahead, "I am not comfortable being near the officer with whom I was recently in an argument which caused my suspension. I will wait outside your office until you can speak to me privately." He reached for the doorknob, glaring at Hanson and pulling the door shut.

"No, wait, we're done," Officer Gerard said. "Hanson, you can leave and follow up on your lead. Let me know when you have something. No more false arrests!"

Randy winked at Hanson as he left the office, slamming the door shut after him. It was comforting to know Gerard was bringing Hanson down a peg or two. "We have a problem!"

"Yes, you are damn right: we have a problem!" Gerard barked, standing up and leaning his hands on his desk. "I told you to curb your attitude. You have been doing a good job. You will make a great detective one day, but since Jeffery Hanson joined our station, you have had a little chip on your shoulder."

Randy bit his lip, exhaling. Hanson was one officer he would prefer to avoid. "That's not what I was talking about. I have to tell you about the kid I just brought in for some traffic violations and suspected drug charges."

"What are you doing in uniform making arrests? I said you needed to report to me before your shift began. I was going to put you on desk duty to clean up your files. This new case doesn't sound like something that needs discussing, but I will assign another officer to handle it. File your other reports and I will let you know when you are off desk duty." Gerard sat down, dismissing Randy from his office.

"It's about Amy Young," Randy whispered, looking toward the closed office door, knowing anyone could be eavesdropping. He didn't want anyone to overhear what he now suspected.

Leaning forward, Gerard whispered, "What did you hear? Does this new arrest have something to do with it? Who did you bring in? Tell me everything that you know." Gerard reached for his pocket, pulling his notebook to write notes.

Randy pulled a chair from the corner up to the other side of Gerard's desk, opening his case files and referring to his notes. "These two cases I have been working on have led me down a rabbit hole. At first, I didn't think they were connected other than they both involved drugs, but the more information I dug up, the more I started to wonder if it was all related to the victims found in the freezers. Amy is connected as the witness who found all three of the bodies, but I need to let you know that she is not a suspect like Officer Hanson wants you to believe. I don't think it's a coincidence that she is missing; she knows something important. I also believe the person behind the drugs and the poisoning is the same person who kidnapped Amy, possibly to prevent her from revealing what she knows. Her friend Sarah's abduction is probably a coincidence, a result of being in the wrong place at the wrong time."

"What does this have to do with your traffic violation? I'm not following how you are connecting the dots."

"Okay, so let me start at the beginning. I answered the request from Hank at the impound lot about a gold Lincoln Continental Mark III with expired plates, loose pills, white powder and some prescription bottles in the trunk. I filed those drugs into evidence and issued a warrant for the vehicle's driver. My investigations revealed that someone was parking the Lincoln in the alley behind the pharmacy."

"The driver is who you brought in?" Gerard interrupted. "Have you filed the charges?"

"Well, not exactly. It's a long story," Randy waved, indicating that he was getting to it. "I had a warrant out for the driver because the owner got it out of the impound lot with a forged registration and insurance before I could bring it to the police impound lot. When I saw the gold vehicle driving around, I was headed to the station to report to you about starting my shift early. I followed the car and served the warrant to make the arrest. The kid isn't who I thought I would find in the driver seat, but neither Edith Marshall nor her caregiver claimed ownership of the vehicle. I'm not sure if the old lady is senile or faking it. She seemed pretty coherent today when she yelled at me."

"This all sounds good, except the part where someone kidnapped Amy Young and her friend because Amy somehow knows something about the ice box killer. Hanson has stayed the charges against Ralph Norman. I don't understand what you are trying to tell me."

"I'm getting to that," Randy said, inhaling deeply and trying to stay calm with Gerard's interruptions. "When

I pulled up to where the vehicle stopped, Greg Holman was driving. He is one of the stock clerks at the Family Grocers who I interviewed for the Labrash case. He doesn't want to talk to the police, but wait until you hear his story. He has a bleeding lip and the start of bruising on his cheek from fighting against the person who took the girls."

"So, does he know where Amy and Sarah are?"

"Well, not exactly, but he suspects he knows who does, and he has a good idea why a killer is plaguing this town with frozen bodies," Randy paused, waiting for Gerard to understand his meaningful stare.

"You have got to be kidding me! Your report sounds like gossip and rumours," Gerard said, padding his pockets until he remembered he was already holding his pencil.

"I can't ignore what Greg said. Anna Labrash is alive and in danger," Randy said, cautiously gauging Gerard for his reaction.

Grimacing, Officer Gerard sucked in air through his teeth. "That is something you need to keep close to your chest. Is that it?"

"There is even more to what he told me. The biggest problem is that Greg still needs to tell me the whole story! He doesn't know everything, but he did suggest that we can't catch the killer because a police officer is protecting someone he is related to. I want to say it is the same police officer messing with my evidence collection and the one who knows that Anna is still alive."

"Shit."

Randy nodded in agreement, knowing a dirty police officer complicated everything. He thought one or more of the police officers at this station could be receiving a payout for protecting a killer moving drugs around in the neighbourhoods of their seemingly quiet little town. Which police officers were trustworthy? Who knew Anna was still alive?

"How long can we stall on holding and questioning Greg Holman?" Tapping his pencil on the legal pad while he paused to think, Gerard continued, "We need to keep the rescue operation as a missing persons case without hinting about the drug or murder charges. We will verify Greg Holman's confession once we move the girls to a safe location to hear their stories. He will have to give us more if we want to figure out which police officer to squeeze for a confession, if any. We will dig for the truth until we uncover all of the secrets. Did you get a written statement?"

"I have to telephone a public guardian for the kid. He is going to call a lawyer and arrange for a deal in exchange for testimony. We should focus on our search for Amy and Sarah with the new information Greg provided verbally." Randy could only think of one place where the police should focus their search, hoping to find them still alive before it was too late.

"That will give us some time to determine which police officer is involved," Gerard said, nodding and throwing his pencil on the desk. "We will bring the girls home when we find them. George and Beatrice will keep Amy safe while we question her. I don't want the killer or any accomplices to know we are onto them or trying to connect these cases."

"I agree, George and Beatrice will protect her at home. I can stay with them if you think Amy will be in danger."

Gerard laughed, "Are you kidding me? Beatrice will tear anyone apart trying to protect her granddaughter. She is like a momma bear."

"You are right. So, how do you want to proceed? Do we march out together and start bringing down bad cops? Maybe if we break some fingers, someone will tell us where to find these girls."

Tucking his pencil back into his pocket, Gerard said, "We can't get ahead of ourselves! I want evidence before I accuse a police officer of being dirty. I will join you in about fifteen minutes, give or take. I'll get Gates to continue processing the kid like everything is routine. Don't let yourself have trust issues with the other officers. You have to keep up appearances. I will figure out which officer is involved. Trust me! You will focus on finding the girls and using any available officer for help. Get a few of the experienced officers on duty to help you. Call the radio station asking for public assistance. I'm sure someone out there has something helpful to add."

Nodding, Randy left the office. Trying to be casual, he stopped at the front desk. "Gladys, would you please hold these files for me? I will be right back, thank you."

"Sure, I will leave them right here," she indicated to a spot on her already crowded desk. "Where are you headed?"

"Oh, you know me. I'm off to save yet another cat from a tree," Randy answered, smiling nervously and picking up keys for a police cruiser. He casually studied the chalkboard, checking which officers were on duty to gather for his search and rescue. At first glance, three officers were available: Hanson, Trussell and Gilbertson. Only one had connections to special K-9 units. Randy sighed, putting his mistrust aside and deciding to do what he needed to find Amy.

Chapter 33

Groaning, Amy pushed the board off her back, sitting and stirring up more dust and debris. She coughed, wiping her eyes. She called back, "I'm alright! Just give me a second."

"What happened? Is there someone else there?" Sarah yelled through the door.

Rubbing her head, Amy winced, "The door was stuck. A piece of wood fell and hit me on the head when I pushed it open! This place is falling apart."

"Are you alright?"

Slowly, Amy stood and squeezed her eyes shut, willing the room to stop spinning. "I'm okay, but my head hurts. Give me a minute, I'm dizzy." She brushed dirt from her ruined uniform. Looking around the dilapidated house, she noticed it was sparsely furnished with broken furniture. The pink floral wallpaper was peeling.

On one wall, someone had graffitied crude pictures with red spray paint. "I don't think anyone has lived here for a long time. It looks like the family abandoned the house twenty years ago."

"Hurry and open this door! We have to leave this dump before someone comes back."

Amy rushed over to the basement door. She couldn't see any locks on the outside. The doorknob desperately jiggled from the other side. "Look for the key!" Sarah suggested, calling through the door. "I would leave it somewhere close if I knew I was locking someone up where no one would come looking."

Amy stood on her toes to feel around the top of the doorframe, brushing dirt into her eyes. She sputtered and said, "I can't see!"

"Look around. I'm sure there is a key somewhere," Anna pleaded.

Amy used the back of her sleeve to wipe the dirt from her eyes and face, moving closer to the mid-century modern wooden dresser near the cellar door. She started opening the sticky dresser drawers, which took a lot of work. As Amy finally coaxed one of the drawers open, she heard the unmistakable sound of metal hitting and bouncing across the floor. Abandoning her task and dropping to her stomach, Amy pushed aside old papers and cobwebs between the legs of the dresser until she found a worn key. "I found it!"

"Try it in the lock!" Sarah called, banging on the other side of the door.

Wiping her dirty hands on her torn blue uniform pants, Amy inserted the key into the lock, but it wouldn't turn. "It fits, but it doesn't turn. Give me a minute! The doorknob to my grandma's room at the farm would get stuck and needed a little jiggling to force it open." With one hand on the doorknob and the other on the key, Amy wiggled the knob and the key until the door finally unlocked and opened.

The other two girls stepped back down the steps to the basement, allowing the door to swing open fully. Sarah rushed up the stairs into Amy's arms, almost knocking her over. "Thanks for getting us out of there! Maybe, next time, kick it. Any idea where we are?" Sarah asked, handing Amy's jacket to her.

"No, I didn't look around. I could use some water, but I want to save time. Let's go," Amy answered, pulling her jacket over her dirty uniform.

The three girls rushed into the yard, following the overgrown driveway to the gravel road. They stopped and looked both ways, listening for sounds of traffic or homes nearby. The sun was hanging low in the sky, casting long shadows. "I don't recognize this road. Do either of you?"

"No," they replied.

"Which way should we go? Left, or right?" Sarah asked. "What if we go in the wrong direction, taking us further away from town?"

Amy considered their options, realizing it didn't matter which way they went, as long as they found a farmyard where they could use the telephone to call the police. She had yet to determine which direction would lead them back to the main highway or the closest farmhouse. "Um, right. I can see a rooftop in the distance across that field."

"Do we run or walk?" Sarah asked.

"Let's walk. It's probably much further than it seems and we haven't had any food or drink. I'm a little bit dizzy from being hit on the head again during our escape," Amy replied, rubbing her head. "The temperature will start dropping as the sun sets. I don't want to be walking in the dark. We need to find help at someone's house soon."

The dirt was still soft with recent moisture, making the trek across the field slippery and muddy. Amy felt like her shoes were five pounds too heavy with caked mud. Her uniform pants, now wet to her knees, were getting dirty along the hem. She shivered and pulled her denim jacket tighter around her body, wishing she had her vest for added warmth. Hope fueled each step as the girls neared the trees surrounding their destination. Amy's stomach growled, thinking about her granny's table piled high with food and drink.

"It's not much farther! I'm so cold and tired," Sarah complained, tucking her head against the biting wind. "I just want a warm bath to soak in for hours. Do you think they will offer us food? I feel like it has been days since we last ate."

"You will have to go to the hospital for X-rays. Doesn't your arm still hurt?" Amy asked, sniffling. She tried blowing on her fingertips, numb with cold, to warm them. "You will have to eat hospital food! Do you feel like it could be only sprained?"

"I don't feel anything right now," Sarah said, frowning. "I can't even feel my fingers anymore."

"We have to get you inside where it's warm and dry. I think you are more injured than you think," Anna said, squinting her dark brown eyes at Sarah and Amy.

"Let's hurry!" Amy and Sarah said simultaneously, making them all giggle.

"You are both delirious," Anna laughed, shaking her straight black hair.

Finally, the teenagers rounded a large hedge serving as a windbreak, stopping to look at the buildings within the farmyard. There were four little sheds and a small farmhouse frozen in a time long forgotten, sheltered from the harsh wind. No one spoke. A coyote howled in the distance. The waning light cast eerie long shadows, emphasizing the scene of neglect and abandonment. Amy's eyes roamed over the peeling siding paint on the abandoned buildings, surrounded by long tangled grasses and dead wildflowers, an old tractor long since rusted all of its colours, and an old tricycle leaning haphazardly against a dilapidated shed. The chicken coop, once full of the chatter of chickens and the crow of a rooster, stood in silent vigil of life that was no longer there. A family lived and prospered here some time ago.

Amy's heart broke with the realization that no one was here to help them. There would be no warm beds, piping hot soups, delicious cookies or fuzzy pajamas tonight. Amy blinked away her tears, swallowing and trying to stay calm. "Well, that's depressing."

Sarah sank to her knees in the prickly grasses, picking up a rusty tin can and throwing it at the siding of the old wooden shed. The sound echoed against the empty buildings, startling small sparrows. "I just can't do this! We are going to die! They should have just killed us and moved on!"

Wiping her tears out of her eyes with the back of her sleeve, Amy exhaled, "I think we need a break. We are all exhausted. Let's go inside one of the buildings where it will be warmer and rest. We can talk about our next move while we wait for the morning. I don't think our captors will look for us here."

The small farmhouse, once a cozy four-roomed haven for a small growing family, was eerily quiet. A crooked weather vane squeaked quietly with the slight breeze. "Let's go inside," Amy mumbled, feeling her weariness and despair wash over her. "The home is old enough to have wood stove heating. We will be warmer if we can start a fire." Slowly, the three girls entered, pushing past the creaky wooden door. The family boarded up most of the windows, creating a dark interior smelling of must and mildew.

Sarah leaned against a wall with stained flowery paper, sliding down to sit on the floor. "I don't suppose there is a telephone?"

Disappointed, Amy looked at the hole in the ceiling stuffed with rags, suggesting someone had removed a stove pipe and a wood-burning stove from the small kitchen. Disappointed, Amy said, "No. Just rest a few minutes."

"Hey, guys!" Anna said, poking her head into the room. "There is a fireplace in this other room. I found a lighter on the mantle. I will see if I can start a fire to warm us up." The metal flue clanged and screeched with protest, followed by the unmistakable flap of wings from a small bird escaping its nest. "Whoa! A sparrow."

Ducking and covering her head, Amy called out, "Do you need my help?" She heard banging noises coming from the other room.

"No, I can manage. I'm going to use the bird nest as a fire starter. There are a few pieces of wood. We will be fine. Do you hear me, Sarah?" Anna insisted, stopping in the open doorway to look directly at her. "We will be fine."

"Yes, I hear you," Sarah said, lacking enthusiasm and giving Anna a thumbs up sign.

Amy knelt before Sarah, reassuring her; she said, "It will be okay. We're going to be okay. We will find help in the morning."

Chapter 34

Patting his breast pocket, Randy assured himself he had secured the gold earring and its photo before stepping into Officer Gerard's office. "I brought what you asked for."

"You found the missing evidence from the Labrash case?" Gerard said, raising his voice.

"Not so loud, I don't want anyone to overhear. I still think we have a member of this police station stealing the evidence from the locker. I don't want to get blamed for it going missing again."

"Okay," Gerard whispered, leaning forward. "Is this the photo you left at George Petersen's home?"

"Yes, I picked it up before I showed up at the station with Greg Holman."

"Where did you find the gold earring?" Gerrard asked.

"I didn't. Officer Trussell was helping me organize my case files. He found it in the case file for the homeless guy, Ronaldo Baysic."

"Did you put the evidence into that case file?"

"I don't remember, but I have caught officers messing with my files," Randy said, trying to be vague.

"Who do you think is messing with your evidence and case files? Or do you think that you have just been careless and unorganized?"

Randy swallowed and cleared his throat. "I may be disorganized, but Officer Hanson has been messing around my desk. The fight between him and I was over him messing with my case reports. He is my best guess. When I think about it, he was an officer in the big city, but now he is working in our small town and trying to prove himself. I'm sure he thought he could pull the wool over everyone's eyes in this case. Why else would Hanson move to Glenmere except to be closer to his family?" Randy said, raising his eyebrows and tossing the evidence on the end of Gerard's desk. "Greg said the crooked cop was related to our killer. I think the killer and kidnapper are the same person and they are trying to keep from revealing their secrets."

Gerard tucked his pencil into his shirt pocket, leaning back in his chair. "That's a big accusation. Did you ask Hanson if he had any relatives in town? I'm pretty sure he would tell you if he did. The guy brags about everything."

Randy was at a loss for words, knowing he hadn't asked Hanson that simple question. He mentally kicked himself, continuing with his argument. "No, but he has been giving me a tough time and I have caught him messing with the files on my desk more than once. He even tried to arrest Amy!"

"Speaking of Amy, how is the investigation going with the two missing girls? Who do you have helping you on the missing person cases?"

"I'm still working on it," Randy said, trying to keep his voice neutral. He wanted to track down the dirty cop but knew he also needed to redirect his efforts to find Amy and Sarah. "Lloyd Trussell and Harvey Gilbertson have been helping me trace their last known whereabouts. We haven't got any big leads yet, but we think we are looking in the right direction. We knocked on most of the doors in the neighbourhood where George and I found their bicycles. I asked Gilbertson to phone the radio station with their descriptions and ask people to telephone the detachment or our tip line with any information to help us find them."

Officer Gerard leaned back in his chair, sighing, "Are those officers both here?"

"Yes."

Gerard straightened the blotter on his desk, taking his time to decide on Randy's orders. "Have Trussell file the evidence for the Labrash case while you and Gilbertson ask Hanson about his family. I'm sure you will find that Hanson is a good police officer. He has connections with special units that might be useful in your search for the girls. He has worked alongside the K-9 units in Saskatoon. It would help if you talked to him. I'm sure you will find things will work out if you can knock the chip off your shoulder."

Sliding the photo and the bagged jewelry off the desk, Randy walked back into the roll call room in search of Officer Trussell. He was shuffling papers on his desk, motioning Randy over, anxiously waiting to talk to him. "Did you hear any news from Gerard about the missing girls? Does he have any information?"

"No, but I talked to Gerard about the missing evidence from the Labrash case. I had to find it as part of my return-to-work agreement. I don't doubt for a second that Gerard has only let me back on duty to help search for Amy. Where's Gilbertson?"

"He's at the front desk answering phones for Gladys. She needed a ten-minute break and he volunteered," Trussell said, shaking his head in disbelief. "What do you need?"

"Can you do me a favour and log this into the evidence locker?" Randy said, holding up the Labrash evidence. "It keeps getting misplaced."

Trussell eyed the evidence wearily before grudgingly accepting it. "How do you know it won't go missing again?"

"We don't! I know you hate paperwork as much as I do, but I hope you can make an exception this time."

"Okay, but this is the only time I'm going to help you with paperwork," Trussell teased, taking the evidence. "Do you think someone keeps messing with your evidence? Does Gerard know what's happening?"

"He doesn't know, but I am suspicious of Officer Hanson," Randy sighed, looking over his shoulder and checking to ensure no one was listening. "There is something off about that guy. I need to question him about his family and have Gilbertson witness the exchange. You can find us up front, waiting to see if the tip line turns in anything on our missing girls."

"I think Hanson left for lunch. You might try Frankie's Diner."

"Thanks," Randy replied, going to the front desk to check on Officer Gilbertson. To his surprise, Officer Hanson stood at the front desk talking to Gilbertson. Randy would have preferred to have the opportunity to discuss his suspicions with Gilbertson before questioning Hanson. Still, time was running out! He needed to find Amy and Sarah before it was too late.

"Any luck tracking down the missing girls?" Hanson asked.

Randy glanced at Gilbertson, wishing he could read his thoughts about Hanson. "No, not yet, but we are really on to something. We have been canvassing the neighbourhood where the girls left their bicycles. Gilbertson has phoned the radio station."

"I have some connections. Do you need me to take over the case?" Hanson offered, casually shuffling his pink message slips. "I can call in a friend of mine from K-9. I could have those girls home in no time."

"Don't get ahead of yourself! Until we get a strong lead, I won't need the K-9 unit. I think the Tylers and the Petersens want to know the police are doing everything possible to find Sarah and Amy. Family is important to our townspeople," Randy said, seeking an opportunity to dive casually into his line of questioning. "Do you have family in the Glenmere area?" He flinched, thinking his awkward question may have seemed to come out of nowhere. What could he say: are you the one stealing evidence to hide a killer who is kidnapping teenagers?

"No, I don't. It would be nice if I lived closer, but I'm not ready to transfer yet," Officer Hanson replied, putting the pink slips on the desk. "I have a few minutes if you need the advice of someone more experienced. Where are you looking right now? I could give you good pointers."

Randy was momentarily distracted from whatever Hanson said next as he watched Trussell breeze past the front desk, not stopping to talk, giving Randy the thumbs-up sign on his way out of the heavy main doors. "Did you say you don't have any family connections in town?" Randy asked again, narrowing his eyes. "Isn't that why you came to Glenmere? To be closer to your aunt?"

Shaking his head and chuckling, Hanson replied, "No, I'm not small-town. I'm a city boy from Calgary. I transferred here to help establish a major crimes unit after the murder case this summer. The detachment thinks there may be more crime lurking behind these white picket fences than everyone likes to think."

"Glenmere isn't that bad," Randy defensively replied, trying to ignore Hanson's ego stroke.

"Obviously, with the recent poisonings of two teenagers and my CI, crimes are happening under our noses,"

Hanson said, pointing to himself. "I think it will only take a few months to clean up this pint-sized town and be out of here."

"Wait! Who was your CI?" Randy said, tilting his head to the side. *What did he miss?*

"Ronaldo Baysic was our CI for the drug trafficking we were looking into before we started finding bodies in the freezers around town. The guy was feeding us information in exchange for hot meals. I can't say that the information was always helpful to make a case, but Gerard said it didn't hurt to feed the hungry homeless guy."

"Ronaldo was yours and Gerard's CI?" Randy asked, trying to remember what his file stated.

"Gerard signed him as a CI on the drug trafficking case. When Gerard realized that Baysic was a drug user and not the dealer, he put Trussell and me on the case to keep an eye out for anything that would leave us a clue. I was surprised we didn't find anything and stopped getting information from him. Now he's dead and we can't even pretend he was a valuable informant."

Slapping himself on the forehead, Randy said, "Lloyd Trussell has family in town. He has an aunt."

"This isn't new information. Trussell is probably on his way over there for lunch right now," Hanson said.

"If Trussell knew that Baysic was a known drug user, then why did he keep asking about the guy's death, wanting to know what the blood test confirmed? Don't you think he would assume Baysic overdosed?" Randy asked, frowning and trying to make a connection.

Trussell had to know Ronaldo Baysic was a drug user. Baysic may have already named the drug dealer. Could Trussell be protecting the dealer? Why would he do that?

"That's kind of weird!"

"Weird isn't what I would call it. It's suspicious. The blood test linked the homeless guy's death to the ice box murders. Why would he need to confirm that?" Randy exchanged concerned expressions with Gilbertson and Hanson, realizing he might have been suspecting the wrong police officer all along.

"I wonder what he knows about the poisoned victims?" Hanson asked.

"I don't know, but I've already told Gerard these cases are linked to my case of the parking violation and suspected prescription drug selling case. Do you think Trussell is involved in this?" Randy asked, using Hanson as a sounding board to further his ideas.

"I don't see how Trussell could have planned any of those murders. He was with me gathering evidence against the school janitor when the Hildebrandt boy was poisoned and disappeared," Hanson replied, shaking his head. "I'm sure Gerard said he was at his desk the entire shift on the day the Labrash girl was poisoned. How could he be involved? I don't think you can accuse him. You are grasping at straws! There must have been a file error on the blood sample report you checked."

"Unless he is working with someone else or disposing of evidence to obstruct justice?" Gilbertson added, joining the conversation.

Gilbertson's statements forced Randy to create a theory and basic timeline of events, but so much information was only speculative. Gerard warned Randy against jumping to conclusions and accusing his colleagues without substantial evidence. "Maybe," Randy hesitated, leaning on the desk and wondering if he mixed up the blood sample reports in his disordered files. "Is Trussell's aunt on a lot of prescription drugs? Does she have dementia?"

"His aunt is old. I'm sure she takes a lot of meds. I don't think his aunt fits the profile of a killer and kidnapper," Gilbertson smirked, leaning back in his chair. "I don't recall Trussell mentioning a senile aunt."

Looking at his watch, Hanson asked, "What should Trussell be working on right now? I thought he was helping you find Amy and her friend. Didn't the three of you already have a lunch break?"

"Yes, we did," Randy agreed. "I don't know where he is, but I gave him the evidence for the Labrash case just before he left."

"To do what with?"

"To file into the evidence locker," Randy supplied.

"Are you sure he filed it into evidence? Maybe he didn't do it," Hanson said, rounding the front desk toward the evidence room. "He is a lazy son of a bitch. I wouldn't trust him to fetch me coffee."

Randy and Gilbertson followed him, watching Hanson search the evidence log for an entry. "Here it is!" Hanson exclaimed. "Trussell wrote one photo of a gold earring. I guess he logged and filed my case evidence for you! How did you manage to make Trussell do police work?"

"What? I gave him the earring, too!" Randy yelled.

"Next time you have evidence for my case, tell me directly. You might make me look bad," Hanson said, pushing past Randy on his way out of the evidence room. "Now, I have to waste my time looking for evidence I already thought I had."

Randy turned to Gilbertson, mentally slapping himself. "Shit! Trussell may not be the scum behind the killings, but he knows something! The question is: what? Who would he be protecting?"

"Girlfriend?" Gilbertson suggested questioningly. "Did he have one? Would anyone date his lazy ass?"

"If he has a girlfriend, then it is a well-kept secret. Come on, I think we need to go look for Trussell and his dear old aunt," Randy said, throwing the evidence log back on the shelf. "Let's see if a gold earring leads us to the truth about what's happening in this little town."

Breezing into the room, Hanson tossed the evidence bag containing the gold earring at Randy. "There it is," Hanson said, his arrogance dripping from his words. "Next time, do the log entry yourself! Trussell left this evidence at his workstation. I told you he's lazy." Shaking his head, Hanson left the evidence room, leaving Randy and Gilbertson dumbfounded.

Crinkling the plastic bag in his fist, Randy sighed. He thought he was onto something, assuming Lloyd Trussell was the police officer protecting a killer, but he seemed to be wrong again! First, he thought Hanson was tainted, and then he wanted to accuse Trussell. Where did this leave the investigation into the death of three people and the missing teenagers? Randy tossed the evidence bag on the counter, pulling the logbook off the shelf. He knew it was time to stop trying to connect the cases and focus on his main objective: finding the missing teenagers.

"We got something!" Officer Gerard exclaimed, rushing into the evidence room. "Grab your gear! An anonymous tip came in regarding Amy Young and Sarah Tyler. The tipster said a rusty white sedan pulled up to a stop sign with someone yelling inside the trunk. The tipster followed the car west on the old highway until the car turned left on Grid 846. It is a solid lead!"

Chapter 35

Wednesday, October 09, 1985

"Doyle! The K-9 team is here!" Officer Gerard yelled through the open doorway of the abandoned house, exposing the trail of large booted footprints made by the comings and goings of several police officers on the dusty wooden floor, covering over the ones left behind by the teenagers fleeing captivity. Photos and evidence were being collected in the house and on the grounds since the anonymous tip led the police directly to an abandoned home twenty-four kilometres from Glenmere. Officer Gerard ordered the K-9 unit from Saskatoon as soon the officers found Amy's blue Family Grocer's uniform vest covered in oil and dirt in the basement.

"I'm coming!" Randy replied from the dirt cellar, turning off his flashlight. He was confident he was missing nothing. He had searched the basement several times looking for clues and confirming without a doubt that Amy and Sarah had been held there by their captors.

Handing the 35mm Canon camera to Officer Gilbertson, Randy watched the K-9 unit's van roll up the dirt driveway of the property. Patrol cars were still out, searching the gravel grid roads in all directions from this location. Hanson patted Randy's shoulder, encouraging him, "Don't worry. I've worked with this team before. They can track them down using the scent from Amy's vest. We will have them home safely in time to make tonight's breaking news story!"

Randy nodded, watching Hanson cheerfully greet two K-9 handlers. He could see two determined German Shepherds in protective gear, eagerly waiting to spring into action. Officer Gerard joined the reunion, motioning for another officer to bring the evidence bag with Amy's blue vest. Randy felt his chest tighten, his heart hammering in his chest with worry. He frowned, questioning whether they would find the girls in time.

"Doyle! Hanson! You two men are with the K-9 unit on foot," Gerard called, barking orders and assigning job duties. "Trussell and Dillion will follow with patrol cars as a backup. The rest of you are here with me at the centre of operations. Let's get them home! Use extreme caution. We don't know if the girls are by themselves or with their captor."

The K-9 handlers riled up their partners, giving the dogs Amy's vest to smell. The dogs sniffed the roadway briefly and began the chase, the officers running behind them in pursuit along the gravel road.

Adrenaline surged through Randy's veins as he found a comfortable rhythm in his stride. He followed behind the officers leading the hunt with their loyal four-legged partners. He focused on steadying his breathing and trying to conserve his energy. Suddenly, the dogs stopped, circling both sides of the ditch before veering across a field. Randy lifted each leg to stretch his tight hamstrings while he waited for the dogs to pick up the trail. The dogs raced through the ditch where three sets of footprints marked a definite trail leading into a field.

Officer Hanson unclipped the walkie-talkie from his belt, pressed the button, and instructed the patrol cars, breathing heavily. "We found three sets of footprints. Trussell, advance north on the next grid road to see if you can see anything on the other side of this section of land, over."

"Copy, over," Trussell's voice confirmed, followed by static and two beeps.

After another beep, Officer Gerard's voice crackled, "Because we don't know who the third set of tracks belongs to, I am sending Gilbertson and Whitfield in another patrol car to wait on the road where you turned into the field just in case you come out again on the same grid. Over." The radio emitted static and beeped.

"Copy, over."

The mud was slippery, making Randy slow down in a few places to secure proper footing. "Look! The tracks are leading us to those buildings," Randy smiled, hoping they would find the girls alive.

Eventually, the officers reached the overgrown hedge, blocking the team from advancing. The dogs zig-zagged around before leading the team through an opening in the dense brush. Pushing himself through tangled branches to the other side, Randy emerged onto an abandoned homestead with confusion. The German Shepherds pushed through the tall weeds, tongues lolling out with exertion, tracing curious scents. The weeds were trampled in various places but didn't go in any particular direction. Confused by the erratic scent pattern, the dogs pulled their handlers in opposite directions.

"I think the girls explored each building, looking for shelter. Look around! The girls could still be here," Hanson commanded, directing Randy to spur into action.

Randy walked ahead, following the trampled grasses and listening for movement. A bird flew out of one of the little house's windows, startling Randy. Watching it fly around curled shingle roofing, Randy realized that there was a wisp of smoke emanating from the blackened chimney. Inhaling the faint smoke, Randy pointed at the chimney and said, "Chimney smoke!"

"Okay, I see it. I will lead us inside; you follow. We will clear the building and search for them," Hanson said, motioning Randy to unholster his gun, leading them up the steps and counting down to three on his fingers before kicking open the door. "Police officers! We are coming in!"

Randy followed Hanson through the first room and into the next. Bleary-eyed teenagers sat up, looking bewildered at the sight of the two officers who had burst into the room with their guns drawn, awakening them. Randy glanced over at Hanson; his eyebrow raised. Holding his palm toward the girls and listening closely, Randy calmly instructed, "Stay where you are while Officer Hanson clears the rest of the building. Is anyone else here?"

"No," replied Amy, smiling with relief.

"All clear," Officer Hanson announced, returning from the two bedrooms and waiting for Randy's explanation.

Swiftly unclipping his radio and pressing the button, Randy announced, "We have them secured. Send emergency vehicles."

Officer Gerard's voice clicked over the static, "Good Work! We are on our way. Over."

"Officer Hanson, you know Amy, Sarah and Anna," Randy stated, bracing for Hanson's reaction to using Anna's name.

"Anna Labrash," Hanson replied, narrowing his eyes and questioning Randy's identification. "I know. How do you know?"

"That's not the point. You are aware Anna was not the first victim! You knew her sister, Leah Labrash, was the first victim," Randy realized, shaking his head. "I was under orders by Gerard to keep that information close, but I am guessing this was your idea."

"I wasn't aware that you were privy to confidential information," Hanson said, shifting his weight and holstering his weapon. "When did you find out?"

"Yesterday," Randy said, defensively stepping closer to Hanson. "According to what my suspect in custody told me yesterday, Anna has been hiding out. She can confirm information about the drug dealers killing people in Glenmere. The dealers planned to poison Anna and Liam after they witnessed an exchange between the dealer and a drug user, but they accidentally poisoned Leah instead. The two girls look a lot alike."

"Who did you arrest?" Anna asked, frowning. "Did you arrest the killers? Our kidnappers?"

Randy hesitated, wondering how much information he should reveal. "Greg Holman is in custody."

"You have to let him go!" Anna protested, jumping up and pacing. "He was helping me! Greg is innocent. He even tried to fight them off when they grabbed me near the funeral home."

"Calm down!" Randy said, raising his hands in defence and trying to maintain his suspect's cover story. "I think we know Greg was not dealing on his own. He had to have help. If you can tell us who put you in that filthy basement, then we can make another arrest."

"Well, we can't be sure," Amy said, biting her dry lips. "There was a woman at the house where Sarah and I followed the vehicle that they took Anna to. She must have been the person who knocked me out and put me in the trunk."

"That's right, except there were two women. I saw them both when I walked into the house. Amy was already lying on the floor. One of the women was dragging her across the floor," Sarah explained, acting out the scene in dramatic fashion. "The other was just standing there yelling orders."

"Wait! Who was with you in the car? Did Greg Holman set you up to be kidnapped?" Officer Hanson asked, looking at Anna. "Were you with him of your own free will?"

"Well, there is a lot to the story that you don't know," Anna said, biting her fingernails. "Greg is a friend of mine. He was helping me move from place to place. I could only couch-surf my relatives' homes for a short time before I started getting restless; I was trying to help plan my sister's funeral. I didn't realize it was still so dangerous. I guess I wasn't careful enough."

"The vehicle Greg drives isn't registered to him. During an impound, I had seized evidence that gave me a reason to issue an arrest warrant for the driver," Randy informed everyone, wondering if he was revealing too much. Switching to the cover story, Randy continued to fill everyone in on the fake arrest. "I found Greg Holman leaving the vehicle and executed the warrant. Greg admitted to several traffic violations, but he hasn't provided his entire statement yet. We still need to question him to determine his involvement in this criminal investigation." The distant sounds of police sirens broke the stunned silence of the smoky room, their cries of urgency slowly growing louder with each passing moment.

Shaking her long black hair, Anna yelled, "No! You got it all wrong. Let me talk to him. He will tell you the whole story. He's just scared to say anything! He's trying to protect me."

Nodding in agreement and approaching Randy, Amy said, "I know I told you Greg threatened me, but after talking to Anna, I realized that he was warning me away from getting hurt. I have to talk to him, too; I just want to be sure he wasn't trying to hurt me."

The sirens seemed to intensify outside in the overgrown yard, the sound broken only by the bark of the K-9 dogs. "Well, it sounds like our rescue is here!" Hanson exclaimed, rubbing his hands. "We will get you to the hospital for medical help and then take you to the police station for your statements."

"But what about Greg?" Anna asked.

"He will remain in custody until we have reason to release him," Randy sighed, inspecting the girls' disheveled appearance. "I may permit you to talk to him once we interview him. More importantly, our office dispatcher will call your families while we drive to town. I'm sure that they will join you at the hospital. All of you are dehydrated and have injuries; after some food, a warm bath and a rest day, I will let you talk with Greg at the station."

As everyone started to leave the room, Officer Hanson held up his arm, blocking their exit. "One last thing, the police dogs need to sniff you so they know they have found you. They will be looking forward to it. Don't deny the dogs their rewards," Hanson said, grinning as girls filed past him to greet the awaiting K-9 unit.

"There are big holes in your case, Doyle," Hanson said, grabbing Randy's arm and preventing his exit. "I'd keep your head down and mouth shut!"

Randy shook his arm free of Hanson's grasp, scowling. "Don't touch me! I am looking for a connection between my drug dealer case, the kidnapping and the murders. I ordered blood work on Ronaldo Baysic. He died of thallium poisoning! It seems like more than a coincidence, don't you think?"

"Not really. There has to be a mistake. Why do you think the dealer would poison a junkie?" Hanson asked, mocking Randy's theory. "Why would a dealer want to kill someone they are dealing drugs to? It doesn't make any sense."

Randy considered various theories regarding the homeless man's death, but he only had a hunch. "Ronaldo Baysic was a drug addict, but he also relied on the generosity of our townspeople and the soup kitchen to feed him," Randy said, stringing his thoughts together. "If we show Baysic's photo to Anna, she can confirm whether or not he was the junkie she witnessed in the drug deal."

"That still doesn't explain why a dealer would kill the junkie, let alone a few teenagers. How does a dealer become a killer?"

Randy rubbed his muddy boot across the tattered rug, wondering what would make a dealer start poisoning people. The idea hit Randy with a jolt, bringing a sudden realization. "Of course, that's it!" Randy exclaimed. "The dealer doesn't want to be identified!"

Rolling his eyes, Hanson replied, "That's a given. What drug dealer wants to be identified? Tell me something I don't know."

"A dealer who is good friends with a police officer," Randy stated, revealing his dirty cop theory and hanging it between them.

Wiping the sweat off his forehead, Officer Hanson said, "If a dealer was good friends with a police officer, the only reason the dealer would kill people is to keep other officers from finding out a colleague is looking the other way."

"Damn, it looks like we are working on the same case from different directions," Randy said, cursing what he was about to say next. "Gerard will want us to close this case and make the arrests. Greg Holman said dirty cops were interfering in this case; he didn't say how many officers."

"Get out! Are you suggesting an internal investigation?" Hanson asked, his eyes widening with surprise. "That's a lot of accusations based on drummed-up theories. You should stick to traffic violations until you get a handle on police procedures."

"Are we done here?" Randy asked, trying to control his frustration.

"Yup, I'm going to celebrate finding the missing teenagers," Hanson said, preening his hair and uniform. "This case is closed."

"Just one more thing before you go bask in your glory," Randy said, extending his arm and stopping Hanson from exiting. "Who else knows Anna is alive?"

"Lots of people: the family, your guy Greg, and a few officers," Hanson said dismissively, pushing Randy's arm aside.

"Which officers?"

"I don't have to tell you, but it was me, Gilbertson and Gerard. If Gerard thought you should know, you would know, but I guess it doesn't matter now," Hanson replied, brushing past Randy and leaving the small building.

Inhaling deeply, Randy tried to calm his heart, hammering against his chest. He walked around the small room, ensuring the three girls left nothing behind. He attempted to shake the insistent theory of a dirty cop away, but it kept gnawing at him. Resolved to talk to Officer Gerard about Greg's accusations again, Randy left the old home, relieved the girls would reunite with their families.

Randy smiled and shook his head, watching Jeffrey Hanson celebrate his part in finding the missing girls with the other police officers around them. Someone gave each girl a chocolate bar, which they were practically inhaling. Randy's stomach growled, knowing Beatrice Petersen would have a mountain of food waiting for her granddaughter's return.

Officer Gerard wiped the sweat from his forehead; issuing orders, he yelled, "Okay, everyone. The families want to see their girls. Let's get moving! Trussell and Gilbertson will take the girls to the hospital to reunite with their parents. I have already radioed ahead to have Gladys make the phone calls. Doyle and Hanson will file the evidence and start the reports."

Slapping Doyle on the back, Hanson said, "I'm going to catch a ride with the K-9 unit. You can ride with Gerard and start logging the evidence while I catch up with my buddies."

Randy watched Hanson walk away, frowning. "What an asshole."

"I wouldn't take him too seriously," Trussell said, drawing Randy's attention. "Do you want to ride with Gilbertson to take the girls to the station?"

"Of course! I don't want to let Amy out of my sight until the Petersens know she is safe," Randy responded, feeling his heartbeat quicken. "I'll see you at the station."

"I'm going to stop at my aunt's house to check on her first," Trussell said, looking away to avoid Randy's stare.

"Your aunt?" Randy frowned, feeling prickles run up his spine. "She must be fairly old. Does she live at the nursing home?"

"No, she still lives in her home. She didn't want to go into the nursing home, but I'm starting to think she would have been better off under their supervision."

Randy inhaled deeply, trying to remain calm and aloof, but alarm bells sounded in his head. "No problem," he replied, faking a smile. "I'll go with Gilbertson to bring Amy, Leah and Sarah to the hospital."

"You mean Anna," Lloyd Trussell stated.

"What?" Randy asked, shaking his head and faking confusion. "Oh, yeah. Anna. See you later." Randy stood unmoving as his eyes followed Trussell's retreat into a police car. The gravel spewed from the car's tires as Trussell sped away in the Gran Fury, heading to town. Randy watched the police car until it disappeared around a corner. He flexed his hands, listening to the blood rushing in his ears.

Gerard stepped up beside Randy. "What's on your mind, Doyle? You look like someone pissed in your Corn Flakes."

Randy blinked rapidly, trying to gather his thoughts. "It's Trussell," he growled through clenched teeth. "Somehow, he is the dirty police officer mixed up in the killings, the kidnapping, and the drug dealings. I know it!"

Gerard moved closer into Randy's confidence, whispering, "What exactly did he say to you?"

"He just identified Anna as Anna, correcting me when I called her by her sister's name."

"Shit! He isn't supposed to know. Do you know where he was going?"

"He said he was going to check on his old aunt. He wished he had put her in the nursing home instead of letting her live in her own home."

Gerard nodded, backing away. He quickly yelled new orders, "Dillion and Nelson, bring the girls to the hospital! Hanson, Gilbertson, Hunter and Allen are my backups! Doyle, you are with me! Trussell is our suspect. We need to chase him down and bring him in! Stay off the radios until we have him in our sights."

Chapter 36

"You'll drive so I can coordinate," Gerard said, tossing Randy the keys. "Let's move it! No sirens until it's vital."

Randy caught the keys, rushing to get behind the wheel of the Plymouth Gran Fury police unit. In his urgency, the seat belt locked when he tried to put it on. Pushing it aside, Randy started the vehicle and shifted into reverse, firmly pressing his foot on the gas pedal and kicking up mud and gravel. Shifting into drive, Randy floored the accelerator again. The backend of the car fishtailed until Randy steered out of it. He followed the rutted road, ignoring the mud slapping against the wheel wells.

"Easy, Doyle! We know where he is going. Let's take this one step at a time," Gerard said, trying to calm Randy.

Randy inhaled deeply, easing off the accelerator and gaining more control over the vehicle. He knew it wouldn't do anyone good if he rolled the car before they got to Trussell. "What's our plan? Trussell is driving a police car. How will we chase down another police car without using radios?"

"While we were waiting for you and the K-9 unit to track the girls, I had the station find out who owned the abandoned homestead where the kidnapper held the girls."

Glancing at Gerard and back on the slippery road, Randy asked, "Whose is it?"

"The homestead used to belong to Howard Marshall. His wife sold the land and moved to town after he died."

"Edith Marshall? I knew it!"

"Do I need to tell you where she lives now?" Gerard asked, smirking like he already knew the answer.

"Nope! We found Amy and Sarah's bicycles across the street from her house. I arrested Greg Holman on the front lawn!" Randy exclaimed, slapping his hand against the steering wheel. "The drugs in the trunk of the old green beast, the caregiver, the old lady and a dirty police officer! Damn it! That's the connection I was trying to make. I couldn't get it together in my head!"

"Slow down," Gerard casually stated, grabbing the handle above the door. "We need to turn onto the highway in four hundred metres. We will get Lloyd Trussell at his aunt's place. Lloyd and the caregiver will both be under arrest for kidnapping, drugs, and murder until we can sort this out."

The tires squealed on the pavement as Randy maneuvered the vehicle onto the highway, throwing mud and gravel onto the paved road. Randy looked into his rearview mirror, confirming the presence of two police officers backing up the pursuit. "The guys are right behind us. We need to communicate with them to organize ourselves. How are we going to do that?"

Reaching for the radio receiver mounted under the dashboard and pressing the button, Gerard said, "I think I'm going to go to Frankie's for something to eat. I could probably eat five pancakes in a matter of minutes. Does anyone want to join me? Over."

Randy frowned, glancing at Gerard. "Will they get the message?"

Soon, Hanson's voice crackled across the radio; he replied, "I could use some pancakes. Over."

"That's my boy! He caught on quickly. One more to go," Gerard exclaimed, excitement mounting. "I used something similar with Hanson not that long ago."

Randy listened, waiting expectantly until the radio crackled again. "Count me in, too," Officer Hunter's voice chimed in from the other car.

Gerard changed the radio to channel five and pressed the radio's handset button. He called out, "Follow me to Fifth Street. Be on the lookout for Lloyd Trussell and a middle-aged woman. Arrest both of them for kidnapping and murder. Assume they are armed and dangerous."

"This is Hanson. We copy. Over."

"What about Trussell's auntie? Over," Hunter's voice snapped over the radio.

Gerard raised his eyebrows, waiting for Randy's clarification. Shrugging, Randy replied, "She is an old senile woman. Trussell hired Loretta Flatiron, a caregiver for his aunt."

"The older woman is senile and may be acting against her will. Take caution, but handle her with care. The middle-aged woman is Loretta Flatiron. Over," Gerard responded, releasing the talk button and returning the radio receiver to its hook. "We are almost in town. Turn on your lights, but leave the siren off until you see Trussell."

Randy flipped the switch on the console, turning on his flashing lights. Vehicles began to move aside, providing clear passage. Turning onto Fourth Avenue, Randy suggested, "Tell one car to go around from the other direction. We can come to the house from both sides."

"Good idea." Reaching for the receiver and pressing the button, Gerard said, "Hunter, take Fourth Street around the block."

Randy watched the end car turn right in his rear-view mirror. Wiping his damp hands on his pant legs, Randy inhaled deeply, preparing for the showdown with Trussell. He slowed down for the corner, turning right onto Fifth Street. He spotted Trussell's police car in front of Edith Marshall's home. The passenger door was open.

"Easy. Slow down. Don't get too close too soon," Gerard instructed.

Randy pressed on the brakes, slowing the police vehicle and parking at an angle, blocking the street. He reached for the crank to unroll the window and saw the door of the 1930s home open with a bang. Loretta Flatiron ran out of the house carrying a suitcase, looking over her shoulder and yelling at Trussell. Randy locked eyes at the dirty cop, glaring at his suspect. Slowly, Trussell raised both of his hands in surrender. Loretta stopped, frantically looking around at the flashing lights and the police vehicles blocking the street.

Randy unsnapped the strap on his sidearm with his right hand, his other reaching for the door latch mechanism. He opened his door to shield himself, turning his focus on Loretta, wondering what her next move was.

"Police officers! Don't move! Put your hands on your head," Officer Hanson yelled, crouching behind the hood of his police vehicle.

Gerard opened his door, crawling around to the front fender. He yelled, "We have you surrounded! Drop what you are holding and place your hands on your head!"

Randy held his hand on his weapon and watched Loretta's eyes dart from one police officer to the next. He could see Lloyd placing his hands on his head, speaking quietly to Loretta. She shook her head, dropping her suitcase and scrambling into her white Chrysler Newport sedan. The door slammed shut and the engine rumbled, blowing thick exhaust. The car sputtered as it shifted into reverse.

Randy's eyes widened and he looked across the hood at Officer Gerard, wondering if he should move to a better position so he could see the driver's door of Loretta's sedan. The engine revved, blowing more fumes. Randy blinked, deciding to get back behind the wheel of the police vehicle. He leapt into place, shifting into reverse as the white sedan's tires squealed out of the driveway, Loretta lining up to smash into the front fender of his police vehicle. Randy backed his vehicle up, receiving a glancing blow to the left headlight. The glass popped as metal screeched against metal. The white car changed directions, moving across the neighbouring grass and smashing through a white picket fence to drive around the police car blockade.

Gerard banged on the hood of the car, yelling, "Go! Go! Go!"

Pushing his foot to the floor and accelerating quickly in reverse, Randy yelled, "Oh, shit!" He pulled hard on the steering wheel, spinning the car around one hundred and eighty degrees and coming to a sudden stop. The smell of burning rubber assaulted his nose, making him cough.

Three sudden thumps on the back fender of the car forced Randy to crane his neck to see what he might have hit. Randy watched Officer Gerard run along the side of his vehicle and open the passenger door. "Follow her!" Gerard yelled, jumping into the seat and slamming the passenger door closed.

Thrusting the gear shift into drive, Randy turned on the sirens and stepped on the gas to pursue Loretta's rusty Newport. Loretta made a sharp right turn onto Fourth Avenue, bouncing over the curb and grazing a parked car.

Randy's car radio hissed and crackled with static until he realized that it was still on the wrong channel to call for backup. "We are still on channel five!" Randy said, trying to concentrate on his pursuit. "Switch to the emergency channel!"

"Unit 879 is pursuing a dangerous suspect travelling north on Fourth Avenue. Backup needed," Officer Gerard called into the radio receiver.

Randy was relieved when he heard another siren join him in the chase. "I'm right behind you. Over," Officer Hunter replied over the radio. "Hanson is arresting the first suspect, Lloyd Trussell, and securing the scene."

Randy concentrated on weaving around other vehicles and keeping his eyes on the speeding sedan. Loretta turned onto Main Street, hurdling two hub caps onto the sidewalk, narrowly missing pedestrians.

"Watch this corner!" Gerard shouted, holding onto the passenger handle mounted above the door.

"I'm on it!" Randy declared, relentlessly following. He was not going to let her get away from him; he owed it to Amy and the Petersens. No one can mess with his family and get away with it!

Loretta rounded the corner where the red-bricked post office building stood. Her vehicle's tires strained against their rims. People standing on the cement steps of the post office gawked with open mouths at the spectacular scene before them. Randy cranked hard on the steering wheel, following the sedan's blue exhaust. He suspected Loretta might head towards the highway for a clean getaway. "Come on! Pull over!" Randy pleaded, flexing his hands on the steering wheel to ease his grip.

"On the next straight away, try to bump her off the road," Gerard instructed. Randy nodded, watching the white sedan swerve right and then turn left.

Turning left and glancing in his rearview mirror, Randy said, "We have two cars following our pursuit. Tell them I'm going to attempt a maneuver!"

"Hold back! We are going to try to force the car off the road. Over," Gerard announced over the radio.

Gripping the steering wheel, Randy leaned forward and pressed the accelerator to the floor, lining the cruiser up with the Chrysler Newport's bumper. He clipped the vehicle's right rear corner. Randy's body surged forward with the impact. Unfortunately, the heavy car shimmied, but it didn't spin as Randy had planned. "I'll try again. Hold on!" Randy shifted in his seat, preparing for another impact. He pressed the accelerator again, striking the rear end of the sedan. The white car spun to the right, making a U-turn across the intersection and narrowly missing a fire hydrant.

"She's still going for it!" Gerard exclaimed, believing Loretta was still trying to escape the police.

Cranking the car around in the intersection, still in pursuit, Randy braked and slowed his vehicle. He kept his eyes on his prize. The sedan bounced across the lawn and the sidewalk, hitting the street with a loud pop. "She blew a tire!" Randy announced, watching chunks of rubber fly onto the pavement. "Sparks! Sparks! We might have a fire if she doesn't stop driving! Where does this bitch think she's going?"

"We got her!" Officer Hunter's voice crackled over the radio as his unit's Gran Fury drove into the front grill of the Chrysler Newport, finally forcing it to a stop. Acrid smoke wafted around the scene as Officers Hunter and Allen exited their vehicles, drawing guns and calling for compliance.

Randy braked and stopped his police car near the rear of the sedan, opening his driver's door and unholstering his weapon swiftly. Inhaling deeply, Randy tried to slow his heart rate, and steadied his weapon. Aiming his gun at Loretta's left shoulder, Randy shouted, "Put both hands out the window! We have you surrounded! Stop resisting arrest, Loretta!"

Randy slowly advanced closer to the driver's door, swallowing hard and taking another deep breath through his nose. He waited while his heartbeat drummed in his chest. Seconds felt like minutes. Eventually, her shaking and well-manicured hands appeared out of the open window; Randy released his breath.

Tapping Randy on his left shoulder, Gerard said, "I've got you covered. Proceed with the arrest."

Randy removed his support hand from his weapon, reaching for the door latch. "Keep your hands where I can see them!" The door swung open wide, rocking the car with its weight.

"I didn't do anything! Why are you arresting me?" Loretta pleaded, her voice wavering with emotion.

"No sudden moves! Keep your hands up and swing your legs out of the car," Randy instructed, gripping his weapon with both hands. He watched Loretta move into position to exit the vehicle. "Put your hands on your head and kneel on the ground!"

"I don't want to get all dirty," Loretta whined, moving into position on her knees.

"Don't move!" Randy ordered, holstering his weapon and unclipping his handcuffs from his utility belt. "Loretta Flatiron, you are under arrest for resisting arrest, kidnapping and murder."

Chapter 37

Absently clicking the end of his pen, Officer Randy Doyle stared through the one-way mirror into the examination room, focused on the mesmerizing dance between Officer Gerard and his suspect. He studied Gerard's line of questioning, trying to learn from his mentor: calm voice, even tone, patience, and uncomfortable silence.

"We know that you weren't working alone on this, Miss Flatiron," Gerard calmly stated, sifting through the open file on the table between them. He straightened the papers into a neat pile, tapping it against the table. "Let us go over the part about the kidnapping one more time. Explain why you were helping to kidnap Amy Young, Sarah Tyler and Anna Labrash."

"I already told you; Edith forced me to help with the kidnapping of those girls," Loretta snapped, glaring at the officer. Crossing her legs, she tried to lean back in her chair, but she was restricted by the cuffs chaining her to the middle of the table, rubbing across the worn table's surface.

"Um, what my client is trying to say is that she has nothing further to comment at this time," the young court-appointed lawyer said, fidgeting with the cheap necktie that seemed to be strangling him. Randy noticed beads of sweat around the lawyer's clean-shaven upper lip and a small vein pulsing along his damp hairline.

Rolling her eyes and ignoring her counsel's advice, Loretta continued, "It was Edith and her nephew, Lloyd. The police should arrest them. They kidnapped those little girls while I was at the bank. Did you check the security cameras?"

"Miss Flatiron, you shouldn't-" the counsel said, stopping when a swift knock on the interview room door echoed in the sparse room.

The door opened and Officer Hanson strode into the room, dropping another file onto the desk in front of Gerard. Hanson glanced at the lawyer as he left without speaking or showing any emotion.

Gerard slowly opened the file folder and studied it, flipping through each page after carefully reading the contents. His suspect, Loretta, leaned forward, trying to read the file's contents. "I see that we have matched the poison used on the three victims to a sample taken from the supply closet at the school where Ralph Norman works as the janitor. Were you forced to help poison those two teenagers and one homeless man?"

"Allegedly poisoned," the counsel interrupted, unenthusiastically throwing the pencil he was chewing down onto the table. "My client has made no comments or suggestions that she knew about someone poisoning other people; she has only admitted to being forced to assist in the kidnapping of three people."

Turning slightly at the sound of the door to the observation area closing, Randy asked Hanson, "Are you already finished interrogating Trussell?"

"It wasn't difficult. Once Trussell realized he was in the hot seat, he melted. The whole story flowed freely out of him. He had nothing to do with the kidnapping; therefore, he was eager to help us find the girls. He thinks Miss Flatiron intended to kill them and frame him. Trussell is ashamed of everything Loretta manipulated him to do. He didn't realize what was happening until it was too late." Moving toward the one-way mirror and standing beside Randy, Hanson smirked, "Who's the lawyer? Is he even old enough to practice law?"

Chuckling, Randy answered, "Miss Flatiron said she didn't need a lawyer, but Gerard insisted. He had Gilbertson phone every lawyer in the book. This court-appointed lawyer from Legal Aid was the first representative to return the call. I guess everyone else was unavailable this weekend."

Smiling, Hanson replied, "We found the evidence we needed, but I'm hoping the lawyer doesn't suggest Trussell planted it. We have Lloyd Trussell's statement and Edith Marshall's medical report. The case hinges on Lloyd's word against Loretta's. Gerard needs to push for a confession from Loretta to make the case rock solid. Gerard thinks he knows who had the motive to kill, which is what led to the kidnapping. If he can't get a confession, then it will be up to the prosecuting attorney to prove it. Hopefully, for Trussell's sake, it will work out. I would hate to be an ex-police officer inside the prison."

Holding up a piece of paper from one of the file folders, Gerard said, "During our search of your white 1964 Chrysler Newport, we found evidence linking you to the murder of Leah Labrash, Liam Hildebrandt and Ronaldo Baysic."

"I don't see how that would be possible. I have not had the vehicle very long, a couple of weeks," Loretta smugly stated.

Gerard pulled open a file, taking out a single sheet of paper. "This is a photocopy of your vehicle's registration, dated September 28th, after the murder of the first two victims."

"Ha! I told you."

"But that does not mean we didn't find traces of rat poison containing thallium in the trunk of your vehicle; the same vehicle you used to transport your third victim to the walk-in freezer at Frankie's Diner. We also found a gold earring at Frankie's matching the one found with your first victim's body."

"I don't know about any earrings."

"I'm sure your blood sample will be a match to the blood found on the evidence," Gerard stated, sifting through papers and glossy photos. He slid photographs taken at the abandoned house across the table one at a time while he continued to speak. "We also have evidence proving that someone placed Amy Young and Sarah Tyler in the trunk of your white 1964 Chrysler Newport. Miss Young and Miss Tyler both confirm this accusation. Sarah, Anna and Amy were locked up and held captive in the basement of an abandoned house."

Loretta leaned forward, studying the photographs Officer Gerard presented and widening her eyes in surprise.

"We found a piece of one of the girls' clothing in the cellar, which helped the dogs track them. Thankfully, they were rescued. Otherwise, I would be adding three more counts of murder to your charges."

"The old shack doesn't belong to me. It is where Edith Marshall lived before she moved to town," Loretta said, releasing an exaggerated sigh. "She kidnapped the girls to protect her nephew, Lloyd, from being arrested for murdering three people. I have already told you this."

Gerard collected the photographs, placing them inside a file folder. "Do you still want to stick to your statement that Edith Marshall is the mastermind who kidnapped the girls? Your statement suggests that Edith, an elderly woman, put the young girls into the trunk of your vehicle and drove them to the abandoned house, leaving them locked and bound in the dirt basement to die."

Nodding her head, Loretta reiterated, "Like I already told you, Lloyd was helping Edith kidnap the girls. He remembers visiting his aunt at the old shack as a kid. Not me. I've never been there. I was at the bank while he kidnapped the girls."

"There are a few holes in your statement," Gerard replied, setting his pencil on the table. "The security footage at the bank shows you were there the day after Amy and Sarah were kidnapped. The film helps place you in the right place and time for the abduction of Anna Labrash. Her story is collaborated by a witness who has filed assault charges and a restraining order against you, but as a minor, the identity of the witness is withheld."

"Oh, good one!" Randy said, playfully punching Hanson in the arm. "I didn't know Greg Holman filed charges. I'm glad I brought him into the station under warrant. Officer Gates captured photos before administering first aid."

"We have several witnesses at this very police station placing Officer Lloyd Trussell in this building, at his desk doing paperwork at the time of the kidnapping of Sarah and Amy," Officer Gerard continued. Doyle and Hanson waited in the silence stretching between Loretta and Gerard, wondering how she would explain away her involvement in the kidnappings. "How would an elderly woman such as Edith Marshall knock out two young teenage girls, drag them into the trunk of your car, drive them to an abandoned house and lock them in the basement?"

Loretta, sputtering, blinked away fresh tears and replied with ragged emotion, "Edith forced me to help her against my will because Lloyd was unavailable! The old lady insisted that the girls were stealing her medication. She didn't want them to get away with it, so she lured them into the house and hit them over the head."

"You already said you were at the bank when Edith kidnapped Amy and Sarah, yet we have found no evidence to suggest you were at the bank on the day you said Edith took the girls. Are you now saying you were with Edith Marshall when Sarah and Amy entered the home? She forced you to help her knock two girls over the head and move them into the trunk of your vehicle?" Officer Gerard said, placing evidence photos onto the table. "In the trunk of your car, we found Amy Young's hair scrunchie with strands of hair and a few blood spots from rolling around in that big old trunk of yours."

"Again, you don't have to answer that," the young lawyer stated, pulling on his cheap tie. "You have already answered his questions. He is trying to trick you into admitting guilt."

"It's okay. I will argue that Lloyd Trussell was planting evidence at crime scenes trying to frame me," Loretta said, glaring at her counsel. "This is what happened: I went to the bank, *but* I forgot my bank book. I came home to get it when I discovered Edith standing over two unconscious girls in the living room! She forced me to help her put the girls in my trunk and drive them out of town because Greg had her car. Edith directed me to the place where she used to live!"

"I have a hard time believing that Edith Marshall is capable of forcing you to do anything, Miss Flatiron," Officer Gerard said, shaking his head. "She is just a sweet little old lady from Glenmere, Saskatchewan. I also don't believe that Mrs. Marshall can move bodies around, stashing them in freezers by herself. She would need help. Lifting a teenager would take two people, especially for the boy, Liam Hildebrandt! Are you saying that Mrs. Marshall is the manipulating mastermind of this whole ordeal? An elderly woman forced you to help her with the heavy lifting after poisoning three people and kidnapping three teenagers, all preventing them from telling the police what they knew? Are you sure you were not the one calling all of the shots?"

"She's crazy in the head! I can't believe some of the plans she comes up with," she said, shrugging her shoulders. Loretta rattled the chains across the table as she moved. "Who's to say why she does the things she does? She seems sweet on the outside, but once you get to know her, she is evil and manipulative."

"Well, I agree that Mrs. Marshall is a sweet old lady, but I have medical evidence that shows you are manipulating Edith Marshall." Gerard closed one case file and opened another, withdrawing some papers and placing them over the photos on the table. "I have a statement from Edith's medical doctor and her specialist, a neurologist. She was diagnosed eight years ago with early-onset Alzheimer's disease. Edith Marshall has dementia but has been able to live on her own because she has a live-in caregiver, and her nephew is living nearby. You know her nephew, Lloyd Trussell, the police officer you pursued a relationship with to secure your job as a live-in caregiver to his aunt, intending to manipulate her to your benefit."

Randy shot Hanson a look of bewilderment, asking, "Does she have dementia? I was starting to wonder if it was all an act. I thought she seemed to know more than she was letting on the last time I talked to her, but I wasn't sure. Come to think of it, she knew that Gerard suspended me and she told me that her nephew had a name tag like mine. If Mrs. Marshall was referring to Trussell, she pointed to my police badge above my name tag on my uniform, not my name tag."

"That's how the disease is sometimes. One day the person seems coherent; the next, they are confused. It's hard to know," Hanson replied, nodding as he watched through the one-way mirror.

"Hmm," Randy mused, continuing to listen to Gerard's account of events, waiting for a reaction from the suspect. "I guess that's why seniors are so vulnerable."

Gerard continued his account of events, watching his suspect closely for any reaction. "While you were living in Edith's home, you took her to her appointments using Edith's car, a gold Lincoln Continental. It didn't take long for you to realize that an older person takes many prescription drugs with street value. You have been stealing her money and dealing her medications and other drugs on the streets of Glenmere. Isn't that right?"

Loretta shrugged, rolling her eyes, while her lawyer remained silent and unmoving.

Patting himself on his chest, Randy boasted, "That was my case! A parking violation and tow allowed me to search the vehicle. I had to follow up with the pharmacy with regards to the pills that I found: heart meds, painkillers, unmarked pills and some white powder which turned out to be rat poison."

"Shhh!" Hanson shushed. "I think we are getting to the good part. Wait until you hear what I solved with my superior investigative skills!"

"But then a couple of unlucky kids witnessed you selling those drugs to an addict from the trunk of your car in the back alley behind the Family Grocers. That's when you decided to use thallium poison to kill Anna Labrash and Liam Hildebrandt. You used your past relationship with Ralph Norman, the high school janitor, to gain a visitor pass so you could deliver a poison-laced drink to Anna during school hours. You didn't have a chance to push your second drink on Liam because the class bell rang, so you threw it in a trash bin near the front doors. Knowing that the poison would kill the girl in about eight hours, you stuffed some paper inside of the door jam at the Family Grocers while the store was still open so that you could come back later that day to stash the dead body. Everyone in town knows the layout of that store! It would have been easy for you to sneak into the back room and exit out the back door. Unfortunately, the police misidentified Leah for her sister, Anna, but you made the same mistake. Once you realized your mistake, you target Anna, looking to make her disappear before she could identify you as a drug dealer and murderer. How am I doing so far?"

"It's quite a story," Loretta supplied, her facial expression remaining stoic. "Except, you meant to say that Lloyd did all of that. He is Edith's nephew, giving him full access to her home, her medicines and her vehicle. Lloyd sold the drugs for extra money to pay for my caregiving services for his aunt. He used rat poison to spike the slushie. He had a motive: Lloyd didn't want to risk losing his job."

Gerard picked up his pencil, poising it over his legal pad, "I'm sorry, but what did you call the drink?"

Confusion clouded Loretta's eyes; willingly, she answered, "A slushie. You can buy the frozen drink at Circle K. All the kids drink it."

"This drink, a slushie, comes in different flavours?"

"Yes," Loretta frowned, cocking her head to the side.

Gerard made a notation on his notepad in large lettering: *try a frozen drink called a slushie*, aware that Loretta was reading the paper upside down. "Now, where was I?" Gerard paused, looking back in his file folder. "Lloyd had been lending Greg Holman, a friend of the family, use of his aunt's car as well. I'm sure that would get inconvenient at times, when you wanted to access the drugs you stored in the trunk. That's when you got fed up with sharing the vehicle and bought the white sedan, a Chrysler Newport."

"I didn't have any drugs in the trunk of my car," Loretta said incredulously, raising her voice to a higher octave.

"No, you didn't get to them in time because Greg had the car parked illegally behind the pharmacy, something he did repeatedly. The pharmacist had Mrs. Marshall's car towed. While the vehicle was in the impound lot, Officer Doyle searched the vehicle and confiscated the drugs."

"There wasn't any poison in the trunk of my car, either," Loretta frowned, looking sideways at her lawyer.

"The rat poison you bought to kill Anna Labrash and Liam Hildebrandt was not in the trunk of your car. We found the box in the janitor's closet where you put it, framing Ralph Norman. His work area was searched when we arrested him in connection to Anna Labrash's murder, but we couldn't establish a motive. If you remember, Mr. Norman was in police custody when Liam Hildebrandt was poisoned and left in a freezer, giving us reason to doubt he was the prime suspect. After Lloyd Trussell's arrest, we searched Edith Marshall's home and found a second box of rat poison under the sink with your fingerprints on it," Officer Gerard said, pausing for effect. "Care to explain that bit of information?"

"Edith's house has rats," Loretta's eyes narrowed as she tried to figure out what else to say. "I was framed! It was-"

"Trussell? No, it wasn't him; but according to you, he has a motive to poison two teenagers and kidnap three more. You really should check your schedule for murdering and kidnapping kids against your boyfriend's work schedule. We can account for where he was during all of the kidnappings and murders." Gerard said, pulling a photo of Ronaldo Baysic from a brown folder and laying it on the mounting evidence. "Do you think Lloyd had a motive to kill Ronaldo Baysic, a homeless drug addict?"

"Yes! Yes!" Loretta exclaimed, slapping her hands down on the table. "I tried to warn the homeless guy, but he was high on drugs. He wouldn't listen to me. Lloyd killed him and now he's trying to frame me!"

"Is that the conversation Anna Labrash and Liam Hildebrandt witnessed in the alley?"

"Yes!" Loretta said, laughing. "Now you got it."

"Hmm. I have a statement from Anna and Lloyd saying you were having a different conversation," Gerard hinted, feathering a few documents onto the cluttered table.

Loretta leaned forward, frantically looking at the pages. "What? No, I'm telling you the truth! It wasn't my idea."

"According to witness statements, you were threatening Ronaldo Baysic to *keep his mouth shut or the Big Boss was going to deal with him for snitching on his business*." Gerard paused, waiting for a confession; it wasn't forthcoming. "Trussell was one of the new police officers working on Baysic as an informant against the drug dealing in our town. You were worried Baysic would tell the police about your involvement in a drug ring."

Loretta bowed her head, pulling on her restraints to cover her face. She muttered, "I can't believe this."

"You used Edith Marshall's generosity to poison a homeless man with thallium-laced food, but you also needed to dispose of anyone who could link you to him and suspect you of his murder. Anna Labrash and Liam

Hildebrandt overheard your conversation and could identify you. Everything seemed to be going as planned, but Amy Young found one of your earrings at the crime scene; the earring you dropped when you put Leah Labrash's body in the grocery store freezer," Gerard said, sifting through evidence photos and bringing one of the earrings to the top of the pile. "That earring is a key piece of evidence! Trussell confided in you about Amy Young finding your earrings, linking you to the crime. He also told you that the Labrash family identified the victim as Leah Labrash, not her sister, Anna. That is how Anna Labrash and Amy Young became your next targets. Sarah Tyler was just in the wrong place at the wrong time."

Loretta raised her head. Her face changed as a dark presence washed over her features. She leaned over the table's edge, speaking quietly, "You are right about everything except one: Lloyd said the police found the earring near the homeless guy's body. I didn't lose it there! Lloyd planted that evidence to frame me. I will demand for a mistrial!" Loretta said, twisting her body, attempting to put her hands in her sweater pockets. "I don't see how this is going anywhere. Release me and save yourself the embarrassment."

"We removed an earring from that grey sweater you are wearing. Amy Young wore it the first time she was in this interrogation room. Officer Hanson put it over the back of a chair in the evidence room, but Lloyd returned the grey sweater to you before Hanson could put it into the evidence locker," Gerard stated, sliding a photo of her grey sweater onto the growing pile of evidence.

Furrowing her brow, Loretta asked, "How would my sweater end up at the police station? I never lost it."

"It's the same grey sweater that Amy Young was wearing the night police officers arrived at Frankie's Diner, where you dumped Liam's body. Moving an almost fully grown teenage boy is more work than you anticipated. When you arrived at Frankie's Diner, you removed your sweater, hanging it near the back door. Lloyd knew Amy was wearing your sweater when he arrived on the scene with the other officers because it was a gift from him."

"Lloyd set me up! Why are we even talking about my sweater?"

"Stop talking!" the young counsel yelled, his eyes bulging. "Anything you say will be an admission of guilt."

"Nah, they still got nothing. It's all circumstantial: an earring and a sweater!"

"We have the matching earring to the one found in the freezer at the Family Grocers," Officer Gerrard smiled, sliding the evidence bag with the two gold earrings in it. "It's funny where a set of earrings keeps reappearing: the grocery store freezer, near the body of a homeless man, at Edith Marshall's home, in your sweater at Frankie's Diner, and in the trunk of your car."

"That's more earrings than the set you have in front of you. The earrings don't prove anything. You have too many!" Loretta laughed, mocking him.

Nodding, Gerard explained, "Yes, thanks to Officer Trussell's tampering, the earring was taken out of the evidence locker and planted at your next crime scene every time it came back to us. Lloyd Trussell wanted to connect the right person to all of the crimes. We know they are the same because Trussell put a tiny mark on each. How's that for planning? Trussell was tired of your manipulation. He was embarrassed to say anything, but his clever plan led the police investigation directly to you. Luckily, Lloyd was very clever with his clues. He explained everything in his statement."

Loretta stood suddenly, knocking over her chair, straining against the handcuffs anchoring her to the table. She yelled, "Lloyd isn't as clever as I am! He couldn't plan a trip to Saskatoon on his own. I don't think he could have figured out that rat poison contained thallium. It's tasteless and easy to mix in with just about anything!"

"Yes, including a slushie. I never told you what kind of drink the killer used, Miss Flatiron," Gerard calmly said. "Only the killer, the medical examiner and me knew about the slushie. Oh, there is also blood evidence on the first earring found that matches your blood type."

The young lawyer quickly stood next to his client, rearranging his pages. "I think that this interrogation is over, along with my career. Miss Flatiron has *nothing* more to say to you."

As the door to the interrogation room burst open, a slick, fancy lawyer breezed in, "I will have to ask everyone to leave immediately for discovery with my client."

Gerard stood, frowning, "Who are you? Miss Flatiron already has legal counsel."

"I am Bert Illingsworth, Miss Flatiron's new lawyer." He looked pointedly at the young lawyer, who was biting his fingernails. "You are dismissed."

Loretta bent over and placed her forehead on the table, an eerie laughter bubbling up her throat. "I think you are too late, counsellor."

"Yes, I think I already have everything I need to charge your client with resisting arrest, three counts of first-degree murder, two counts of indignity to human remains, three counts of kidnapping, six counts of assault and battery, elder abuse, fraud, drug dealing and threatening a police officer. I'll check on that last one and make a longer list. I have no more questions at this time." Officer Gerard stood up, collected his files and strolled out.

"What did you do?" Bert yelled, cursing at his client. "You should have waited for me!"

Chapter 38

"Where are your friends?" Officer Hanson asked, looking around the waiting area.

"Sarah wanted to stay home to answer the telephone. The lines have been steadily ringing since the police rescued us. Everyone in town wants to talk to us about our abduction," Amy replied, vacating her seat. "Anna is helping her family prepare for Leah's funeral."

"Okay, Miss Young. Right this way," Officer Hanson instructed, turning and walking in the direction he wanted her to follow.

"Are you sure you want to do this alone?" George Petersen asked his granddaughter, resting his hand on her shoulder. "I will sit quietly in the corner and watch over you if you want."

"No, I need to do this," Amy said, squeezing his arm to offer him reassurance as she walked past. Quickening her step, she hurried to catch up to Officer Hanson as he made his way down the hallway to the interview room where Hanson had interrogated her after finding the body at the diner.

Hanson opened the door across the hall and they entered into a brightly lit room; her uncle Randy stood up from the table. He looked refreshed in his carefully pressed uniform. Amy wondered if Randy had discarded the muddy uniform he was wearing when he rescued her yesterday, like she had done with her ruined Family Grocers uniform.

"Amy, thanks for coming. You look well rested after your ordeal," Randy smiled, collecting his paperwork and notepad. "This is unusual, but we will give you time to speak with Greg. You can have as much time as you need. Call out to me when you are finished."

"Thanks," she said, clearing her throat. She watched her uncle leave the room, winking at her on the way out. "Greg, I don't know what you have told the police and what you haven't, but I need to talk to you about what happened to me."

Greg sat back in his chair, crossing his arms and flicking his matted, colourful hair out of his eyes. "You shouldn't be here. Why don't you go home? I don't need to talk to you. I have told the police everything that they need to know."

Unconsciously, Amy pulled a strand of her brown hair out of her ponytail, twisting it around her finger. Swallowing, she continued, "Where is your lawyer? Don't you have someone here to help you?"

"I don't need them anymore. I sent them away," Greg scowled, running his fingers through his hair. "Officer Doyle told me you were coming. Why do you want to talk to me?"

Amy approached the table, but stayed standing. "Did you write me the threatening note Carly gave me at Frankie's Diner? Were you trying to hurt me?"

Frowning, Greg shook his head and said, "I don't know why you would think I was trying to hurt you. I was the one who called the ambulance when you fell in the park."

Amy's eyes grew large as her brain registered what he was saying. "What were you doing in the park that early morning?" she asked.

Shrugging, Greg answered wearily, "I was passing through the park on my way to meet someone. My vehicle had been towed. I had to walk."

"Did you tell Officer Doyle? I'm sure he would want to know, because I have already told him you threatened me."

"Stop! Why would you tell him I was threatening you?" he said, uncrossing his arms and gesturing with his hands.

Slamming her fist down on the table, Amy raised her voice, "What was I supposed to think? I felt threatened by you! You kept telling me to go home!"

"I was just trying to help you!" he yelled back.

"By telling me to quit my job and go home? That makes no sense to me," Amy shouted.

Standing up, leaning over the table to come eye-to-eye with Amy, Greg quietly said, "I knew you were looking for Leah, and I knew she was dead because both you and the killer mistook her for her sister, Anna. If you kept looking for Leah, you might have found Anna, and then you both would be in danger. I wasn't far off. You got yourself, and Sarah kidnapped, for Christ's sake!"

"I was following you! You had Anna. She got kidnapped too, no thanks to you!"

"She would have been fine if she hadn't insisted on helping her family with funeral plans. She made me drop her off at the funeral home. When I came to get her, Anna was outside talking to Edith."

"Who is Edith?"

"She is the lady who lets me use her car to get around in exchange for making pickups and deliveries for her. She is an honorary aunt, my mom's friend."

"Is she the kidnapper?"

Laughing, Greg stood up. "No, she's a harmless senior, a family friend. She didn't kidnap you, but I know who did."

"Who?" she asked.

"Ask me something else," Greg demanded.

"The morning you found me in the park, were you following me or making a pickup for the old lady?"

Greg looked away, answering quietly, "No, it was a delivery."

"That makes no sense," Amy said, raising her voice. "What were you delivering? In the park? In the dark?"

"Drugs. You got me. My mom sent me to Glenmere to get me away from the drug scene, but it didn't work. I was meeting a drug user, hoping to score." Greg shook his head, smiling sarcastically. "Only he was dead and you were lying on the sidewalk."

Amy thought about her encounters with Greg at work and school. She could not remember a time when she noticed Greg acting like he was using drugs or acting strangely, but then again, she didn't know him well. "You are using drugs?"

"No. No! Edith sends me to meet this homeless guy in the park to give him a sandwich. She leaves the sandwich wrapped on the table for me to take. I know what Edith wants me to do when I see them. She left sandwiches two days in a row for the homeless guy. She's awesome when other people aren't manipulating her."

"Wait, the dead guy who froze to death? That's who you were looking for?" Amy shuddered, remembering the cold frosty morning, slipping on the icy sidewalk, the red and white shoes. Anna peeked under the table, looking at the black marker-covered shoes with a tiny bit of red revealed near the toes.

"Yeah, I was supposed to bring it to the homeless guy the night before, but I didn't get there in time to meet him because someone towed my ride. I went back in the morning hoping he would be around, but instead I found you unconscious and the guy was dead. I called the ambulance and police from the payphone down the street. I didn't tell anyone."

Amy struggled to see how feeding a homeless man in the park had anything to do with the events leading up to her kidnapping. "How did you get involved with hiding Anna?"

"Edith found the earring at the house. She gave it to me, said that I should return it to my girlfriend," rolling his eyes, Greg sighed. "I tried to tell her that my girlfriend didn't wear those earrings, but I pocketed it so she would stop repeating herself. Sometimes she gets a little confused and fixated on things." He took a deep breath and continued, "Look, I already told the police what I know about the earrings! They kept making me repeat the part about the sandwiches and the jewelry. It's weird. I don't like repeating myself."

"I don't know what you did. Tell me about the earrings," Amy said. "I have to know or I won't be able to sleep at night. I found them twice!"

Greg ran his hands through his messy hair, trying to smooth it. "I was in the pharmacy to pick up some supplies for Edith when I heard Officer Doyle asking questions about earrings and Edith's prescriptions. I went back to ask Edith where she found the earrings. Edith said something about telling her nephew to get an earring from the police station trash can so I would have the matching set," Greg said, inhaling dramatically before continuing. "Like I said, she does get confused. I would have dismissed the idea, but I couldn't stop thinking that a cop was involved with Leah's death. Edith couldn't remember which police officer and I didn't want to upset her by asking her too many times. I knew

Anna was in danger because everyone had mistaken her as already dead! I couldn't ask the police for help, so I was looking for Anna alone. When I found her, she made me promise to help her stay safe, but I failed."

Greg was presenting a lot of information to process, but Amy still had to have one question answered, "You said you knew the person who kidnapped us?"

"Yeah."

"Who?"

"The same person who killed Leah."

"I'm still not following you."

"Edith's friend, Loretta. She's been manipulating and stealing Edith's money and pills. I don't know for sure, but somehow Anna found out. Didn't she tell you?"

"I think Anna saved most of her story for the police, but yes, she told us that the kidnapper grabbed her outside of the funeral home while she was distracted by an elderly woman," Amy replied, twisting a strand of her hair. "Are you under arrest?"

"I don't think so. Officer Hanson and Doyle told me they were only keeping me here for my safety until Loretta could be placed behind bars," Greg said, shaking his head. "I don't know how or why Loretta used poison to kill people! The police can only use some of my information because I got my facts third hand. I have no proof to offer! I think they've got their confession because my mom is coming to get me."

"So, you aren't facing charges?"

"As long as you dropped your charges involving uttering threats, which I didn't do, I have no charges. They were warnings," Greg replied, sighing heavily. "Well, I have one traffic ticket for parking in a no-parking zone behind the pharmacy, but the rest have nothing to do with me. I'm not the owner of the vehicle. It's all circumstantial."

"This is the longest conversation we have ever had," Amy smiled nervously, sensing an awkward moment. "I'm going to leave now. Thank you for speaking with me."

Chapter 39

Turning on the hot water, Amy added the dirty plates to the kitchen sink. "So, the police officer was dating the killer who kidnapped us? Was he in on everything from the beginning?"

Opening a drawer, Randy slowly pulled out a clean dish towel before answering, "Well, Lloyd thought he was dating her, but she was using and manipulating him. He thought he would need to move Edith Marshall into a nursing home, but Loretta sweet-talked him and told him she would be a live-in caregiver. He knew Loretta was stealing and dealing, but he didn't have anyone else to help with his aunt. She pressured him to bury the evidence of her crimes. I guess he couldn't take it any longer."

"What will happen to his aunt now? Who will care for Mrs. Marshall while Officer Trussell is in jail?"

"Mrs. Marshall has already been moved into the nursing home on Second Street. She will have other seniors to interact with and full-time nursing care to help her. She seemed happy about her move when I checked in on her."

Amy reached for the tap, stopping the water before the bubbles overfilled the sink. "Does Mrs. Marshall remember helping Loretta move the bodies or kidnap us girls?"

Shaking his head, Randy pressed his lips together. "It is a real shame that Loretta used her that way. With her mental state, she had no idea what Loretta was really up to. Lucky for us, Loretta confessed to everything, hoping to lessen her sentence."

"And the old abandoned farmhouse where we were held captive was Mrs. Marshall's old place?"

"Yes."

"How did you know to start the search for us there?"

"That one was easy, although it would have been easier if you were still there when we arrived!" Randy cleared his throat when he caught the glare from Amy. "Trussell figured that you might be at the old house when he realized that Loretta was behind the kidnappings. He recalled telling Loretta about the abandoned homestead. Lloyd jumped on the opportunity to telephone the anonymous tip line as soon as he learned Officer Gilbertson had phoned the radio station asking for public assistance. The tip was detailed enough to lead us to your uniform vest and the cut ropes in the cellar. The Family Grocers logo was an obvious clue that it belonged to you. Officer Hanson immediately called in the K-9 unit, leading us directly to you. We weren't expecting to find Anna with you, but I hoped the third set of prints were hers and not the kidnapper's."

"What is going to happen to Officer Trussell now? He didn't kill anyone or kidnap us. What did he do, exactly?"

"Once Trussell figured out what Loretta was doing, he kept stealing evidence and planting it at crime scenes and in the trunk of the cars Loretta was driving. He hoped we would figure it out and arrest her. Lloyd didn't plant the drugs or the poison, but he planted the gold earrings at Ronaldo Baysic's crime scene and in the trunk of Loretta's car before he called in the tip. Lloyd said he recognized Loretta's grey sweater on you while you were standing in the doorway at the diner. He slipped an earring in the sweater pocket while you were still at the crime scene."

Amy reached into the hot, soapy water, methodically washing each plate and putting it into the rinse water for her uncle Randy to dry. Her mind raced with questions she wanted to ask, but she sensed the window of opportunity closing fast. "What was the poison that Loretta used to kill Leah and Liam?"

"Thallium poison is odourless, tasteless, and difficult to detect. It makes people very sick for up to eight hours before it kills them. Once we found out the cause of death, we knew that finding out when the killer administered it was the most important because without that, the time of death only implicated you and Sarah."

"And you believed me when I said I didn't do it," Amy said, sliding another plate into the rinse water.

"Yes, I believed you, but I must admit, the evidence did implicate you until we gathered more information. Still, I have a lot to learn when it comes to solving crimes, but Officer Hanson had to follow procedure while we waited for the bloodwork to come back and rule you out as a suspect. The lab has confirmed that Loretta's blood was on the earring you brought me. Hanson's not my favourite person, but I could learn from him. Gerard is putting us together as a team."

Amy hesitated, concentrating on the casserole dish that she was washing. "Do you think Loretta planned to poison us after she kidnapped us? She didn't give us food or water, at least not while we were there."

Swallowing, Randy answered cautiously, "Maybe. It's hard to know because we didn't give her the chance. Hopefully, we would have found you in time and given you an antidote, but I think she decided it would be less work to leave you to starve to death in the cellar."

Reaching back into the hot, sudsy water, Amy let it chase away her chills. It was warm and humid standing in front of the sink at her grandparent's home - her home. It was good to be back, warm and safe again. Tomorrow, she would return to school like nothing had ever happened, because nothing ever happened in this little town of Glenmere. Did it? Life seemed to be changing in this peaceful town filled with idyllic white picket fences. She would do anything to return to the fairytale, back when she lived with her grandma Dorothy in the little farmhouse thirty-five kilometres out of town.

Staring out of the kitchen window, she imagined the farmhouse, her farmhouse, and the young family signing a five-year lease. She smiled, imagining the joy of children's laughter returning to her childhood home. Life in Glenmere would return to its leisurely pace; hopefully she would finish high school without another incident.

The End

If you enjoyed The Ice Box, please leave a review on Amazon, Goodreads or the author's website.

Thank you for your support!

Continue reading for an Anecdote from the author. Your favourite characters from the Glenmere Box Mysteries will return in Book #3 (sneak peaks and updates will be emailed to her monthly subscribers). Follow author Lisa Adair on social media and sign up for the monthly email to learn more!

https://www.booksbylisaadair.com
http://www.linktr.ee/booksbylisaadair

Anecdote

6 Dead Hookers

I was right in the middle of writing an exciting chapter when I realized that I needed a good car for the scene. In my manuscript, I wrote the words 'insert a car with a big trunk here' and highlighted them to make the spot easy to find later when I went back to add in the details. Luckily, I knew I would have the opportunity to attend a few car shows before my book was done, so I wasn't worried. I always use car shows to 'shop around' for inspiration.

While attending the August car show in Prince Albert, Saskatchewan, I found the ideal vehicle to use in a fascinating chapter in my manuscript for my book. It was big, white and rusty in all the right places. I noticed that the sign on the windshield read '1964 Chrysler Newport.' I walked a circle around my glorious find, trying to memorize every detail and taking the odd photo. The middle-aged man, who I assumed was the owner, started the motor of his magnificent beast, revving the engine and blowing blue smoke while he talked about engines and exhaust with another car enthusiast.

I smiled. Perfect!

Walking up to the man sitting in a lawn chair under a temporary shelter beside the car, I tried to put my introverted tendencies aside, asking, "Excuse me? Are you the owner?"

"Yup, that's me."

"Do you mind if I ask you a few questions about your car?" I asked, trying to raise my voice over the noise of the live band, the chatter of the crowds, and the occasional revving of classic car engines.

"What?" he leaned closer, almost falling out of his lawn chair.

With my husband off mingling in all his glory with the other attendees, talking about restoration, engine blocks, custom paint, and all the different topics that might be related to anything on wheels, I knew that I would have to repeat my request. Trying to be heard over the chaotic activity typical of every car show I have ever attended, I yelled, "Can I ask you a question?"

"Ask away!" He grinned, spreading his arms wide, reminding me of a game host displaying sought-after prizes.

"How big is the trunk?"

Without hesitation, he answered, "Big enough to stack six dead hookers side by side; four if you left the spare tire in it."

I laughed. The man had no idea why I needed that information. "Would you mind popping the trunk so I can see? I'm an author writing a murder mystery novel. I think your car would be great for my book."

He rattled off other facts and stats about his prized car that I didn't understand as we walked around to the back of the vehicle. I assume he thought I knew a lot about cars, but that would be my husband's domain. I don't think he heard what I said. The man unlocked the trunk while he continued to tell me a story about fitting an entire outdoor patio set into the trunk. I peered in, smiling. It was gloriously big! There was more room than I could have imagined, had I just picked the car from a photo on Pinterest. "Where's the spare?" I asked, realizing that I couldn't locate the tire.

"Don't have one, but it would go right back there." He pointed far into the back of the trunk.

"Thanks," I said, wondering if someone would have to crawl into the trunk to remove the spare tire. "It's awesome! I will be putting your car into my novel."

And I did!

-Lisa Adair

The Glenmere Box Mysteries: Book Blurbs

The Puzzle Box, book 1.

In the small 1980s Saskatchewan town of Glenmere, sixteen-year-old Amy Young wants to save enough money from her summer jobs to build a future for herself somewhere else. Anywhere would be better than living with Aunt Jeannie, who took her in when her grandmother, Dorothy, died unexpectedly, leaving behind a puzzle promising to reveal the secret to everything Amy had ever wanted. Amy hopes for a small inheritance that might help her leave Glenmere, a sleepy little town where nothing ever happens. That has been changing as of late: The gossip mill is churning with talk of an unusual rash of break-ins, theft and a shady character hanging around town. Everyone is on edge.

The search is on for Amy's Uncle John, her grandmother's only living child and one of the primary benefactors. John is a known gambler who no one has seen in years. Unfortunately, the estate lawyers aren't the only people looking for him. John's old friend is also in town, hoping to cash in on John's inheritance before his past catches up to him and takes him out. The past is closing in fast. With every answer that comes to light leading only to more questions, Amy's usually boring small-town life is turning on its head, with secrets, murder and mystery around every turn.

About the Author

Author Lisa Adair was born and raised in a small Canadian town in the heart of Northern Saskatchewan's forestry region. Using her own experiences there as inspiration, in 2023, Lisa released her debut adult-fiction novel, *The Puzzle Box (FriesenPress),* the first installment of "The Glenmere Box Mysteries."

With degrees in science and English from the University of Saskatchewan and a diploma from Saskatchewan Polytechnic, Lisa has always enjoyed writing about positive role models and personal growth. In 2023, she also authored a children's fantasy series about urban fairies and mythical creatures, *Blaze Peppergrove to the Rescue (Lisa Adair),* the first installment of "*The Blaze Peppergrove Adventures.*"

When not writing, painting, scrapbooking, or playing the guitar, Lisa enjoys camping and hiking in and around her beautiful Saskatchewan home, where she lives with her husband, children, and their beloved rescue dog.

Printed in Canada